W9-BLD-024

MAX ALLAN COLLINS

THOMAS & MERCER

The characters and events portrayed in this book are fictitious. Any similarity to real persons, living or dead, is coincidental and not intended by the author.

Text copyright © 1999 Max Allan Collins
All rights reserved.
Printed in the United States of America.
No part of this book may be reproduced, or stored in a retrieval system, or transmitted in any form or by any means, electronic, mechanical, photo-copying, recording, or otherwise, without express written permission of the publisher.

Published by Thomas & Mercer
P.O. Box 400818
Las Vegas, NV 89140

ISBN-13: 9781612185194
ISBN-10: 1612185193

*For Stephanie Keenan—who is
under the mistaken impression that
anyone could ever forget her*

Though this work is fanciful, every character in these pages existed, and an underpinning of history supports their characterizations. No disrespect is meant to these real people, or to the tragic event that engulfed them. Our interest in the *Titanic*—and the enjoyment taken in traveling back to that simpler, grander time—must always be tempered by the knowledge that men, women and children died on that night we still remember.

"There was not the slightest thought of danger in the minds of those who sat around the tables in the luxurious dining saloon of the *Titanic*."

—May Futrelle

A TRIP TO SCITUATE

From the beginning, mystery and controversy have been stow-aways on the *Titanic*'s crossing into history. The world's largest, most luxurious steamship—with a First-Class passenger list that was a Who's Who of its day—the R.M.S. *Titanic* began her maiden voyage midday April 10, 1912, and ended it prematurely in the midnight hours bridging April 14 and 15, after brushing an iceberg designed by God or fate to challenge the naively arrogant men who had deemed the ship unsinkable.

But no one is certain how many died on that clear starry night in icy Atlantic waters. The American inquiry into the disaster came up with 1,517 dead, the British tallied 1,490, while the British board of trade said 1,503, and various respected authorities today cite figures that range as low as 1,502 and as high as 1,523. What none of these authorities, past or present, cites are the two deaths aboard the *Titanic* that preceded the sinking.

The two murders.

Before this tale begins proper and I take my proper place next to the Wizard of Oz—behind the curtain—I would like to share with my readers how I came to learn of the *Titanic* murders, and how this fascinating historical footnote came to elude those far better, and more knowledgeable, *Titanic* scholars who have preceded me.

It began, as does so much in modern life, with a phone call.

Like most authors, I am frequently contacted by strangers, would-be collaborators who have a wonderful idea, or a fascinating life story, and all that's left for me to do is write it up. Everyone who has ever been involved in a crime (as a victim or a perpetrator) or who has survived a war (World War II or Vietnam, most frequently) is convinced that theirs was a unique experience, and that New York publishing and Hollywood studios are clamoring for the opportunity to throw money at them for sharing their story with a lucky, waiting world.

This is rarely the case, of course, and these individuals would have a better shot at fame and fortune by telling their timeless tale to the convenience-store clerk while scratching off "instant win" squares on lottery tickets. Besides, authors usually like to cook up their own ideas and, anyway, as a mystery writer, I'm not really suited to ghostwriting someone's military memoirs or turning Great-Aunt Ida's fascinating life on the prairie into a manuscript for the Christian bookstore market.

So I was skeptical when I received the phone call, late that Sunday evening, at my Muscatine, Iowa, home, from a would-be collaborator who refused to even identify himself by name.

"You were recommended to me," the male voice said, a reedy baritone. A hint of an accent was in there, somewhere—French? French-Canadian?

"Recommended how? By who?"

It wasn't a great connection; obviously long distance, as scratchy as an ancient phonograph record.

"Mutual friend."

"What mutual friend?"

"I have an idea for you. It'll make a great book, a great movie."

I rubbed my eyes. "Really."

"I read your novel."

"Which one?"

"The Lindbergh-baby book. Very good. Thorough job."

Well, now he'd bought himself a little time with me; he had just been about to land in that same limbo where my household dispatches phone solicitors. But compliments, like royalties, are immediately embraced by all writers.

"Thanks," I said. "I worked hard on that."

"Interesting case. You think you solved it, the kidnapping?"

"I think my solution holds up as well as anything anybody's come up with, yeah."

He paused; while static filled the empty air, I was imagining a face to go with the voice: thirtyish, rugged, smugly smiling....

"You like history. You like to find the mystery in history, don't you?"

"Yeah, it's kind of a speciality.... Well, listen, it was nice of you to call. I got one on Amelia Earhart in the works. You might like that, too—you might want to watch for it."

This is where a fan calling would have asked what the name of the new book was, and when was it coming out. But my vaguely French long-distance caller had an apparent non sequitur for me, instead.

"What about the *Titanic*?" he asked.

"What about it?"

"Lot of interest. Many books. TV specials. Videos of Ballard's dives, big sellers."

I knew, vaguely, what he was talking about. Dr. Robert Ballard's discovery of the shipwreck on the ocean's floor had been big news, not long before, and generated big dollars. Even before Ballard, interest in the *Titanic* never seemed to wane, and I'd known about the famous disaster at sea since childhood. My generation of kids was big on Walter Lord's book *A Night to Remember*, and I'd seen the movie version at a matinee in a majestic theater long since torn down.

Also, my anonymous caller had touched a distant nerve. While I did not have an interest in the *Titanic* in general, I had a specific interest in one of the ship's notable passengers....

So I said, "The *Titanic*, right, right ... is that your idea? Something about the *Titanic*? New theory on why and how it sank or something?"

"You know, Ballard, he called us grave robbers."

"Called who grave robbers?"

"Ballard thinks the wreck, it's like an undersea cemetery."

"Well, it is sort of a grave site."

"More than you know."

"Look," I said, interested but irritated, "what's this about? Were you on one of Ballard's expeditions?"

"Not Ballard's."

"Whose, then?"

I was aware the French Oceanographic Institute—INFREMER—had ignored Dr. Ballard's wish that the *Titanic* be left undisturbed, that no salvage or recovery be pursued, no artifacts removed, and had undertaken several expeditions to do just that. The artifacts salvaged, mostly from a debris field between the two sections of the sunken ship, had been hyped on a tacky television production hosted by Telly Savalas, and then treated rather more respectfully and responsibly, in museum exhibitions around the world.

He was saying, "You know, they get away with this, Ballard too, 'cause they found no bodies."

Though no expert, I remembered from documentaries I'd seen that most scientists and explorers had expected to find the *Titanic* more or less perfectly preserved, a virtual Edwardian time capsule, due to the coldness at that depth of the ocean, and the lack of oxygen—furniture, clothing, even human bodies, showing little or no decomposition.

This theory, like so many about the *Titanic*, had proved wrong. Deep-sea organisms had eaten away fabric and wood—and flesh, and for that matter, bone. An empty pair of shoes, the feet eaten right out of them, was as close as anyone had come to finding the remains of a *Titanic* fatality.

And, as my anonymous caller indicated, the various visits to the *Titanic*, whether for purposes of shooting documentary footage or salvaging artifacts, were acceptable to society at large only because no human remains had been viewed by the explorers, or their cameras. The ghostly majesty of the rust-encrusted wreckage would have turned ghastly had its decayed decks been littered with human rubble, had bones mingled with the bottles, bedsprings, dishes and dolls of the debris field.

"Listen," I said, close to hanging up, "you're going to have to give me your name."

"I don't know you, yet. Don't trust you, yet. This is big money. Dangerous, too."

"Why's it dangerous?"

"I signed papers not to tell. I took money."

"What for? Who from, damnit!"

"… I can't say."

I held the phone away from my face and glared at it; then I brought it back to my ear and mouth and said tightly, "Then why are you bothering me?"

Silence on the line, staticky silence.

"… They thought the galley area would be a good place to look. For the kind of things easy to take, still in nice shape … dishes, silverware, pots, pans … you know what a White Star dish from the *Titanic* would be worth?"

Had my anonymous caller been on a salvage expedition to the Titanic, *with modern-day pirates?*

"I'm sure a lot," I said.

"They had huge refrigeration on that ship. Very modern for back then, condenser-coil water system. Separate cold rooms for different perishables, you know, meat, vegetables, wine and champagne … and on the orlop deck, a cold-storage cargo hold, for other things … away from the food."

I didn't know what an orlop deck was (it's the lowest deck of a ship with multidecks, in this case right above the *Titanic*'s three immense propellers) but I did have a question. It's the kind of question a mystery writer would ask.

"This cold-storage hold—would that be where they'd put somebody who died?"

There was a nod in his voice. "That ship had everything—swimming pool, squash court, barbershop, Turkish bath, operating room, everything—except a morgue."

The staticky silence seemed to need filling, before he would go on; so I said, "I see."

"You're right—the cold cargo hold, in through number-five hatch … that's where we found them."

"… Bodies?"

"We didn't know that's what they were at first. They were just big canvas bags, sewn shut ... beautifully preserved. The submersible brought the bags up, we hauled them out on deck, and we cut one of them open ... the stench was like a sewer...."

"I don't need details."

"Have you read Poe?"

"Of course I've read Poe."

"Have you read the story of the sick man who is hypnotized?"

"Yeah, and I saw the movie." He was referring to "The Facts in the Case of M. Valdemar."

"Then you remember the hypnotized man, he finally collapses in an oozing pile of putrescence, melting from the bones—"

"Okay, okay," I said. "I may want to eat again someday."

"It's not what *National Geographic* wants for a Discovery Channel special, I can tell you that much. We never opened the other bag, but there was a body in it, all right."

Staticky silence, as if some distant telegraph message were going unanswered.

I asked, "And no one knows of this?"

"Only those on deck that day."

"On what deck? What ship, what expedition? You sound French."

"Oh? I thought my English was very good."

"Berlitz would hire you in a heartbeat. What about the bodies?"

"We buried them at sea. We swore not to talk of it, we were paid handsomely ... I'll tell you one thing about the body in the bag, the bag we opened?"

"Yes?"

"Its skull had been crushed. Caved in."

"Couldn't that have happened when the ship went down?"

"I don't think so. I think this was death by violence, man's violence, not nature. Murder. Isn't that what you write about?"

"I do, but I'm not really a nonfiction writer. I mean, I research real, unsolved crimes, but then I write a fictional work around the facts I uncover."

"That's why I called you. I can't risk a true treatment of this, but if you could devise a fiction story around it ..."

"I don't know. You're not giving me much to go on ... I'm afraid a nonfiction treatment would be where the interest, and the money, is. Hey, come on, pal—what *is* your name?"

"Are you interested in my story?"

"Yeah, I'm interested. Mildly. But interested."

And he hung up.

Perhaps I hadn't shown sufficient enthusiasm, and if you'd had as many crank calls, relating to your work, as I've had, you'd have been at least as skeptical as I was. Still, the notion of a murder—of *two* murders—on the *Titanic*, before she went down ... that was intriguing.

And it did tap into my very narrow, specific *Titanic* interest, an interest I'd carried since childhood....

Among the *Titanic*'s famous passengers, hobnobbing with John Jacob Astor, Molly Brown, Ben Guggenheim and the rest, was one of the most celebrated and popular American mystery writers of his day, Jacques Futrelle, creator of Professor S.F.X. Van Dusen. Futrelle's creation, also known as the Thinking Machine, was a cerebral sleuth whose exaggerated cranium housed a formidable brain, a dabbler in detection who refused payment for his crime solving, displaying a cold, imperious attitude (and devotion to pure logic) that made Sherlock Holmes seem warm and fuzzy.

Despite the French ring of his name, Futrelle was an American journalist turned fiction writer. His tales of so-called "Impossible Mystery" were a major influence on Agatha Christie; there is much of Professor Van Dusen in her Hercule Poirot and his celebrated "little gray cells." The Thinking Machine's first case remains his most famous: "The Problem of Cell 13," in which the detective, on a bet, escapes from a death-row cell. This tale remains one of the two or three most reprinted short stories in mystery fiction, and is the first detective story I remember reading.

And the brief biography of Futrelle included in the preface to the Scholastic Books' collection of "Thinking Machine" stories was where I first heard about the *Titanic*, and the sad news that Futrelle—and a number of unpublished Professor Van Dusen stories—went down with the ship.

I'd always been interested in Futrelle, and loved his stories, but little of his work was in print and coming by editions of his handful of novels was difficult. Consequently I hadn't given him much thought in perhaps twenty years when the Robert Ballard–stirred revival of *Titanic* interest sent journalists scurrying to talk to survivors of the tragedy, and even relatives. A wire-service interview with Futrelle's daughter Virginia made me recall how, as a boy, I'd enjoyed Jacques Futrelle's fiction.

Now, ironically, from a single wire-service story, I knew more about his grown daughter than I did about Futrelle himself; and she'd had quite a life of her own.

Born in 1897, Virginia had been an operatic prima donna featured in musical revues, frequently sharing the bill with young Cary Grant's acrobatic act at the Hippodrome in New

York. She toured Europe, consorted with show business roy-
alty (she was Barbara Stanwyck's bridesmaid) and eventually
married Charles F. Raymond, an eminent New York theatrical
manager, living with him in London and, after World War
II, in Johannesburg, South Africa. Later in life she worked in
broadcasting, in production, winding up back in Massachusetts,
where she'd grown up.

Virginia Futrelle Raymond, interviewed about her father and
his death on the *Titanic*, passed along to interviewers a number
of fascinating stories told to her by her late mother, May, who
had survived the disaster. I noted that Mrs. Raymond, now a
widow, lived in Scituate, Massachusetts.

And since I had a book tour coming up that would take me
through Boston—twenty-five miles from Scituate—I made my
own impulsive, out-of-the-blue telephone call to the daughter
of Jacques Futrelle.

"I'm a fan of your father's work," I told her, "and I'd consider
it a great honor if you'd consent to meet with me."

She was easily ninety years of age, but her voice had the
no-nonsense quality of a businesswoman, tempered by the
musicality of a former professional singer.

"I'd be delighted," she said. "I adored my father, and it's a
pity his memory, his work, has been so neglected."

"I couldn't agree more."

Her next remark seemed intended to set the tone for our
meeting to come: "It will be nice to talk to someone more interested in my father than the tragedy that took his life."

I asked where we might meet, wondering to myself if it
would be a nursing home of some kind, although the fact that
her number had been listed should have told me she was in her
own home or anyway an apartment.

"It's beautiful here this time of year," she said.

It was April.

"And," she continued, "you should have the pleasure of enjoying our lovely harbor. So—I believe I'll let you take me out to lunch, young man."

It was nice being called "young man," even if I had to hang out with women in their nineties for that to happen. My wife accompanied me on the drive down Massachusetts State Route 3A, which was mostly inland and not terribly scenic.

But Scituate itself provided all the scenery landlubbing midwesterners like us could drink in, even on a cool overcast afternoon. Nestling on four cliffs, looking down on a gentle curve of coastline, Scituate was a small, quaint community whose antique Cape Cods and Colonial homes had us immediately discussing relocating.

Virginia (on the phone she had made it clear she was "Virginia," not "Mrs. Raymond") had suggested the restaurant—Chester's at the Mill Wharf—which was on Front Street, on the town's picturesque sheltered harbor, overseen by a nineteenth-century lighthouse. We were early, and sat in the rustic, nautically themed restaurant at a table by the window looking out on the busy harbor—bobbing with pleasure craft and a working fishing fleet—and an ocean so smooth and gunmetal gray it nearly blended with the overcast gunmetal sky.

When the daughter of Jacques Futrelle entered, there was no mistaking her. I had seen Futrelle's photograph—he had a John Candy–like, round, boyish face, with dark wide-open eyes behind wire-frame glasses, and seemed at once alert and childlike, scholarly and cherubic, and was apparently rather thickset though by no means obese.

Based upon the one known photo of Futrelle aboard the *Titanic*, a full-figure shot of him on deck in a three-piece suit, his hair ruffled by wind, the author appeared to be fairly stocky, even short.

But Virginia Raymond was tall, close to six foot, with the big-boned frame of her father and a handsome face that echoed his, as well; at ninety, she still cut a commanding figure. She wore a dignified suit—a lavender pattern on top, with a solid lavender skirt (which my wife later described as "very Chanel")—and she used a cane, though she strode otherwise unaided through the mostly empty restaurant. (We had chosen to dine mid-afternoon, when we would have the place mostly to ourselves.)

We rose, and I introduced my wife and myself, mentioning that both of us were writers.

"Ah, like my parents," Virginia said, allowing me to help with her chair. "You didn't know Mother was a writer, too? She and Papa collaborated only once, on a short story that frankly wasn't very good. Well, of course, they collaborated on my brother and me, too."

We laughed at that, as I took my seat right across from Virginia. Soon we ordered soft drinks, and chatted about the drive down, and this lovely scenic little city, and explained that we were in Boston making appearances at several bookstores, promoting my latest historical detective novel and an anthology my wife had coedited.

"Look how smooth it is today," Virginia said, gazing out at the calm gray ocean. "That's how they say it was, you know. My mother said the ocean was like a millpond, that Sunday night."

I said nothing, exchanging nervous glances with my wife; we'd agreed to avoid the *Titanic* in conversation, as on the phone Virginia had made such a point of her willingness to spend time with a Futrelle fan, as opposed to a *Titanic* buff.

"You know, it's close to that time of year, isn't it?" Virginia asked.

Again, I said nothing, just smiled a little—I knew damn well the anniversary of the sinking was days away.

"Each year, on April 14, for as long as she was able, my mother held a private memorial service to my father, and the others who lost their lives that night. She would stand alone on Third Cliff here in Scituate, looking out over the open sea, a fresh bouquet of flowers in her hands ... and she would sprinkle the flowers with her tears, and then would toss them, into the water."

"That's lovely," my wife said.

The handsome, deeply grooved features formed an embarrassed smile. "Well, my mother did have a terrible streak of melodrama, I'm afraid. But she loved Papa; I don't think she ever really fully accepted his death. She and I didn't really get along very well, you know...."

This private piece of information coming along so early in our conversation was startling; but I managed to say, brilliantly, "Really?"

Virginia sipped her coffee, which she was drinking black, and nodded, saying, "She favored Jack, my brother ... she had quite an ego, Mother did. When she lost Papa, she lost the one person in the world she loved more than herself."

A waiter came over and we ordered lunch; wood-grilled fresh fish of every variety—not exactly midwestern fare. Then when the waiter had gone, Virginia turned toward the gray, gently rippling landscape and spoke again.

"I wasn't on the ship," she said. "I was in school—I went to private school, up north—yet memories of the *Titanic* sinking have been with me most of my life. Mother relived the sheer terror of that experience, from time to time, nightmares mostly, and sudden stabs of memory. She lived to be ninety-one ... I intend to outdo her, on that score."

Thinking of my anonymous phone caller, I said, "You seemed to have a positive opinion of Dr. Ballard's expedition, uh ... when you were interviewed. But what do you think of these later expeditions, recovering—"

She interrupted sharply: "Ghoulish. Simply ghoulish. I've always thought of the *Titanic* as my father's grave. I hope they'll let her be—she's at rest, a memorial in herself."

"Oh, I agree with you," my wife said. "This awful talk about trying to 'raise' the ship ..."

Her brown eyes, which were lovely, pressed shut. "I pray nightly that the ship will be allowed to remain where she lies. Anything else is exploitation. It seems only ... honorable, respectful, to leave the ship and its victims in their final resting place as was God's will."

I thought of those two canvas bags, sewn shut, in the cold cargo hold.

But then we spoke of her father, and she told anecdotes about him, warm funny stories of his playful practical jokes, such as the time her mother had "gussied herself up" for a party that her father wanted to skip. May Futrelle had approached her husband, who was tarrying with yard work, watering the lawn, and prodded him to come inside and put on his evening wear—he had instead hosed her down, in all her finery, and after her fury turned to laughter, they'd spent a quiet romantic evening together.

"They were a love story, Mama and Papa," she said rather wistfully. "A real-life love story."

"You know, I'd really like to see your father's work get back into print," I said. "Maybe if I could interview you, in depth, I could put a biographical piece together that would spark some interest."

I was putting a toe in the water, because my real intention was to seek her cooperation in writing a book-length biography of her father.

"I'm afraid that wouldn't be possible," she said, as if reading my mind. "I'm already working with two friends of mine, women I worked with in broadcasting, on creating a book about Papa."

I tried not to show my disappointment, although such a project—even if not written by me—was good news to this Futrelle fan.

That left me with nothing to say, or to ask, and I awkwardly changed the subject back to the *Titanic*.

"You know, these people *are* grave robbers, quite literally," I said. "Anyway, they are, if this phone call I received recently wasn't just a crank."

"How so?" she asked.

And I told Jacques Futrelle's daughter about the cargo hold, and the pair of bodies that had been stored there, years ago, only to be recently disturbed.

"Is that right?" she said. She was smiling, a strange smile, a young smile in the old face. "And here I thought Mother was spinning one."

"Pardon?"

"Well, you have to understand, my mother had major writing ambitions herself. She published several novels, both before and after Papa's death … wrote a sequel to one of his books, in fact. But when times changed, her writing style didn't, and that was the end of it."

15

"I see," I said, not really seeing, not really following any of this.

Virginia was rattling on: "Not long before her death, in 1967, she told me a story, an elaborate story, a detailed story ... and she claimed it was true. But I didn't know what to think. Why hadn't she told me before? She had no explanation for that."

"What sort of story?"

But Virginia didn't answer, not directly: "Mother was an adult when the *Titanic* went down. She was in her mid-thirties. Most of the survivors giving their eyewitness accounts these days were children at the time—some of them babes in arms!"

"And she was a writer," I said, nodding. "So her memories would be vivid, and credible, in a way the average person's might not."

"That's what you'd think, but sometimes I discounted her. She could be self-serving, Mother could, and she had a good imagination, a writer's imagination, and some of what she recalled about the *Titanic* didn't match up with other people's recollections."

"Really? What, for instance?"

"Well, for one, she insisted the band didn't play on deck— she said it was bitter cold and the violin strings would have snapped, and besides, they were playing indoors. All the eye-witness testimony to the contrary wouldn't sway her. She also said the band was German, and it's well-known it was a group of English musicians."

"Perhaps they played German selections and that confused her."

"Perhaps. She also insisted the iceberg was a 'growler,' a small berg, not the towering monster of ice so many others recall seeing. So, all things considered, I didn't pay much attention to her story, fascinating as it was. But now … what you say seems to confirm it."

"Virginia, what are you—"

"Here's our food," she said, and indeed the waiter was bringing it. "We'll speak of lighter subjects while we eat … and afterwards, if you like, if you have the time, I'll tell you about the murders."

And for three hours that afternoon, never seeming to tire, never missing a beat, she did.

What you are about to read is based upon Virginia Futrelle Raymond's recollections of the tale her mother told, supplemented by research and imagination.

Bon voyage.

DAY ONE

APRIL 10, 1912

ONE

A BIRTHDAY PRESENT

IN A SEA OF TOP hats, bowlers and Chesterfield topcoats, Jack Futrelle, bareheaded, felt damned near dowdy in his three-piece tweed, the soot-flecked breeze mussing his brown hair. His wife of nearly seventeen years, May, standing beside him on Platform 12 at Waterloo Station, was a Gibson girl come to life in her tailored shirtwaist, leg-of-mutton sleeves and long black skirt, made stylish by her elaborate black-and-white feathered chapeau.

Futrelle had the towering, burly build of a waterfront plug-ugly, but the kind, regular features of his round face, and the pince-nez eyeglasses his brown eyes nestled behind, gave him a professorial demeanor. Though a successful author, even a celebrity (the London press insisted on referring to him as "the American Conan Doyle"), Futrelle knew he was out of his league, financially speaking.

The boat train he and May were about to board would be carrying First-Class passengers to the brand-new dock built by and for the White Star Line at Southampton. He had booked Second-Class passage on the *Titanic*—it had been widely pub-licized that Second Class on this new luxury liner was designed to surpass First Class on the rival Cunard Line—but, somewhat mysteriously, had received First-Class tickets.

A note from J. Bruce Ismay himself—the son of the White Star Line's founder, and currently its managing director—had enigmatically stated only: *Please see me at your convenience, after boarding*, signed with *Regards—Bruce*. Regards from a man Futrelle had never met....

May, of course, had been delighted.

They had found the tickets waiting in their mail slot at the Savoy yesterday morning, and over a magnificent luncheon, May had sipped champagne and said, in a Georgia lilt that years of living in Massachusetts had done nothing to allay, "Perhaps Mr. Ismay knows it's your birthday."

And it had been Futrelle's birthday: his thirty-seventh. But Ismay was a stranger, and Futrelle, mystery writer that he was, viewed this unexpected, undeserved kindness with suspicion.

"We have a suite on C deck, darling," he told her. Born in Georgia, years of newspaper work up north had whittled his Southern accent away, leaving only the faintest hint. "Do you have any idea how much that costs?"

She shrugged, her features soft in the cool shadow of her wide-brimmed, large-domed, lilac-banded hat. "It's not costing us anything more than our Second-Class fare, is it?"

"Twenty-three hundred dollars."

Her blue eyes flared, then settled into their hooded, deceptively languid state in the smooth oval mask of her face. "Must you look every gift horse in the mouth, dear?"

"Everything has a reason," Futrelle said, nibbling an impossibly hard roll—the only food the British had mastered, in his opinion. "And nothing in life is free—particularly on the *Titanic*."

She reached across the fine-linen tablecloth to touch his hand with her gloved one. "You have a right to travel First-Class. You're Jacques Futrelle!"

"If you add 'the American Conan Doyle' to that, I'll..."

Her pretty mouth formed an insolent pucker, a kidding kiss. "Knock me into a cocked hat? My hat's cocked already, Jack.... Don't you think a second honeymoon would be fun?"

She was a pretty thing, and smart as a whip, too—probably smarter than he was, he'd always felt. Even now, in her mid-thirties, the mother of his two teenaged children, the former Lily May Peel was as beautiful as the day she'd stood beside him in her parents' home on Hilliard Street in Atlanta when the couple had said their vows.

But God help any man who married a Southern belle.

"Darling," he said, "traveling First-Class is not a privilege of celebrity. I may have achieved fame and success, but we are still resolutely a part of the middle class."

"The *prosperous* middle class."

"Undoubtedly. But not the wealthy upper class. You read the article in the *Times*—you saw the names of those who've booked First-Class passage on this monster ship."

She shrugged again, sipped her champagne. "We've never had any trouble fitting in with the high hats; you know that, dear. No one's more charming than my Jack."

He shook his head. "I'm just afraid this is Henry's work. He and René are traveling First-Class, you know—in point of fact, they're on C deck, themselves."

New York stage impresario Henry B. Harris and his wife Irene (René to her intimates) had been friends of the Futrelles for over ten years, dating to the period Jack had managed a repertory theater company.

"And what on earth is wrong with Henry giving you a birthday present?"

"Just because we're friends, he shouldn't make me beholden to him. That's the kind of kindness that has a business sting in its tail."

"What's wrong with that, Jack? He's been after you for years to write him a play."

"I'm not sure my work is suited for Broadway. There are precious few locked-room murders in *Naughty Marietta.*"

"You could do a mystery for him. Look how well Henry did with *The Third Degree.*"

May had a point, and doing a play for Henry was certainly not out of the question; but the puzzle of their elevation to First-Class status nagged at him.

Now they were waiting for the Harrises on the platform at Waterloo Station, that Victorian jumble of smoke-stained ancient buildings under an absurdly new steel-and-glass roof. Among millionaires British and American alike, he felt decidedly like a poor relation. A dozen men, divided between this boat train and the similar one departing from Paris to Cherbourg where the *Titanic* would make a brief stop, netted a total worth approaching $600 million.

Futrelle, on the other hand, at the conclusion of this European trip, was bringing home $30,000 in cash advances and contracts from publishers in Holland, Germany, France, Sweden and England. To the likes of John Jacob Astor or J. P. Morgan, this sum which seemed so grand to Futrelle would be pocket change.

Acting as his own agent, Futrelle had for a number of years been making regular trips overseas to maintain his contacts (and contracts) in European publishing. Many transatlantic travelers were the free-spending nomad rich with their endless retinue of maids and valets; others were captains of industry to whom North Atlantic crossings were business necessities. Futrelle liked to think of himself as belonging to this second group.

"Jack!"

The gruff voice was a familiar one, rising above the top hats and bowlers; but Futrelle at first did not place it.

Then, cutting a path through the crowd, the man who belonged to the voice revealed himself: in a long black topcoat with an appropriately military cut, and a black garrison cap, came the formidable form of Major Archibald Butt, a tall broad-shouldered figure in his mid-forties, trimly mustached, with dimpled, jutting jaw. Even out of uniform, he was the exemplar of the military man.

Archie's hand was extended as if he were charging with a saber. The Georgia-born major's Southern accent was gently intact: "Jack! Jack Futrelle, is it really you, old man?"

"It's me, all right." Futrelle shook the major's hand, and said, "Like you—older, fatter, no wiser. I don't believe you know my wife...."

Introductions were made and Archie, admiring May, said, "She's a lovely bride, Jack. How *did* you manage it?"

"No earthly explanation can cover it."

May was atypically speechless. Major Archibald Butt's household-name fame had nothing to do with wealth; he was the military aide to President Taft, and had been Roosevelt's aide-de-camp prior to that. Diplomat, soldier, novelist, Archie Butt moved in the highest circles, politically and socially.

Finally May managed, "Jack, you never mentioned that you knew Major Butt ... that you were friends...."

Futrelle, his arm around May, said, "Archie and I were coworkers at the *Atlanta Journal*, years ago, before you and I met … and before he traded journalism for the army … hell, man, should I be calling you Major Butt?"

"No, no … we'll not stand on formalities at this late date. I take it you're boarding this boat train, for the Southampton dock?"

"Yes. You're taking the *Titanic* as well?"

Archie nodded. "Heading home after a little mission to Rome for the president."

"Do tell! The Vatican?"

"Delivered a letter to the pontiff thanking him for creating those three American cardinals."

Futrelle laughed, shook his head; his friend had been pompous and puffed up with himself even before his celebrity. "To think I beat the pants in poker off such a high mucky-muck as you."

Blustery as he was, Archie could still take a jest. "Perhaps aboard the ship you'll have another opportunity—but I may have improved in the intervening years."

"I doubt it," Futrelle said.

May shot her husband a look for taking such liberties with so important a personage, unaware of the nights he and the major-to-be had closed down any number of Atlanta saloons.

Something about Archie did strike Futrelle as changed, however—of course, no one was impervious to the passage of time, but the weariness, the sadness in the eyes of the seemingly cheerful major did give Futrelle pause.

Through the crowd of swells another figure emerged, a distinguished-looking gentleman in a dark gray Chesterfield and top hat. In his middle sixties, his hair white, his generous mustache salt-and-pepper, he carried himself with an easy grace in contrast to the martinet movements of Archie Butt, whom he approached with a gentle smile.

"All the baggage is aboard, Major," he said in the cultured manner of an American who had spent considerable time in England. "Our compartment is ready."

"Frank," the major said, "I'd like you to meet Jack Futrelle and his lovely wife, May ... Jacques Futrelle, the detective writer, that is."

The major's traveling companion turned out to be Francis Millet, the celebrated painter. Futrelle told Millet how much he loved his famous painting *Between Two Fires*, a gently comic slice of life and love among the Puritans, and Millet praised "The Problem of Cell 13." May oohed and ahhed over the artist; though the Futrelles had traveled in circles of celebrity since their Gramercy Park days, during Jack's tenure on the *New York Herald*, May remained girlishly impressed by the famous.

"Oh, how we've enjoyed your paintings in the Metropolitan, Mr. Millet," she burbled. "And at the Tate Gallery, here in London!"

His smile was shy, his eyes twinkling with pleasure and embarrassment. "Call me Frank, please, Mrs. Futrelle."

"Only if you'll call me May."

As they stood chatting, a rather bizarre figure rolled through the crowd like a cannon on wheels, a figure so out of place in this posh company he seemed designed to make Futrelle feel more at home here: wearing a gray suit that seemingly had been slept in, a shapeless brown hat whose brim was as crooked as a beggar's smile, came a potbellied cross between a hobo and Saint Nick, with wild sky-blue eyes in a splotchy visage adorned with a full nest of snow-white beard that all but blotted out his string tie. He was probably in his mid-sixties, as was the rather ordinary, heavyset woman trailing along after him.

"My word," May breathed. "Who is that creature?"

"A colleague of mine, madam, unlikely as it may seem," the major said, "though we've never met."

"That's William T. Stead, dear," Futrelle told his wife. "One of the world's foremost eccentrics."

"I'm afraid I've never heard of him."

"Well," the major said, "you'll undoubtedly *hear* him on the ship—he's quite vociferous, one of the most notorious of the muckraking journalists of Britain, lately an outspoken pacifist, and a devoted spiritualist."

"What an outlandish combination of interests," May said.

Futrelle could see that his wife's initial unfavorable reaction to Dr. Stead's appearance had already been overcome by her native curiosity in the complex package that was this strange man, who the mystery writer knew to have been an influential, even pioneering newspaperman in his day.

But Futrelle was puzzled about something, even as he watched the burly bearded figure board the train, the elderly woman seeing him off. "And how is it that Mr. Stead is *your* colleague, Archie?"

"I understand the president has invited him to speak at the international peace conference, later this month in New York."

"Who else is appearing?" Millet asked dryly. "A trained bear?"

"Don't underestimate him, Frank," the major said to his friend. "He has an evangelical background—they say he's a mesmerizing speaker."

A diminutive figure, dapper in a single-breasted fine-striped sack suit and pearl-gray fedora, topcoat over one arm, swaggered up with a gold-topped walking stick and removed his hat, nodding to May. He had gone to some trouble to present a handsome appearance, an effort undercut by his narrow ferret's face, intense unblinking dark eyes and an oversize, overwaxed handlebar mustache.

"Good morning, Major," the ferret-faced man said in a voice as oily as his black hair. "Bit of breeze, carrying soot, I'm afraid."

"One never knows what rubbish a breeze will blow in," the major said. His eyes were tight.

"I was hoping you'd introduce me to your famous friend"— and the little man nodded to Futrelle—"the great author, Mr. Jacques Futrelle."

A smile twitched under Archie's mustache. "If you already know who he is, Mr. Crafton, why bother?"

The awkwardness of the situation—and such seemingly rude behavior coming from the supremely social Archie Butt (who, in a single hour at a reception given for members of the judiciary, had once introduced over a thousand guests to President Taft)—prompted Futrelle to act.

He stepped forward, presented his hand to the ferrety little man. "Jack Futrelle at your service, sir. And you are?"

He cleared his throat, touched his breast with a gray-gloved hand. "John Bertram Crafton, Mr. Futrelle. Traveling to the States on business." He had a crisply British accent, but just a hint of the lower class was in it, a Cockney in the woodpile. "We'll be fellow First-Class passengers on the *Titanic*. I hope you'll allow me to buy you a drink aboard ship."

"I think I could be tempted. This is my wife, May …"

As introductions were made, Archie glowered on; even the urbane Millet seemed made uneasy by Crafton's presence.

Finally, Crafton tipped his pearl-gray fedora, and strutted aboard the train, swinging his walking stick.

"Cocky little bastard," Futrelle said.

"Jack," May scolded; but her eyes agreed with him.

Archie's face was frozen in a scowl. "Stay away from him, Jack. He's a bad egg."

"Care to be more explicit, Archie?"

"No."

And it was left at that.

Soon, the major and Millet had boarded and the crowd on the platform was thinning out. The Harrises were late; but, then, they were theatrical people.

"Perhaps we should go ahead and board, dear," Futrelle was saying, when suddenly the remaining crowd parted like the Red Sea and the Harrises, in all their good-natured show-business vulgarity, made their entrance.

"Okay, okay, so we kept you waitin'!" Henry said, as the couple approached. "But you'd be out of business if there wasn't a little suspense in life, right, Jack?"

Henry—his red bow tie incongruously peeking out from under an Inverness cape that was an apparent London souvenir—was a big man with a big voice, the hair receding on a bucket head with bright dark beads of eyes barely separated by a prominent nose. His wife, René—that she used the masculine form of her first name betrayed her ignorance of French and a certain lack of breeding, which Futrelle found endearing—was comparatively petite, a dark-haired woman in her mid-thirties with a sunny disposition matching her yellow linen hip-length jacket, with its tan linen ankle-length flared skirt. Her cute features peeked out from under a pale green large-crowned felt hat, its wide brim turned jauntily down.

"You know, Henry," Futrelle said to his grinning unapologetic friend and his giggling wife, "some people think you're a loud overbearing Hebrew jackass ... but I stick up for you."

"No kiddin', Jack?"

"I say I don't find you all that loud."

Henry roared with laughter, hugged his friend in that theatrical manner Futrelle had long since come to accept, and René and May huddled together and moved toward the train, chattering about whatever women chattered about.

"How do you like my cape, Jack?" Henry asked, as they followed their wives onto the corridor train.

"You look like the Yiddish theater version of Sherlock Holmes."

"I might just bring a Sherlock Holmes play to Broadway, Jack, if you don't write something for me."

"You really think Victor Herbert wants to write a song for Professor Van Dusen to sing?"

"Stranger things have happened."

Shortly after boarding, they were caught behind a couple whose considerable retinue required the private compartments on either side of the aisle; the husband and wife were a handsome pair in their late twenties, Futrelle guessed, American or possibly Canadian, judging by their accents. A nanny carried a babe in arms and the mother held the hand of a beautiful little girl of three or four with eyes as blue as the light blue bow in her golden hair. A maid was with them, too, a plump pleasant woman in her twenties, helping them jockey the children and themselves into opposite compartments.

Like the little girl, the nanny had beautiful blue eyes, though a different shade, a dark blue that bordered on cobalt; the nanny would have been a stunning beauty—she had an hourglass figure wrapped up in her dowdy black livery—but her otherwise lovely features were distorted by a nose that had been rudely broken. She was like a follies girl with a prizefighter's proboscis.

Henry noticed Futrelle staring at the girl and whispered, "You've got better at home, Jack."

Futrelle glared at his friend, who despite his good nature apparently thought tact was something you put on the teacher's chair.

"I'm a writer," Futrelle whispered defensively. "I observe."

"Just as long as May doesn't observe you observin'," Henry said.

René looked back and said, "What are you two whispering about? Henry B.! Be good."

Then the family had managed to get themselves into their opposing compartments, and the two couples moved down the train corridor toward their own compartment.

They were nearly there when a door opened and a loud male voice from within said: "Out! We'll hear no more of this, sir! And kindly keep your distance in future!"

Then, shoved unceremoniously into the narrow corridor, there suddenly stood Archie Butt's acquaintance—the ferret-faced John Bertram Crafton, awkwardly snugging his fedora back on, and attempting to maintain his balance, and his dignity.

"You may wish to reconsider, Mr. Straus," he huffed. "I suggest you do."

Into the aisle, and into Crafton's face, came a bald, spade-bearded compact gentleman in his late sixties; his eyes were slits of fury behind pince-nez glasses not unlike Futrelle's own. The old gentleman wore a conservative, but expensive, dark suit and had a genteel manner, even under these circumstances.

"If you bother me aboard ship," the old boy said, "I'll report your conduct to Captain Smith. On a vessel as completely fitted out as the *Titanic*, I feel certain a brig has been included."

And the door slammed shut, leaving Crafton with the sudden realization that he was blocking the aisle—and that this exchange, the last part of it anyway, had been overheard.

Crafton smiled stiffly, tipped his hat to the ladies, and said to the men, "In business, emotions can run away. My apologies, ladies ... gentlemen. Good day."

And he disappeared down the aisle and into the next coach.

"Who is *that* character?" Henry wondered aloud.

"A disagreeable acquaintance of my old friend Major Butt," Futrelle said. "And that's about all I know of him ... except I believe the older gentleman may be Isidor Straus ... I noticed his name on the passenger list."

"Oh!" René said, as if she'd been pleasantly struck. "He owns Macy's department store! Let's get to know him, shall we, May? A friendship with Mr. Straus may lead to getting our fall fashions wholesale."

May laughed, as if René had been joking, though Futrelle was pretty sure she wasn't.

The compartment was upholstered in a deep blue gold-braided broadcloth, with lush mahogany woodwork, a nice promise of luxury to come. Futrelle and May settled into the comfortable cushioned seats and the Harrises took the opposite seating.

Promptly at nine-thirty the boat train rolled out of Waterloo Station, its chocolate-brown coaches pulled by a green locomotive, beginning an eighty-mile journey that gave the Americans a picturesque tour of the English countryside. Slate-roofed, red-brick town houses marked Surbiton, Woking and the rest, tidy rows of tidy structures each with its own back garden bursting with blossoms. The countryside was ablaze with color: daffodils, tulips and narcissus, brilliantly green hedgerows and flowering cherry trees, all flourishing in the April sunshine of a spring that had come early.

"We're tickled you decided to go First Class," Henry said, settling back. He had hung up the silly Inverness cape and his considerable girth was encased in brown tweed. "You know how these liners segregate the classes."

"I'm glad you two are willing to put up with riffraff like us," Futrelle said.

"We'll force ourselves," Henry said with a grin.

"This wasn't your doing, was it?"

"How so?"

May flashed a look his way, but Futrelle pressed on just the same: "You know, Henry, I do turn an honest dollar, now and then. I haven't been reduced to taking charity."

"What the hell are you talkin' about?"

Futrelle told him about the unexpected gift from Ismay.

"I had nothin' to do with that," Henry said with a dismissive wave. "But it doesn't sound like Ismay's style, either—I've been on White Star liners he was ridin' before, and he's one rude, arrogant son of a bitch ... pardon my French, ladies."

Soon the train was traveling through Surrey, domain of the landed gentry with their cottages of dressed fieldstone, half-timbering and thatch, where fields of grass and heather stretched endlessly, interrupted occasionally by clusters of birch, oak, spruce and beech.

"How did your trip go, Jack?" Henry asked. "Come back with some nice fat contracts for stories and books?"

"Be good, Henry B.," René scolded mildly. "It's none of your business. *Did* you, Jack?"

Futrelle chuckled. "I did very well, actually. I've contracts enough to hold me through the next year, easily … but I've had to revive my old nemesis."

"More 'Thinking Machine' stories?" Henry asked, eyes laughing. "I thought you'd sworn off that cranky old egghead— like Doyle dumping Holmes off that cliff."

Futrelle worked up half a smile. "Yes, but like Sherlock's papa, I'm afraid, Mammon tempted me back into the fray."

May said, "Jack's written six new 'Thinking Machine' stories on this trip—heaven help us if our steamer trunks are lost!"

"How about you, Henry?" Futrelle asked. "Find any British plays worth producing? Got your next *Lion and the Mouse* lined up?"

"I've got a couple honeys under option. But I'm branching out, Jack, into the future."

"What future would that be?"

"In my steamer trunk are a couple of tin cans that set me back ten thousand pounds."

"Tin cans?"

"Of motion-picture film, Jack—I've got Reinhart's *The Miracle* in kinemacolor! Just spoke with Oscar Hammerstein yesterday, and he's interested in going partners."

Futrelle made a face. "I'm not an admirer of the cinematograph. I believe in words not pictures."

"You sold *The Hidden Hand* for filming," René reminded him.

"Yes, and they butchered it."

After a while the landscape rolling by the boat-train window shifted from idyllic rural to harsh urban, sprouting not flowers but corrugated-iron factory roofs, the forests not trees but smokestacks of textile mills and steelworks. Much as he admired the captains of industry, like those on this train, Futrelle could not reconcile their capricious leisure with the quiet desperation of workers such as those who dwelled in the dingy rabbit warren of squalid red-brick row houses gliding by the window like an admonishing vision courtesy of one of Scrooge's ghosts.

Henry, with that good heart of his, must have felt a twinge himself, because he suggested they repair to the smoking car, where shortly Jack was lighting up a tailor-made Fatima from a gold-plated cigarette case and Harris a Cuban cigar.

"It's that unpleasant fellow again," Henry said, waving out a match, nodding toward a table by the window where indeed the ferrety Crafton was seated with none other than that great unmade bed of a man, William T. Stead. The two men had their heads together, Stead listening intently, frowning, Crafton whispering, his smile lifting the ends of the handlebar mustache into black angel wings.

"Not interested, sir!" Stead said suddenly.

Banter in the smoke-filled car fell to a hush, as the white-bearded, massively bellied Stead stood and berated his fellow passenger in a bellow.

"To the dogs with you, sir! The dogs!"

Embarrassed, Crafton smiled nervously, shrugging to the other men in the smoking car and nodding toward Stead, with an expression that encouraged their common knowledge that the old man was mad as a March hare.

Stead understood this patronizing gesture and grabbed Crafton by the front of his striped sack suit and lifted him from his chair like a naughty child.

"Fortunate for you, sir," Stead said, nose to nose with the frightened little man, "that I am a pacifist!"

And then Stead tossed him back onto the chair, storming out of the car, leaving a smoldering stogie and a chagrined Crafton behind.

"Fella seems to make friends everywhere he goes," Futrelle said to Henry.

"Maybe I should follow him around with a motion-picture camera," the producer said.

Soon they were back in the compartment with their wives. The train had begun its long downhill ride to Eastleigh, doing better than sixty miles per hour, shooting like a bullet through the hill tunnels of Hampshire Downs, past Winchester, into Southampton, sailing like a ship through Terminus Station and across Canute Road.

Finally, just before 11:30 A.M., the boat train moved down the side of Central Road and took a slow turn to the right onto the track flanking the platform built on the White Star Line's ocean dock. Nearby loomed the massive pair of long, narrow sheds, their corrugated steel painted green, where Second- and Third-Class passengers and cargo were processed.

But the boat train delivered its First-Class passengers dockside; they stepped out into the crisp sea air, where the port side of the giant ship towered before them, filling their sight like a vast cliff of steel.

May squeezed her husband's hand, craning her neck back, still not able to see the sky: just the freshly painted black hull and, straining, the gold-trimmed white band above. To left and right, the *Titanic* filled their eyes. Around them fellow passengers were swarming about the pier, parents struggling to keep track of children, porters and deckhands lugging luggage. But May seemed oblivious to this chaos, her attention seized by the Promethean vessel that was making scurrying ants of them all.

"Jack—it's endless...."

"Four blocks wide, dear. Eleven stories tall—not counting the four funnels. The literature says you could drive twin locomotives through one of those glorified smokestacks ... but who'd want to?"

"I can't even *see* the funnels...."

"Step back, just a little."

"There! There they are—they're golden, Jack! Oh, and there's the sky, at last."

Futrelle, overwhelmed by its looming enormity, was nonetheless impressed by the vessel's racing-craft-like sleekness.

"I think that's the way!" Henry Harris, a giddy René on his arm, was pointing to the gentle slope of a gangway that led to the main entrance on B deck. They trundled that direction.

"Shall we go aboard, dear?" May asked.

"Why not?" Futrelle responded.

TWO

A CLOSE CALL

INTO THE ENTRYWAY OF B deck, with its gleaming white walls and gleaming white linoleum, trooped the elegant army of First-Class passengers. They were met by a gaggle of ship's staff—the chief steward and his assorted minions, and the purser's clerk, who saw to it that tickets were quickly processed, names jotted in a ledger book, keys dispensed, directions to staterooms given, with smiles and courtesy and efficiency that boded well for a pleasant voyage to come.

In the entrance hall beyond, the opulence of the ship first made itself known to the Americans: gold-plated crystal teardrop light fixtures, polished oak paneling, gilt-framed landscapes in oil, Oriental carpet, horsehair sofas, silk lampshades, caneback chairs with red velvet cushions....

The abundance of it all assaulted their senses, stopping them in their tracks. May gasped, René began to laugh, and both women did pirouettes, looking all about with the wide, innocently greedy eyes of children in a lavishly stocked toy store.

To the right rose a magnificent marble staircase enclosed by a grand framework of wood sculpture, its carved walnut flowers running floor to ceiling, with exquisitely sculpted oak balustrades bearing wrought-iron and gilt-bronze scrollwork.

Henry put his hands on his hips and laughed. "And I thought *I* was a producer! This makes the *Lusitania* look like a garbage scow."

Futrelle was admiring a beautiful bronze cherub perched on a pedestal at the center of the foot of the flight of stairs. "Well, I heard White Star planned to leave speed to Cunard, and concentrate on luxury—apparently it wasn't just the bunkum."

Only the relative lowness of the ceilings in this reception area provided a hint that this was anything but the finest land-based hotel. Behind them, the next group of First-Class passengers was traipsing in, to be similarly bowled over by this opulence.

The two couples made their way around and down the staircase to C deck, and were soon padding along a wide, blue-carpeted, brass-railed white corridor on the port side of the ship, where other First-Class passengers were following the path to their staterooms, as well. Up ahead was that family from the boat train, the handsome couple with the lovely little golden-haired girl, shapely blunt-nosed nanny with babe in arms and plump maid. They had paused and the young husband was speaking to someone.

John Crafton.

"Is your friend making friends again?" Henry whispered, walking just behind Futrelle and May.

Actually, he seemed to be. Crafton's pearl-gray fedora was in his hands and he was smiling pleasantly, or at least as pleasantly as possible for him, and both the husband and the wife were returning the smile, with no apparent strain.

Only the nanny was frowning, and seemed nervous, but then again the baby in her arms was squirming and fussing.

As the Futrelles and Harrises approached where the little group clustered, blocking the way, Crafton noticed and said,

"We seem to be holding things up … I'm so pleased to have run into you, Mr. Allison, Mrs. Allison. Until later, then."

Crafton tipped his hat and—the Futrelles and Harrises standing aside for him—swaggered past, cane in hand, nodding and smiling as he did.

René twitched her nose. "Why does a smile from him make me crave a bath?"

This required no answer, and anyway, they were up even with that family, now.

"I'm afraid we always seem to be in the way," the young husband said, turning toward the two couples with an embarrassed grin. "I'm Hudson Allison, this is my wife Bess, our daughter Lorraine … Alice, there, has little Trevor."

Introductions were made all around, hands shaken (though of course the maid was not mentioned, and nanny Alice only that once in passing); but more passengers were coming up the corridor and the baby was crying, so further information, getting better acquainted, would have to wait. It was time for everyone to move on.

Heading aft, making a left turn down a hallway (for all its length, the ship wasn't all that wide—perhaps ninety feet), the Harrises finally found C83, their cabin. Before pushing on to find their own quarters, the Futrelles peeked in at the lovely little room with its graceful, even dainty Louis XVI styling, exemplified by walls of white-and-green-and-gold brocade with whitewashed waist-high walnut trim.

"Oh, René," May said. "It's simply beautiful!"

"Step inside, you two," René said.

A gilt-adorned carved walnut bed with silk-damask-upholstered head- and footboard dominated the room, that same upholstery carried to a plump sofa and a padded walnut armchair.

A basket of fresh flowers adorned a rosewood-and-walnut dressing table, and more flowers waited on the marble-topped mahogany nightstand. A small black fan was ceiling-mounted, perching like a big out-of-place bug in all this elegance.

"I guess our baggage will be delivered later," Harris said, taking in the posh little room with a big grin.

"Wrong again, Henry B.," René said—she'd been exploring. "Here it all is!"

In a spacious trunk closet, as if they'd materialized magically, were neatly stacked the array of steamer trunks and bags.

"Can all the rooms be this marvelous?" May wondered.

"Let's find out," Futrelle said, and to the Harrises added, "We'll probably head up on deck to take in the departure."

"We'll find you up there, or see you at luncheon," Henry said. René waved, saying, "Toodle-oo, you two!", and the Futrelles pressed on.

The numbering of the rooms was confusing and inconsistent, and by the time they found theirs—C67/68—the Futrelles were not far from where they'd started, the area near the C-deck entrance hall and the grand stairway.

"We're going in circles already," Futrelle said, working the key in the door, not sure if the size of this ship was to his liking.

But May's eyes glittered with girlish anticipation. "Let's see if our accommodations measure up to Henry and René's."

They did, and then some.

The Futrelles found themselves in a suite that made the Harrises' quarters seem like a plush closet: awash with the elegance of Louis Quinze stylings, the oak-paneled suite consisted of a sitting room adjoining a bedroom (off of which were both a bathroom and a steamer-trunk closet—their things, too, had been delivered). The carpeting was a deep blue broadloom.

"Oh Jack," May said, breathlessly. "This is too much...."

"The last time I saw a room like this," Futrelle said, "a velvet rope was keeping me back, and a tour guide was nudging me on."

The sitting room was almost cluttered with fine furnishings with their typical Quinze cabriolet legs and ebony wood—replete with rococo carvings, in a shell motif—and upholsteries of delicate shades of blue: a sinuously contoured sofa, a round table with a damask cloth, corner writing desk, assorted formal chairs. A large gilt-framed mirror leaned out over the white-and-gold sham fireplace with an ornate gold clock on the mantel; on either side of the mirror were windows—not portholes—blue-striped satin curtains gathered back for ocean views.

"How can I make myself at home in this showroom?" Futrelle asked May, thinking she was beside him, but she wasn't.

Glowing, she leaned out from the adjacent room. "Jack, come take a look at this bedroom—"

"Now this *is* starting to sound like a second honeymoon," he said, joining her, but she wasn't paying any attention to his flirtation. She was caught up in the grandeur of their sleeping quarters.

Ebony woods and the rococo shell motif continued, but shades of rose had taken over the fabrics, and the carpeting was a cream-and-rose floral that Futrelle hesitated to set foot on with his lowly shoes. Like a child in a flower garden, May flitted from furnishing to furnishing—mirrored dresser, table with lamp and chairs, pink-and-white striped chaise lounge—touching each as if to test its reality. A four-poster brass bed with plump pillows and pink quilted bedspread nestled to the right of the adjoining room's door.

"I wonder what we did to deserve this," Futrelle muttered, mostly to himself.

May was peeking in the bathroom, saying, "Before we go up on deck, I'd like to freshen up."

He checked his pocket watch. "We're supposed to shove off at noon—that's fifteen minutes from now."

A shrill ringing caught both their attentions.

Futrelle, frowning, turned in a half circle, as the ringing continued. "What the hell … is that some kind of ship's signal?"

"What do you think it is, silly?" She smirked prettily and pointed to the marbletop nightstand, and the telephone there, from which the ringing emanated. "Some detective you are."

"Telephones?" Futrelle said, going there, not sure whether he was impressed by the extravagance or offended by it. "The cabins on this ship have *telephones*? Amazing … Futrelle, here."

The voice in his ear said, "Mr. Futrelle, J. Bruce Ismay, chairman of the White Star Line."

Futrelle had to smile; as if Ismay needed to identify himself as such …

"Yes, Mr. Ismay. To what do I owe this pleasure? I refer to both this call, and this sumptuous suite we find ourselves in."

"The White Star Line believes that celebrities like yourself should travel in style. If you could spare me five minutes, in my suite, I can explain further, and properly welcome you to my ship."

May was already in the washroom.

"Certainly," Futrelle said. "Can I get there without a taxicab?"

Ismay laughed, once. "You'll find all the First-Class cabins and facilities on the *Titanic* are rather conveniently grouped together. I'm just a deck above you, sir—almost directly above you, in B52, 54 and 56."

"That's even one more number than we have."

Another laugh. "You know what they say about rank and its privileges. Can you come straightaway?"

"Delighted."

A minute later, more or less, Futrelle knocked once, at the door of Suite B52, and almost instantly, the door opened. Futrelle had expected a butler or valet to answer, but it was J. Bruce Ismay himself, a surprising figure, in several ways.

First, he wore a jaunty gray sporting outfit—Norfolk jacket, knickerbockers and heavy woolen hose—where Futrelle had expected something more pretentious of the man.

Second, Ismay was the rare human who towered over Futrelle, a man who himself had been described by one reporter as a "behemoth." Ismay topped six feet four, easily, although the narrow-shouldered man lacked Futrelle's massive build; in fact, he looked slight and soft, for as tall as he was.

But Ismay did cut a fine figure in his sports clothes: a handsome devil, in his late forties or early fifties Futrelle judged, trimly mustached, with bright dark eyes in a heart-shaped face, his healthy head of dark hair touched here and there with gentle gray.

In a tenor voice, confident and cutting, his host announced himself: "J. Bruce Ismay."

Somehow Ismay had resisted the urge to add: "Chairman of the White Star Line," and somehow Futrelle had resisted the smart-aleck urge to utter it, himself.

"Mr. Ismay," Futrelle said, with a little nod.

Ismay was extending his hand; and Futrelle took it, shook it—a firm enough grasp. "Bruce, please, call me Bruce."

"Jack Futrelle. Call me Jack."

"Do come in. I had hoped you'd bring your lovely wife along."

But of course Ismay hadn't mentioned to Futrelle that he should bring his wife; and Futrelle already had the firm idea that Ismay wasn't the sort for such an oversight—this was meant to be a private meeting between the two men, as the absence of any servant or secretary augured.

"May's settling in, in our suite, before we go up on deck for the waves and cheers."

"Mustn't miss that."

Ismay's sporting attire—apropos for the great ship's departure as it might be—seemed suddenly absurd in the ostentatious suite with its French Empire decor. If the Harrises' cabin had paled next to the Futrelles' stateroom, Ismay's suite of rooms reduced them both to shanties.

The parlor into which the two men had entered was white-painted oak with a beamed ceiling and built-in fireplace, an oblong gilt-framed mirror over its mantel. The mahogany and rosewood furnishings, sometimes ebony-punctuated, reflected the straight and curved, ponderous and heavy, construction of a style dictated by the Little Corporal himself: the Napoleonic paw and claw feet, the brass and ormolu mounts, carved winged griffins and pineapples. No sissy stripes or floral patterns adorned the rich, heavy upholstery: strictly royal blue, like the carpet and sofa, or deep red, like the gathered curtains on the windows that looked out not onto the ocean, but a private, enclosed promenade deck.

A door stood open onto a similarly grand bedroom, and a door in that room onto another.

"Impressive digs," Futrelle said. "Remind me to acquire some rank so I can get privileges like these … not that I'm complaining about my own accommodations, mind you."

"Sit, please," Ismay said, gesturing to a round, blue-damask-clothed table in the center of the parlor. Futrelle did, and Ismay, not sitting yet, asked, "Too early for a drink? Some lemonade, perhaps?"

"Nothing, thanks."

Ismay sat across from Futrelle, and smiled shyly, a smile Futrelle didn't fully believe. "Normally I wouldn't travel in such a highfalutin fashion ... not on my company's dollar, at any rate." Ismay gestured about him. "This parlor suite was reserved for Mr. Morgan, but he took ill at the last moment ... so why let it sit empty?"

By "Mr. Morgan," Futrelle took that to mean American financier J. Pierpont Morgan, the *Titanic*'s titanically wealthy owner, the man who'd acquired the White Star Line from the Ismays a decade before.

"Actually," Ismay said, a smile lifting his mustache, "you and Mrs. Futrelle are in *my* suite."

"So we benefited from Mr. Morgan's illness as well. But why did you choose us with whom to be so generous, Mr. Ismay?"

"Bruce! Please."

"Sorry—Bruce. Or should I say Saint Nick?"

He smiled again, shrugged. "As I indicated on the phone, we like our celebrity passengers to travel in style. You'd be wasted in Second Class."

"Wasted how?"

Ismay folded his hands, shifted in his cushioned chair; his expression shifted, too: serious, businesslike. "This is the *Titanic*'s maiden voyage ..."

This was news on the order of learning that Ismay was chairman of the White Star Line.

"… and it's important to us that our First-Class passenger list resembles the audience at a gala theater opening … I'm sure your friend Mr. Harris would understand the importance of salting notables among that first-night crowd."

"Well, obviously, I'm happy to offer whatever small prestige my presence might provide. But I think you rather exaggerate my importance."

"Not at all. We have a number of authors aboard, but none of your stature, your popularity, on both sides of the Atlantic. My understanding is that your books sell just as well in England as in the United States."

"Perhaps a little better," Futrelle admitted.

His eyes tightened. "This is … if I may be frank, knowing that you will be discreet … a somewhat troubled first crossing for us."

Now Futrelle shifted in his chair. "How so?"

"Oh, oh, it's nothing to trouble yourself over … from the standpoint of technology, this is the safest ship on the ocean, the finest achievement shipbuilding has yet realized." He frowned, shook his head. "But this recent coal strike has thrown a veritable wrench in the works … other transatlantic lines have idled their vessels—thousands of crew members, dockworkers, are out of work. We even had to cancel crossings for a number of our other ships."

"I know," Futrelle said. "When we decided to come home a trifle early from our European tour, the *Titanic* was really our only option."

"Well, we transferred bookings from half a dozen of our other liners onto the *Titanic*, and without this tactic, frankly, we'd have been embarrassingly underbooked for our maiden voyage. Even so, we're only 46 percent of capacity in First Class and 40 percent in Second Class ... though steerage is 70 percent capacity." He chucked dryly, adding, "Finding poor people who want to go to America is never much of a problem."

"This is a stumper." Futrelle adjusted his glasses on the bridge of his nose. "The maiden voyage of the world's largest liner—that should have attracted ticket buyers like bees to honey."

"Oh, we've a respectable booking, but the damned strike's damaged the entire shipping industry ... with cancellations and postponements making travel so unpredictable, leaving passengers stranded, bewildered, disenchanted.... People just aren't traveling at this particular time, a time which is so crucial to us with the launching of this ship."

"You may have been up against another problem, Mr. Ismay—Bruce."

"Yes? What would that be?"

"Fear." Futrelle raised an eyebrow. "Aren't there those who feel that your 'monster ship' is simply too big to float?"

Ismay sighed. "Unfortunately, Jack, you're right—though that's such sheer poppycock it barely merits a response. This ship is the last word in modern efficiency, every expert considers it literally unsinkable. It's utter ignorance, and the pity is, it's not just coming from the great unwashed, but from intelligent, educated people, as well."

"And what can be done about that?"

He leaned forward. "Reeducation. This is where you could be of service to the White Star Line, Jack."

Futrelle sat back. "To repay my luxury suite, you mean?"

"No. There are no strings attached to that, other than the right to inscribe you upon our glittering First-Class passenger list. But I understand you and Mrs. Futrelle make at least one European crossing, annually ..."

Futrelle nodded, folded his arms. "It's the nature of my business. You indicated yourself, I have a following on your side of the pond."

"Exactly. How would you like to have free annual passage on any White Star liner, a permanent open ticket—First Class?"

"Is that a rhetorical question?"

"Not at all. It's a business proposition, actually."

"How so?"

"Mr. Futrelle—Jack ... if you could concoct a novel, with the *Titanic* as its setting ... a mystery ... an adventurous romance ... detailing the lovely surroundings, the fine cuisine ..."

"I'm not an advertising writer, sir."

Ismay held up his hands, palms out, as if Futrelle were a highwayman he was facing. "Please! I don't mean to offend you. But isn't a vivid, intriguing setting for his story something any good writer of popular fiction strives to achieve?"

"Yes, of course ..."

Ismay shrugged again, risked a small smile. "Well, then. The White Star Line would simply like to see you use our magnificent ship as the backdrop for your next exciting novel."

"Bruce ... Mr. Ismay. Frankly, what you suggest strikes me at first blow as distasteful ... and yet I admit I really can't see a reason not to at least consider your suggestion."

"Good!" He leaped to his feet, quick as a jack-in-the-box; this response from Futrelle was apparently enough for Ismay to consider this phase of the negotiations closed. "Your consideration is all I ask, at this point."

Almost reeling from the suddenness of this, Futrelle rose, and Ismay cheerfully took his elbow and led him to the door. "... Now, in the meantime, please enjoy your voyage. I've arranged for you and Mrs. Futrelle to sit at the captain's table, tomorrow evening—that should be a nice way to start off our first evening out at sea."

"Well, uh … thank you, Bruce. I know my wife will be pleased."

Ismay opened the door. "Ah, I only wish I could have brought Florence and the children along, this time. They came aboard this morning, for a tour of the ship…. You should have seen my Tom, George and Evelyn, running up and down the private promenade."

"I have a girl and a boy, both teenagers," Futrelle said politely.

"I'm always at your service," Ismay said, and shut the door.

And Futrelle stood staring at the portal to B52 for a few moments, and was bemusedly heading back down to his own stateroom, wondering whether he should tell his wife about Ismay's slightly unpalatable offer, when he noticed another passenger in the corridor.

Swinging his cane, pearl-gray fedora cocked to one side, John Bertram Crafton was coming Futrelle's way.

"Mr. Crafton," Futrelle said. "We meet again."

Crafton, without pausing, nodded, touching his hat, saying, "We'll have a chance to get better acquainted soon, Mr. Futrelle, I assure you."

Futrelle kept walking, but glanced back, and hell and damnation, if Crafton hadn't stopped at Ismay's door—where he was knocking!

The little scoundrel did get around.

As departure time approached, Futrelle and his wife were among many other First-Class passengers making their way to the uppermost deck of the ship, the boat deck. There they stood at the rail near a davit-slung lifeboat and looked down at the crowd of citizens, from Southampton mostly, who appeared tiny indeed with the massive White Star sheds looming behind them and gigantic loading cranes towering above them—yet both the sheds and cranes were dwarfed by the *Titanic*.

At the stroke of noon, a measured, deafening blast from the full-throated, triple-toned *Titanic* steam whistle announced imminent departure. May pointed down and Futrelle's eyes followed: like the drawbridge of a castle, the gangway was raising, to the frustration of what appeared to be a clutch of tardy, frustrated crewmen, literally missing the boat.

Another deafening blast from the steam whistle, and the immense mooring ropes that held the ship to the pier went splashing into the water, to be drawn quickly ashore by dockworkers. Rude little snorts from the horns of the tugboats moving into position made an almost comical contrast with the hollow power of the *Titanic*'s steam whistle.

From elsewhere on deck—Futrelle couldn't be sure, exactly—a small orchestra was playing selections from the operetta *The Chocolate Soldier*, only to be momentarily drowned out by the final blast of the steam whistle, announcing that, finally, the great ship was in motion, easing gently, quietly from her berth, not under her own steam as yet, but propelled by those half a dozen tugs.

The unseen orchestra was playing "Britannia Rules the Waves" now, while everyone on the boat deck waved down to the strangers below, who waved back, hankies fluttering; some of the passengers, May among them, cast flowers into the water. As the massive liner began to slide from the dock, the crowd down there ran alongside, keeping pace, shouting farewells, cheering.

"Oh Jack," May said, her face aglow, eyes glittering with happiness, "it's all so exciting!"

And it was—there was an epic sweep to it, the mammoth ship, the crowd waving from the dock, the orchestra playing, the pungent smell of burning coal, the billowing of smoke from the stacks of the tugs pulling, pushing, prodding the so-much-bigger ship out of the dock area.

It was a storybook departure, until—expertly maneuvered into the channel in a turn to port by the tugboats, who then cast off—the *Titanic* gave a faint tremor, telling the more seasoned passengers that the great ship was at last getting way under her own power, however tentatively. Moving at a modest six knots, the liner steamed past two ships—the White Star Line's *Oceanic* and a smaller American ship, the *New York*, moored at the quay, two of the liners put out of commission by Ismay's coal strike.

The side-by-side mooring of these ships made a narrow channel more narrow; the quayside was lined with spectators, and still more people leaned at the rail on the deck of the *New York*, where they had boarded to get a good look at the greatest ship in the world as she started her maiden voyage, gawking and waving at the *Titanic*'s lucky passengers from a mere eighty feet away.

"I don't like this," Futrelle said, standing back from the rail.

May, who was returning waves to the spectators on the *New York* deck, asked, "Why? What's wrong, dear?"

"The way those liners are bobbing," he said, nodding toward what he was talking about. "This big ship of ours is displacing too much water ... causing too much turbulence...."

"Oh dear, I'm sure the captain knows what he's doing ..."

What might have been a gunshot cracked the air. Then another sharp crack!

And four more reports, as if every chamber of a six-gun had been emptied into the sky.

"Jack!"

The *New York*'s massive metal mooring ropes had snapped like cheap shoelaces.

Futrelle put his arm around his wife and held her close. "It'll be fine, darling ... don't worry...."

The metal ropes arced and coiled in the air like lasso tricks gone awry, sending spectators scurrying and shrieking, quayside. On the deck of the *New York*, the people who'd boarded for a better look were scattering and screaming, quickly abandoning ship, or trying to.

And on the boat deck of the *Titanic*, the clanging of bells from the bridge providing accompaniment, counterpointed by the sirens of tugboats rushing to attempt rescue, the passengers were frozen in disbelief—no screams, just occasional gasps and outcries, as couples (like the Futrelles) embraced, witnessing the *New York*, loose now, begin to swing, like an awful gate, stern first, toward the *Titanic*.

Ismay's assertion that his ship was unsinkable seemed about to get an early test.

The *Titanic* picked up speed, slightly, and her wake seemed to push the smaller ship back, but as close as the *New York* was, this didn't seem to be enough; the bigger ship moved forward, and the smaller ship swung toward it, stern toward stern....

Agonizing seconds that seemed like minutes dragged by, as the two ships seemed about to touch, and as the passengers braced for the screech of steel, hugging each other desperately ...

... the stern of the *New York* missed the *Titanic*'s stern by inches.

Around the boat deck, sighs of relief and some laughter and even some applause and cheers floated through the air, aural confetti being tossed; and the orchestra began to play a catchy ditty that Futrelle later learned was "The White Star March."

In the meantime, the *New York* was still drifting free; however, the tugboats were steaming into position to take care of that, and the *Titanic* was coming to a premature stop, till all this could be sorted out.

"You're right, dear," Futrelle said.

May looked at him, relieved but dazed. "Pardon?"

"This *is* exciting."

She smirked and hugged him, but Futrelle—writer of suspense that he was—could not shake a sense of foreboding. This near miss—actually, it was a near hit, wasn't it?—was an inauspicious start for such a grand voyage.

On the other hand, if he ever wrote that *Titanic* mystery for Ismay, he had a hell of a first chapter, didn't he?

THREE

SUNSET OVER CHERBOURG

SUN SPILLED LIKE MELTED BUTTER onto the boat deck, but top-coats were needed. The nip in the air came as a shock, though Futrelle—typically bareheaded—found it bracing, and May, swaddled in her black beaver coat, wanted to take advantage of the nice spring day, since the weather would only grow colder as they crossed the North Atlantic.

During the hour's delay caused by the incident with the *New York*, the First-Class passengers had been summoned to luncheon by the ship's bugler, who passed from deck to deck playing the White Star's traditional call to luncheon, "The Roast Beef of Old England." To American ears, it was like a cavalry charge.

Shortly after, D deck's elegant First-Class Dining Saloon—its patrons looking decidedly underdressed in their departure attire in the massive white wedding cake of a room—had served up orchestra selections from *The Merry Widow* and a sumptuous buffet. May warned her husband not to overdo—the evening meal was reserved for that purpose—and Futrelle had passed up the exotic likes of corned ox tongue and galantine of chicken for some rare roast beef of old England (not wanting to disappoint the ship's bugler).

Conversation in the Dining Saloon ran largely to talk of the *New York* incident, and of course introductions—the Futrelles sat with the Harrises and two of the latter's Broadway investors, Emil Brandeis from Omaha, department-store magnate, and John Baumann from New York, a rubber importer. Rounding out the table for eight was the dignified old couple, Isidor and Ida Straus.

These were the assigned tablemates for all meals in the First-Class dining room (though the Futrelles would be guests at the captain's table tomorrow evening), and it was no accident that these passengers—but for the Harrises' traveling companions, the Futrelles—were all Jewish (though only the Strauses ordered the special kosher meals made available).

"That was a close call," Brandeis had said, referring to the *New York*. He was a pleasant heavyset fifty with a walrus mustache and healthy appetite.

"I was impressed by how skillfully Captain Smith averted disaster," Baumann said, touching a napkin to tender lips. He was a lean, bright-eyed, clean-shaven thirty.

"I agree with you," Futrelle said, "but I'd be more impressed if they'd anticipated the problem."

"How so?" Baumann asked.

"I fear it's a sobering indication that no one's quite sure what a ship this size can do."

"It wasn't so long ago," Mr. Straus said in his softly resonant voice, raising a glass of red wine near his lips, "that Ida and I took passage on the *New York*'s maiden voyage."

"The last word in shipbuilding, it was, they said," Mrs. Straus added. She had lovely dark blue eyes in a smooth kindly face whose matronly beauty was accentuated by the backward sweep of her still mostly dark hair into a bun. Both the

Strauses were conservatively dressed, but—witness Mr. Straus's golden-brown silk tie and Mrs. Straus's dark blue silk and lace shirtwaist—expensively.

"Did I tell you about that mysterious stranger who accosted me?" René asked suddenly.

"Did some man bother you?" Henry said, looking up sharply from his veal-and-ham pie.

Henry's concern might have been a bothersome insect, the way René waved him off, continuing her tale in wide-eyed animated fashion: "Shortly after the incident, when we were coming down off the boat deck, still in a state of shock, a stranger ... tall, with a trim mustache, and piercing dark eyes ... you'd have hired him at once as a leading man, Henry B.... asked me, 'Do you love life?'"

"My goodness!" Ida Straus said, cutting her corned beef.

May's laugh was a tiny squeal. "And what did *you* say?"

Henry was frowning.

René giggled. "Well, of course I said, 'Yes, I love life.' And do you know what he said then?"

"Go ahead and tell us," Futrelle said. "I can't stand suspense unless I'm dispensing it."

"He said, 'That was a bad omen. There's death on this ship. Get off at Cherbourg—if we get that far. That's what *I'm* going to do!'"

Everyone laughed at this melodramatic story, if uneasily.

"Superstition is the enemy of any thinking man," Mr. Straus reminded them.

"Well, I'd feel better about this trip," May said, daintily cutting her fillet of brill, "if Jack hadn't just finished a tale with a great ship sinking in it!"

"Is that right, Jack?" Henry asked.

"I write about a lot of things," Futrelle said with a shrug, and sipped his iced tea.

"It's his new novel," May said. *"My Lady's Garter—The Saturday Evening Post* has taken serial rights, already."

"Let's not boast, May," Futrelle said, spearing a piece of rare roast beef.

"Will it make a good play, Jack?" Henry asked.

"Don't change the subject, Henry B.," his wife said. "I just want to know if Jack here has psychic abilities."

Over his soused herring, Mr. Straus was studying Futrelle with keen interest, but then everyone at the table had their eyes on him.

"I'm probably no more prescient than any writer," Futrelle said. "I think all of us who write fiction tap into something, if not mystical, certainly akin to the dream state."

Young Baumann, so fascinated with this he'd completely forgotten his grilled mutton chops, asked, "Have you ever made up a story and had it come true?"

Nodding emphatically, May said, "One of the first stories he ever published! Based on the notorious suitcase murder in Boston ..."

"I read about that," Brandeis said, pointing with a knife. "Grisly affair...."

"Don't ask for details over luncheon," Futrelle said, with a smile, but meaning it.

"Sound thinking," Straus said, saluting Futrelle with his wineglass.

May rattled on: "Jack solved the case, completely, weeks before the police, who were holding an innocent man."

"Do tell!" René said. "Jack, how did you do it?"

"No crystal ball—simply logic. Applied criminology."

"Sound thinking indeed," Mr. Straus said.

Henry whispered, "Better not let old man Stead hear them callin' you a psychic, Jack—he'll recruit you for one of his séances."

Two tables over, the white-bearded old boy was hunkered over a huge plate of food, shoveling the fine fare in like so much coal, while his stunned tablemates did their best to avert their offended eyes.

"They say he's half-mad, half genius," Futrelle said.

"Well, he's an entire slob," May said.

May's frank comment elicited an outburst of laughter from all at the table, though Mrs. Straus seemed somewhat embarrassed.

Young Baumann asked, "Would a spiritualist like Stead call a rocky start like this a bad omen? Could we be on an unlucky ship?"

"No, I'd say the odds are in our favor, John," Harris told the importer. "We've already had our accident—whoever heard of a ship havin' two in one trip?"

Sometime during luncheon, the ship's three giant propellers had begun to churn and the *Titanic* set out on the channel crossing, bound for Cherbourg, France. But the diners had been unaware that their voyage was finally under way, so subtle was the motion of the ship and the sound of its mighty engines.

Futrelle and May didn't realize the boat was moving until they were outside, having taken one of the trio of electric elevators ("lifts," in the ship's British terminology)—lavishly paneled in exotic bird's-eye curly maple—up to A deck. They walked up the stairs and out onto the boat deck, where a brisk breeze ruffled the writer's hair and the black and white feathers of his wife's chapeau.

Off starboard the high chalk cliffs of St. Catherine's Bay, the last landmark of the Isle of Wight, were receding into memory.

Futrelle, noting the curving wake of the ship, said, "The captain must be testing his compasses, shaking his ship down after that near collision."

"How's that, dear?"

"He's steering quite the irregular course—S-turns and other maneuvers, trying to get the feel of handling this barge, I'd say."

"Jack, how can you call this lovely ship a barge?"

"Because *that's* a ship," Futrelle said, pointing portside, where a gloriously old-fashioned three-masted schooner with its sails and lines was pitching and rolling, water breaking over her bow. "Probably heading for the West Indies ..."

May hugged her husband, cherishing the romance of that thought. "I never knew the water was so rough, today."

"It isn't. We're stirring up that chop. That schooner'll be fine when we're out of her hair.... Shall we try out the enclosed promenade, before this wind knocks us off our high perch?"

May nodded, and they crossed to port and took a steep flight of metal stairs down into the enclosed First-Class promenade, moving aft down the unadorned deck, their feet echoing off the wood. Navy-blue-jacketed, jauntily capped White Star stewards were setting up the varnished folding wooden deck chairs against the gleaming white walls; the smell of fresh paint mingled with fresh sea air. The deck was fairly deserted, most of the passengers taking advantage of after-luncheon ship tours the purser's office had offered.

Soon they were at the point where the windows of the enclosed promenade stopped and the open promenade began, though steel-beam window frames and a cable for canvas shades would allow this section to be enclosed as well. Fresh salty breeze streamed in, and golden sunshine, while white-touched rippling blue water stretched to forever; it was one of those moments any couple treasures, when the world seems vast and lovely and theirs alone.

The promenade emptied onto the aft end of A deck, where massive cargo-loading cranes bookended the main mast. This small portion of open deck, with its benches and railings ideal for open-air lounging, was unusual in that the First-Class passengers were literally looked down upon by Second-Class passengers, from the railing along the end of their promenade portion of the boat deck.

The Verandah Café was directly under that portion of the boat deck, its sliding glass doors open.

"Is it chilly enough for some coffee?" Futrelle asked his wife, and she nodded.

But when they peeked into the airy café, with its white wicker furniture and ivy-trellised walls, it seemed to have been taken over as an unofficial playroom by nannies and children.

"Or maybe not," Futrelle said, and May smiled and agreed.

Among the tikes scurrying about was the golden-haired Lorraine Allison, while her nanny Alice in black livery sat nearby at a white wicker table, her male infant charge gurgling and capering on his back on a blanket at her feet. Sitting next to the shapely woman with the broken nose was a ship's steward, a towheaded young man in his early twenties, spiffy in his white jacket with its gold buttons, his black tie matching his trousers.

Alice and the steward were smiling shyly, talking the same way, accompanied by some batting of female eyelashes and the steward turning his cap in his hands.

"Shipboard romance?" Futrelle whispered to May.

"Why not?" May asked. "She has a nice smile."

"Almost makes up for the snout."

His wife slapped his arm playfully, and they moved to the bench along the railing.

Futrelle was gazing out at the smooth waters when May nudged him, saying, "I thought your friend was traveling First-Class."

"What friend?" Futrelle asked, turning, looking up at the Second-Class passengers lining the boat-deck railing.

And there he was, the ubiquitous John Bertram Crafton, up at the railing, speaking to a rather handsome, bareheaded black-haired man whose thick though well-trimmed mustache curled up in the continental manner.

In a gray topcoat and a brown suit that were not inexpensive, the black-haired man stood between two young boys in sailor suits and knickers, his boys apparently, one lad two or three, the other three or four, with full heads of hair with which the wind was playing havoc. He had an arm around either boy, holding them to him, protectively, eyeing Crafton—who leaned forward with the skin-crawling smile of a rake selling French postcards—regarding the ferrety little man with suspicion and even scorn.

Futrelle heard neither Crafton's words, nor the black-haired man's response.

But the pantomime they acted out indicated a response that was incensed to say the least, and apparently included enough blasphemies to justify the apparent father to draw his boys closer to him and cover their ears with his hands and the press of his body.

The emotion of the black-haired man was palpable, and so was his disgust for Crafton: his eyes flared, his face reddened, his body trembled, though his head was held high.

Whirling, his gray topcoat spreading like a cloak, the black-haired man gathered the boys and receded onto the Second-Class boat-deck promenade, out of view.

Crafton took the rejection in stride; he sighed, shrugged to himself, and then he noticed Futrelle below, looking up.

Crafton called out: "Beautiful day at sea, Mr. Futrelle, don't you agree?"

Futrelle stepped closer, until he was directly below the ferrety little man in the pearl-gray fedora. "Some of us are more at sea than others."

He shrugged again. "Mr. Hoffman is emotional—you know how Frenchmen are."

Futrelle wasn't sure he did know how Frenchmen were; but he did know they weren't often named "Hoffman."

"Are those his boys?" Futrelle asked.

"Oh yes. He does love his Lolo and Momon. He loves them more than anything."

"And how is it, Mr. Crafton, that such a First-Class individual as you finds himself in Second Class?"

The ship was strictly segregated—the First Class was no more allowed in Second or Third than vice versa.

"Just slumming, Mr. Futrelle. I wonder—could you find some time for me? Just a few short minutes? I have a business proposition."

"What sort of business, Mr. Crafton? Are you a publisher?"

"One of my interests is publishing, yes. Could I have just five minutes? No more, perhaps less."

May had come up next to her husband; he glanced at her, and she was frowning, shaking her head, no, almost imperceptibly.

"All right," Futrelle said.

May sighed.

Crafton called down: "Shall we say the A-deck balcony in
… ten minutes? Would that be agreeable?"

"I'll be there, Mr. Crafton. Then we'll see how agreeable it is."

Crafton tipped his fedora and withdrew.

May said, "Why are you giving that awful little man the
time of day?"

"He's been making people angry all day," Futrelle said. "Why
should I deny myself that pleasure?"

"You've seen how people react to his 'business propositions,'
whatever they are. He's obviously an odious creature."

"I know. I'm just eager to find out how, exactly."

Futrelle and May walked down the portside promenade,
and he used the few minutes before his appointment to tell his
wife about the offer Ismay had made.

"Well, I think it's a wonderful idea," she said, as they walked
arm in arm.

"You don't find it the least bit … base? Using the pages of a
novel to advertise Mr. Ismay's ship?"

"It would make a wonderful setting for an adventure story
… maybe something about a jewel thief, perhaps international
intrigue.…"

"He's suggesting I use my fiction to advertise his product!"

"You sell stories to magazines all the time, and newspapers—
and the editors pepper ads all around your tales, don't they?"

"But you can tell where the story ends and the ad begins."

"Don't be stuffy, Jack. We could write it together."

He and May had collaborated on one "Thinking Machine"
short story, and it had been successful enough, appearing in
Sunday supplements all across America. And May had published
her first novel, *A Secretary of Frivolous Affairs*, last year, and it
had sold well in both England and America.

"We *have* been looking for the right idea to do together, as a novel," he admitted.

"Well, then," she said brightly, "let's at least consider this one. We don't need to give Mr. Ismay an answer just yet—but as we enjoy ourselves on this wonderful ship, we'll just keep a keen writer's eye on the possibilities it presents."

They entered the A-deck reception area, where natural light was filtering down through an immense domed skylight, a marvel of wrought-iron scrollwork and white-enameled glass with a crystal chandelier at its center. This sifted sunlight reflected off the polished oak-wall paneling and the gilt-decorated wrought-iron balustrades of the balcony and Grand Staircase, giving the room a glow at once romantic and ghostly.

Futrelle walked May to the electric lifts behind the staircase, saying, "I'll join you in our stateroom in just a few minutes."

"Now, Jack, don't you strike that blackguard," she said, her expression stern.

Then just as the lift steward was closing the cage door, she added, "Unless he deserves it."

Patting the fanny of the cherub perched at the pedestal at the foot of the middle handrail, Futrelle jogged up the wide marble stairway. He paused on the landing to admire the intricate wood sculpture of the central panel bearing a round Roman-numeral clock, on either side of which leaned a nymph—classical figures carved there by an artisan of unimaginable skill: Honor and Glory crowning Time.

Not the most fitting sentiment to carry into a meeting with John Bertram Crafton, he would guess; the stairs forked right and left, and he went right, because Crafton was standing up there, leaning against the railing.

"How good of you to meet with me," Crafton said as Futrelle joined him on the balcony. A pair of overstuffed chairs and a small table waited by a window that would have looked out onto the boat deck had its glass not been cathedral gray. Swinging his gold-tipped walking stick, Crafton strode there and Futrelle followed, their heels echoing off the fancy cream-colored tile.

"I wanted to find out what makes you so popular," Futrelle said, settling into his chair.

Crafton's smiled lifted a corner of his waxy mustache. "Your sarcasm is not lost on me, sir."

"Why should it be? It's about as subtle as your approach."

Crafton shrugged, began removing his gray gloves, finger at a time; he had set his fedora upside down on the table and filled it with the gloves. "I understand that the service I provide is an ... unsavory one ... destined to make me less than anyone's favorite among their acquaintances."

"Well, don't be proud of it."

His smile lifted both sides of the mustache. "Why not? I have a job to do, a service to perform shall we say, and I do it well. The patient never likes hearing bad news from the physician ... but without knowledge, what are we?"

"Ignorant."

"Precisely. A doctor properly diagnoses a patient, and a favorable prognosis is then possible—*treatment* of the problem.... Wouldn't you agree, sir?"

"Why do I think it unlikely you're a doctor, Mr. Crafton? Unless you perform certain back-alley operations that polite society frowns upon while still finding necessary."

One eyebrow arched. "You mean to insult me—though why you should feel any enmity toward me is a mystery ..."

"That's my line of work—mysteries."

"… I admit there's some truth in what you say. Without the abortionist—let us not mince words, sir, you and I—how many lives, prominent young lives, might be ruined?"

"Well," Futrelle said, patting his stomach, "I may look like I'm in need of an abortion, but I assure you I don't. I'm merely well fed."

Crafton chuckled. "You are a successful man—a noted author.…"

"That's perhaps too generous, sir. I'm a newspaperman who writes popular fiction. Fortunately for me, there's an audience for my foolish tales."

"And we both want that audience to remain steadfastly in your camp, don't you agree?"

"It's blackmail, isn't it?"

The dark eyes flared; the ratlike nostrils, too. "What? Sir— please, I beg you not make rash accusa—"

"Shut up. It's a dangerous game, Mr. Crafton, in company like this. There are powerful men, on this boat—the likes of Major Butt can snap his fingers and you would be nothing more than just an oily little memory … a memory no one will care to cling to, either."

The ferrety face seemed to lengthen into a sinister blankness. "You leave me no choice, but to be blunt."

Futrelle leaned back with a grin, arms casually folded. "What the hell do you think you have on me? I love my wife dearly and would sooner cut off my manhood than philander. My business dealings are aboveboard, and all of my children legitimate."

Crafton's mustache twitched. "I represent a group of investigators."

"What, Pinkertons?"

"Not precisely, Mr. Futrelle. What this group does—both in England and America—is provide a valuable service."

"Valuable."

"Very. They thoroughly investigate the background of a prominent individual like yourself, and in order to *prevent* blackmail, do their best to discover whatever might be ... worth discovering."

"We're back to doctors again. Preventative medicine."

Crafton nodded curtly. "Only by finding out for you, our client, what skeletons in the closet might exist, of a sort that could be discovered by less scrupulous individuals than ourselves, can we protect you—our client."

"Only you do that investigating beforehand—before someone like me is officially a 'client'... just as a time-saving measure?"

"That's well said ... but then, words are your business."

"What happens if a client isn't interested?"

Crafton's expression darkened. "Then we can't protect you. The ... sensitive information might fall into the hands of the sensationalist press, or be placed before business associates, or business rivals, or in some instances law-enforcement authorities.... The consequences could be serious, and unfortunate ... even grave."

"That would make a bully idea for you, Crafton—a grave."

He shrugged. "I'm quite immune to threats, Mr. Futrelle ... though I suppose coming from a man like you, I should take them seriously."

"A man like me?"

"A man with your ... mental aberrations."

Futrelle laughed and it echoed across the balcony and down the marble-and-oak staircase. "Is that what you think you have?"

Crafton leaned forward, his walking stick between his legs, his hands resting on its gold crown. "Mr. Futrelle, in 1899, you suffered a complete mental breakdown. You were unable to continue in your position at the *New York Herald* and were hospitalized. Shortly thereafter you sent your children away, to their grandmother, and your wife and various doctors attended to your needs, in private...."

Very quietly, as if he were speaking to a small child, Futrelle said, "I was the telegraph editor at the *Herald* during the Spanish-American War ... from Manila Bay to San Juan Hill, the news flowed in constantly. I was working twenty-four hours a day, and like many newspapermen, I was a burned-out case, after a time. I spent several months away from the pressures of that job, in a little cottage that belongs to my wife's sister. When I felt up to it, I took a job offer from Mr. Hearst with his new *Boston American*, where I started publishing my 'Thinking Machine' stories and made lots of money ... none of which you and your fellow extortionists will ever see. Not one red cent, sir."

Crafton shrugged slowly, his tiny dark eyes widened. "If you don't feel that your public, your publishers, will be put off by your mental aberrations, sir, your, your ... *dementia*, then—"

"Listen, you damned little weasel—my public and my publishers care nothing about me except that I keep coming up with good stories. If my screws are loose, well then I'm colorful and more interesting—do you know the slightest thing about Edgar Allan Poe? Please, do me a favor, publicize away ... my sales will go up."

"We're not bluffing, sir."

"Neither am I. How can I best make my point? I know ... Please, just for a moment, sir, come with me." Futrelle rose. He curled a finger. "Come along, man—I won't bite. I'm not really a lunatic."

Crafton rose, suspiciously, gathering up his gloves and hat and walking stick.

Futrelle slipped an arm around the much smaller man's shoulders and walked slowly with him toward the balustrade of the balcony. "I think you've misjudged people like myself, and have attracted more trouble than you know."

"Are you threatening me again, sir?"

"No, no! Just giving you some advice. Are you aware that you're being followed?"

"Followed?"

"And by a very unsavory character, at that."

"I've seen no one."

Futrelle moved closer to the railing of the balcony. "He's lurking in the shadows of the reception area, below there...."

Crafton leaned forward, and Futrelle shoved him over, and Crafton's hat and gloves and cane fell from his grasp, gloves spilling and landing in gray handprints on the marble stairs, hat and cane clattering onto the linoleum floor below, pocket change raining, even as Futrelle grasped onto the man's ankles, just above his spats, letting him dangle there like a ripe fruit from a branch.

"Put me down, sir! Put me down!"

Several startled passengers below noticed this bizarre sight, and scurried away.

"Are you sure, Mr. Crafton, that that is what you desire of me? To put you down?"

"I mean, pull me up, at once, at once!"

Futrelle, however, let the man swing there, over the marble staircase and the floor just to the side of it, like a big pendulum.

"Of course, sir, you could be right about me ... I could be quite mad indeed."

"I won't say a word about you! Your secret is safe with me!"

Futrelle dragged the man up and over the finely carved oak railing as if he were hauling a big catch onto the deck of a fishing boat.

Crafton, on his feet again, began smoothing out his wrinkled attire, shaking as if he had the palsy. "That's assault, sir—you could be put in irons! There were witnesses!"

"The witnesses seem to have gone—but we could bring this matter to the attention of the ship's master-at-arms. Since I have no concern whatsoever, whether the information you hold on me is ever released to the public, I'd be glad to bring extortion charges against you."

Crafton, still smoothing out his attire, thought about that, and said, "You may hear more from me later."

"Why don't you keep digging on me? Maybe you'll come up with more. There are rumors to the effect that I have a terrible temper."

Crafton moved down the stairway, at first quickly, then grasping onto the railing, as if afraid of losing his footing, and walking more slowly, if not steadily; he retrieved gloves, fedora, and walking stick, gathered up his change, and disappeared through the reception area, almost running.

Below, several navy-blue-jacketed stewards darted into view. They looked up at Futrelle, who leaned casually against the railing; one of them called: "Is there a problem, sir? We had reports of an altercation."

"Really? I thought it was some sort of acrobatic display. Part of the ship's entertainment." He shrugged, and smiled, nodding to the confused stewards as he strolled down and around the stairs to use the electric lift.

When he got to their stateroom, May was entertaining the Harrises—who pretended to be outraged by the Futrelles' superior quarters—and soon the little group decided to take one of the tours of the ship the purser was offering. The tour began with an inspection of the purser's own office, followed by a look at the spacious kitchens with their modern timesaving devices (including an electric potato peeler), the libraries and other lavish public rooms, peeking in at the squash court, swimming pool and gymnasium. Rumors of a racetrack aboard were entirely unfounded, they were assured.

The purser's Cook's tour even included a quick stroll through the normally off-limits Second and Third Classes. Lounges and libraries that would have been First-Class on any other ship were glimpsed in Second, and the mix of English, French, Dutch and Italian immigrants in Third Class had comfortable lounges and smoking rooms, and a dining room with separate tables and swivel chairs, that were anything but typical of steerage.

After the tour, the Futrelles again climbed to the boat deck, where orchestra leader Wallace Hartley and his little group were giving an open-air concert of ragtime and other lively popular tunes. Before long the sun was low in the horizon.

"Is that France?" May asked from a polished wooden railing. It was just May and her husband, the Harrises having already gone in to get dressed for dinner.

The coastal chalk cliffs glowed in the reddish sunset, as if they had somehow caught fire, and yet the effect was strangely soothing. At the end of a long breakwater, a structure was making itself known as a lighthouse.

"That's France," he told her.

They stood watching the dying sun's rays reflecting across the breakwater's gentle swells. The ship's speed slackened; the great ship would soon be dropping anchor to take on more passengers.

"I'm tempted to get off, and continue our second honeymoon there," she said.

The city of Cherbourg lay ahead, spread along the low-lying shore, dwarfed by the Mount Roule, purple in the twilight. The lights on deck winked on.

"Believing the bad omens, darling?"

"No, no, Jack … France is just so romantic."

The wind was kicking up, waves getting choppier, the sky dark with more than just approaching night.

"I think a squall's coming," Futrelle said. "Let's get inside and change for dinner."

"Oh yes," May said, holding on to her feathered chapeau. "Oh, Jack—what about the terrible man you were going to meet? You didn't strike him, did you?"

"No, dear," Futrelle said. "I didn't strike him."

DAY TWO

APRIL 11, 1912

FOUR

CAPTAIN'S TABLE

LIKE THEIR PREVIOUS STOP, CHERBOURG, the Irish port of Queenstown ahead was too small to accommodate the *Titanic*; so anchor would be dropped offshore, for the arrival of the final batch of passengers and the taking on of mail sacks (the *R.M.S.* in R.M.S. *Titanic* did, after all, stand for "Royal Mail Ship").

From the starboard boat deck, where Jack and May Futrelle sat side by side in deck chairs, blankets wrapped about their already coat-clad bodies, the morning seemed an exceptionally lovely one, blue cloud-fleeced sky, wind rather high but the blue-green waters surprisingly calm. They were unaware of the full Atlantic swell crashing against the ship's port side, deceived by the ship's uncanny ability—even on the boat deck—to emulate terra firma.

Last night, in the First-Class Dining Saloon, the Futrelles and their tablemates had found themselves paying less attention to their plates of endless, wonderful food (course upon course), and more to the new crop of passengers arriving, courtesy of the Cherbourg boat train. The subtle clatter of silverware on fine china was drowned out by the nearby bustle of stewards porting luggage, table talk trumped by the buzz of conversation of new arrivals.

René and Henry would point out this luminary and that one—here John Jacob Astor, his young bride and their rambunctious friend Maggie Brown; there Benjamin Guggenheim trailing behind his mistress, the glamorous French singer Madame Pauline Aubert, as if fooling anyone that they weren't together (an effort that would be short-lived).

But these were just glimpses of famous faces and opera-house fashions, and at the orchestral evening that followed in the lounge (selections from *Tales of Hoffmann* and *Cavalleria Rusticana*), the newcomers were nowhere to be seen. Nor did they appear in the smoking room later, where Astor and Guggenheim might be expected to drop by for a Cuban cigar and a snifter of brandy.

Of course, both millionaires had boarded with beautiful young women, and Futrelle was of the opinion that Cuban cigars and snifters of brandy came in a distinct second and third in a contest involving the late-night company of such beauties.

And none of it seemed to be happening on a ship, rather in some landlocked hotel; only those nearest the windows could have suspected that outside, on deck, a gale was blowing.

Now the gale was a memory, the morning clear, as the Irish coastline showed itself, the gray mountains of Cork bobbing above the horizon.

"There it is!" May said, pointing. "The Old Head of Kinsale!"

The rocky promontory, peaked by a lighthouse, was a familiar and comforting sight to well-seasoned transatlantic travelers like the Futrelles.

"Cork Harbor's just around the bend," Futrelle said.

And, as if at Futrelle's bidding, the great ship began its long, easy turn to port.

The married couple had taken a late breakfast—pressing ten-thirty—in the exquisitely continental à la carte restaurant, nicknamed the Ritz after the Ritz-Carlton dining rooms of White Star's German rival, the Hamburg–Amerika Line. They had spent an at times spirited, at times tranquil morning in their stateroom, doing the sort of things a healthy, loving couple on their second honeymoon tend to do.

Two miles offshore, within the shelter of twin forts guarding the harbor, the *Titanic* dropped anchor, as twin tenders—the *Ireland* and *America*—drew alongside her with passengers and mail. The waterfront of Queenstown—a quaint seafaring village not unlike Scituate, the Massachusetts home of the Futrelles— was lined with sightseers, tiny well-wishers whose waving could barely be made out, whose cheering could scarcely be heard.

"Good morning!"

The voice belonged to J. Bruce Ismay, standing tall and thin, a handsome Ichabod Crane in a dark blue suit with gray pinstripes and matching gray spats, and, brisk breeze or not, no topcoat or hat.

As the blanket-bundled Futrelle and May stirred, Ismay urged them, "Don't get up, please don't get up on my account!" Before Futrelle could make introductions, the White Star Line director bowed to May. "J. Bruce Ismay, madam—I presume you're the lovely Mrs. Futrelle."

"If I'm not," she said, "the lovely Mr. Futrelle has some explaining to do."

Ismay laughed, once—he used laughs as punctuation, having enough of a sense of humor to know where to place them, though no more. "I understand you're an author yourself."

"A novice compared to Jack, here, I'm afraid."

"But published."

"Oh yes. Several times."

"An accomplishment I envy. May I sit?"

"Please," Futrelle said, and Ismay pulled up a deck chair on the husband's side.

"Would it be bad form, sir, to ask if you've had time to consider my proposal?"

"Not at all." Futrelle nodded toward his wife. "I have discussed it with May. She's favorably disposed toward doing a mystery set aboard your ship."

He beamed so widely at her, the ends of his mustache threatened to tickle the corners of his eyes. "I'm grateful, madam. I was not at all convinced your husband would say yes."

"I haven't said yes," Futrelle reminded him.

"I hope that isn't 'no,' " Ismay said.

"I haven't decided, but I am leaning in your direction, sir."

"Splendid! What can I do to aid you?"

"We've had a tour of the ship, thanks to your personable purser, Mr. McElroy."

"Wonderful chap."

"Yes he is. But we may wish to take a closer look at the *Titanic*, from the crow's nest to the boiler room. As a newspaperman turned fiction writer, I find the more truth I can build my tale around, the better."

Ismay was nodding at the good sense of that. "Well, tonight at the captain's table, I'll introduce you to Mr. Andrews. I'm sure he'll take you anywhere on the ship that you wish, and he has keys to everything."

"Thomas Andrews? The master shipbuilder responsible for this vessel?"

"Himself," Ismay said, clearly pleased that Futrelle was this knowledgeable, though Futrelle knew only what a few articles had told him.

A small and colorful flotilla of bumboats laden with local vendors and their wares had followed in the wakes of the two tenders; the bumboats bobbed out there, voices traveling over the water, "Lace and linens!," "Knick-knacks and fineries!"

With comical urgency, May asked Ismay if they'd be allowed to board.

"It's White Star's policy to let the more reputable merchants come aboard," he said, with a tiny shrug, "as a courtesy to our passengers."

Her eyes were bright; shopping was one of May's passions. "Where will they be setting up, and when?"

"On the aft A-deck promenade, madam, and soon."

May turned to her husband, and said, "Jack, I need to get my handbag in our stateroom. Why don't you continue your chat with Mr. Ismay, and I'll meet you down on deck in a few minutes."

Futrelle said that was fine, stood to help his wife unbundle herself from her blanket, they exchanged pecks on the cheek, and she was gone as if fired from a rocket.

"My wife is the same," Ismay admitted. "Someday you simply must visit my wing at Harrods."

Futrelle chuckled; that was a pretty good jest, coming from Ismay. "Actually, Bruce ..." They were on first-name terms, after all; Ismay had insisted, yesterday. "I'm pleased we have a moment in private. There's a subject I need to broach that I'd prefer to keep from my wife."

Ismay frowned in interest, saying, "Continue, please."

And Futrelle told Ismay of his meeting with Crafton on the balcony of the Grand Staircase—omitting, of course, his dangling of the man over the railing.

But Ismay didn't need to be told of the latter.

With a smile and a genuine laugh, Ismay said, "Well, that finally explains it—the rumor I heard that a man of your description had hung a smaller man upside down off the balcony."

"Weren't you going to bring that up, sir?"

"Why? No complaint was filed by Mr. Crafton, and my policy, my company's policy, is to treat our honored guests with … discretion."

"How discreet was I, hanging that bastard over the railing?"

"Not very. Frankly, if I'm not out of line, Jack, I would discourage such practice in future … though that little snake in the grass is worthy of worse."

"I know for a fact that he's approached a number of your other passengers; I've happened upon him in the act, several times."

Ismay's expression darkened. "That is distressing news."

Futrelle ticked the names off on his fingers. "Major Butt, Mr. Straus, Mr. Stead, even a Second-Class passenger named Hoffman … They've all apparently sent him packing."

"Good for them."

"Of course, I have no way of knowing what sort of threat he made, in these individual cases … He clearly represents an international blackmail ring."

"Clearly."

"With what did he threaten *you*, Mr. Ismay?"

Ismay blinked; he hadn't seen that question coming. "Pardon?"

"I saw him knock on your door, shortly after I left your suite yesterday morning … just before noon? And I saw you admit him."

Half a smile settled in Ismay's check, raising one end of his mustache. "You do get around, sir."

"This is a large ship, but a small city. I'm merely more observant than the average person, because of my line of work. That's what you get when you cross a newspaperman with a mystery writer … You're not obligated to tell me, Bruce. I'm just curious, as a fellow Crafton-appointed 'client.' "

Ismay shrugged. "He was simply threatening to widely circulate a certain canard about the building of this ship."

"What canard would that be?"

"A foolish rumor that this ship was built at such a supposedly 'frenetic pace' that a crew of workers were trapped within her hull, and that we simply left them there … to 'suffocate and die.' "

"*Were* there any deaths in the building of this ship?"

Another dismissive shrug. "From keel laying to launch, only two—quite within acceptable standards—the unwritten rule of British shipyards, you know."

"What unwritten rule is that, Bruce?"

" 'One death for every one hundred pounds spent.' "

It was attitudes like that that bred unions and strikes. But at the moment Futrelle was more concerned with blackmail than politics, and said, "Crafton threatened to spread this 'trapped crewmen' tale in the 'sensationalist' press, I suppose."

"Certainly."

"Please tell me you didn't pay him off, Bruce."

"Jack, please do me the courtesy of trusting that I did the right thing."

That was an evasive answer if ever there was one. But Futrelle didn't press it.

He said only, "You now have aboard this vessel representatives of two of America's richest and most powerful families—do you really want this Crafton character working his blackmail racket on Astor and Guggenheim?"

Yet another shrug from Ismay. "What could I do about it?"

Futrelle laughed humorlessly, hollowly. "You could put Crafton off this ship right now—while you still have a chance—here at Queenstown."

Ismay had begun shaking his head halfway through Futrelle's little speech. "I can't do that, sir. Mr. Crafton is, however disreputable a character he may be, a paying customer of the White Star Line."

So Ismay *had* paid Crafton's fee.

"Well," Ismay said, standing suddenly, "I certainly enjoyed meeting Mrs. Futrelle, and I look forward to seeing you at the captain's table this evening."

Then he strode off, heading aft in his quick, martinet's manner. When J. Bruce Ismay decided a conversation was over, it was over.

The aft A-deck promenade had been transformed into an open-air market. This was the same area outside the Verandah Café where yesterday Futrelle and May had seen Crafton bothering Hoffman up on the Second-Class end of the boat deck. Now the relatively cramped area was thronging with First-Class passengers examining the wares of Irish vendors, men in derbies and shabby suits, women in unlikely fine lace like those they were selling from folding-leg tables.

Among the browsing passengers was a particularly striking couple—a slender handsome man in his late forties escorting a pretty, pretty young woman, who could have been father and daughter, but weren't. They were Colonel John Jacob Astor IV and his child bride, the former Madeline Force, fresh from a honeymoon tour of Egypt.

Madeline was said to be as shapely as a showgirl, but that wasn't evident with her navy-blue-and-white pinstriped Norfolk style suit, which even with silk velvet inlay and fancy bone buttons looked a trifle dowdy; even her oversize navy-blue-and-white striped hat was a shapeless thing. Rumors that she was "in an advanced delicate condition," despite her relatively recent marriage, seemed wholly credible.

The lanky Astor sported a boater and a red-and-blue tie that added color and dash to a conservative dark gray suit, and an oversize, dashing mustache at odds with his somber, detached demeanor. His face long and narrow, his chin cleft and rather small, he leaned on a carved ebony walking stick as he paused at a stall, holding his chin high, looking at prospective purchases down the considerable slope of an aquiline nose, peering through small, sky-blue eyes cursed of a world-weariness known only by the impossibly wealthy and the devastatingly poor.

Between the Astors was an Airedale, dutifully keeping them company, no leash in sight; the dog seemed happier than his master, though his mistress was having the most fun.

"This is *very* nice," Madeline was saying at the stall next to the one where the Futrelles were examining some miniature porcelain dolls. The young Mrs. Astor was holding up a lovely lace jacket that didn't look like it would fit her, at least not right now.

"How much in dollars?" Astor asked the vendor, a woman wearing a lovely lace jacket herself, and bad teeth.

"A hundred, fine sir," she said, not missing a beat.

Astor shrugged. "Eight hundred it is," he said blandly, and withdrew a wad of bills as thick as one of Futrelle's novels; the millionaire peeled off eight crisp one-hundreds and handed them to the amazed vendor, who did not correct Astor's mistake, and who could blame her?

Futrelle, arching an eyebrow, exchanged incredulous glances with his wife, who later bought a similar item for twenty-five dollars, which seemed outrageous to Futrelle but May rightly pointed out the savings compared with what the Astors had paid.

Promptly at 1:30 P.M., the *Titanic*'s steam whistles let go three long, mournful blasts announcing departure; the vendors packed up their things and hastened back to their bumboats, and soon gangways were raised, lines cast off, the dripping starboard anchor raised. From the boat deck, the Futrelles could hear and see a passenger on the Third-Class aft promenade, a small mustached man in kilts, playing his bagpipes.

The husband and wife looked at each other, savoring the bittersweet moment: the Irish piper's mournful "Erin's Lament" probably represented its emigrating player's farewell to the beloved homeland he might never see again.

The Futrelles stood at the rail in the cold afternoon, watching the green hills and fields of Ireland slip away, knowing—as the ship made its wide, majestic turn starboard, into the Atlantic's swells—that the next land they would see would have the Statue of Liberty out in front of it.

"It's almost two and we haven't had lunch yet," Futrelle noted, checking his pocket watch. He had seldom missed a meal in his thirty-seven years.

"Let's just get something light," May suggested. "Dinner's not that far away, and we'll be bombarded with one course after another."

The Verandah Café, portside off the aft A-deck promenade, didn't seem as overrun with children as it had yesterday, and the couple ducked in for a snack. The enclosed space conjured the illusion of an outdoor terrace, with its potted palms, white wicker tables and chairs, archway windows and ivy-flung trellises.

The only children today had also been here yesterday: golden-tressed Lorraine Allison and her baby brother Trevor, overseen by the blunt-nosed almost beauty of their nanny, Alice, again holding court at a wicker table.

But this time the parents were here, as well, seated at the adjacent table having petits fours and tea, and in the company of none other than Futrelle's acrobatic partner, John Bertram Crafton.

They were a happy little group, smiling, even laughing, Crafton in a natty brown suit but the same gray fedora, the boyish bespectacled Hudson in conservative gray enlivened by a red tie, the sweetly pretty Bess in a lilac-and-white striped cotton day dress.

The Futrelles sat a few tables away in the sparsely populated café; the same young steward who yesterday had been so attentive to nanny Alice stopped by to take their order.

"A couple of cups of hot bouillon, please," Futrelle said, and the handsome lad nodded and disappeared.

It wasn't until Futrelle had spoken that Crafton noticed the couple's presence. Seeing Futrelle, the blackmailer's face turned as white as the wicker chairs and he swallowed thickly. His smile grew nervous and, rising, he made a hurried good-bye and scurried away, gold-tipped cane in hand, through the revolving door into the smoking room.

As Crafton left, the Allisons noticed the Futrelles, and Hudson called out, "Nice to see you again—other than that crowded corridor! Won't you join us?"

"Thank you, yes," Futrelle said, and he and May did.

Introductions in the hallway yesterday had been exceedingly brief and lacking in detail: the Futrelles soon learned that Hudson was an investment broker from Montreal (a partner in the firm), and the Allisons learned Jack Futrelle was the famous mystery author, Jacques. Hudson admitted he wasn't much of a fiction reader, but Bess was an unrepentant bookworm and had read (and loved) both Jack's *The Diamond Master* and May's *Secretary of Frivolous Affairs*.

The latter made them instant friends: the Hudsons impressed by being in such famous company, the Futrelles flattered by Bess's praise for their work.

At the suitable moment, Futrelle asked casually, "Your friend Mr. Crafton—how did you come to meet him?"

Hudson smiled and shrugged. "Well, sir, we met him just before we met you—in the C-deck corridor."

"He's very charming," Bess said.

The Futrelles exchanged glances; they had been hoping a fan of their books would have better judgment and taste.

"He's an investment broker himself," Hudson said.

"Is that so?" Futrelle said.

"But that's not why we hit it off so well. You see, we have horses in common."

"Horses?"

"Yes." Hudson smiled at Bess, patted her hand. "We've been very fortunate, of late, in business, and recently acquired a farm … the Allison Stock Farm, we're calling it."

"It's always been our dream," Bess said.

To Futrelle the young couple didn't look old enough to "always" have had any dream.

"We built a farmhouse to our specifications," Hudson said. "We'll be moving in, as soon as we get back. Bess decorated it herself. She has a real eye."

But the thread of the conversation had been lost, and Futrelle had to say, "Where do Mr. Crafton and horses come into play?"

"Oh! That's why we were in England. On a horse-buying trip. Mr. Crafton is very interested in horses, and seems quite knowledgeable on the subject."

Probably from the track, Futrelle thought, but only smiled politely.

The steward arrived with the cups of bouillon for the Futrelles. The nanny glanced over and the secret little look she and the steward exchanged was neither as secret nor as little as they thought.

Later, as Futrelle escorted May down a C-deck corridor, back to their stateroom, she said, "You were right about that shipboard romance."

"I hope the lad doesn't get into trouble for fraternizing."

"I should think not. Alice isn't a passenger, exactly. Did you notice the evil eye she was giving Crafton?"

"No," Futrelle said. "Are you sure it wasn't just her natural expression?"

"Now, Jack, she'd be quite an attractive young woman if she hadn't ..."

"Run into a door?"

"You're terrible. What time is your appointment?"

Futrelle was signed up for the full treatment at the Turkish Bath, which was for women mornings, men afternoons.

"In about fifteen minutes. What do you have on for this afternoon?"

"I intend to take a good old-fashioned American bath, in the tub we've been provided thanks to the generous auspices of J. Bruce Ismay. We're sitting at the captain's table this evening, and surely you don't expect me to be ready in a flash."

"No. But I do think that with the several hours at your disposal, you'll be able to make yourself presentable."

She slapped his arm, and kissed his mouth, and—as they had now arrived at their stateroom—allowed her husband to unlock the door for her, before he went off to partake of the *Titanic*'s most arcane ritual.

The Turkish Bath—with its willingly hot steam room followed by male attendants providing full-body massage, exfoliation and shampoo—was an outlandish excess even for this ship. The cooling room was a Moorish fantasy of carved Cairo curtains (disguising portholes), blue-and-green tiled walls, gilded beams, crimson ceiling, hanging bronze lamps, blue-and-white mosaic floor, inlaid Damascus coffee tables, and low-slung couches and chairs with Moroccan-motif upholstery.

It was in this bizarrely exotic chamber that Futrelle again came upon the omnipresent Crafton, this time towel-draped, reclining on a couch next to a similarly lounging and towel-wrapped John Jacob Astor. Whether Crafton was attempting blackmail—as he had with Futrelle—or simply cozying up to the millionaire—as he had with the Allisons—was not clear.

The reason for the uncertainty was Astor himself: his expression remained lifeless, his sky-blue eyes joyless, even bored, blinking only when steam room sweat found its way into them. And as the fast-talking Crafton continued his spiel—telling Astor about the benefits of becoming a Crafton "client," perhaps—Astor remained as mute as the Sphinx he had so recently visited.

Once again, Crafton noticed Futrelle, turned white as his towel, and fled into the adjacent room, where the saltwater swimming bath represented the final step of the Turkish treatment.

Futrelle, pleasantly exhausted from his massage, skin flecked with beads of perspiration, reclining in his own towel on his own Moroccan couch, considered striking up a conversation with Astor. But never having met this man, whose station was so above his own, Futrelle felt uncomfortable doing so, and didn't.

And by the time Futrelle entered the room Crafton had fled into, where the swimming bath—thirty feet long and half again as wide—took up almost the entire space, the little blackmailer had vanished.

At dinner in the First-Class Dining Saloon, the distance between Astor and Futrelle lessened in a number of ways.

First of all, they were seated across from each other at the captain's table, which was at the forward end of the center section of the vast dining room with its white walls and warm oak furnishings.

Second, Astor proved to be a devotee of Futrelle's fiction, and twinkling life found its way into the millionaire's somber eyes when he learned the creator of the Thinking Machine was sitting next to him.

"You combine mystery and scientific thinking in a unique manner, sir," Astor said, in a clipped, oddly metallic voice.

"Thank you, Mr. Astor."

"Please, Jacques," he said, and something like warmth came over the cold features. "Call me Colonel."

Futrelle almost laughed, then realized the man wasn't joking.

"Thank you, Colonel. And I'm not Jacques, to my friends, but Jack."

"Mother-of-pearl, Astor," a raucous female voice asked, "are you tellin' me you're so far around the bend you think 'Colonel' is your first name?"

Eyes turned toward a slightly heavyset, pleasant-looking woman in her mid-forties with beautiful sky-blue eyes almost identical in color to Astor's. She wore a burgundy silk-satin ball dress with glass beading and a feathered hat about the size and shape of a garbage-can lid a milk wagon rolled over. Her name was Maggie Brown, more formally Margaret, more formally still Mrs. James Joseph Brown of Denver, in honor of the gold-mining tycoon husband who cheerfully funded her travels in absentia.

Astor looked momentarily taken aback, then roared with laughter. "Where would I be without you to put me in my place, Maggie?"

And this seemed to be Maggie Brown's function in Astor's life; Futrelle would soon learn that the social-climbing matron who'd traded Denver for Newport had been rejected by much of society, but Astor had adopted her as a sort of mascot, perhaps because the Four Hundred had turned up their noses at him and his young bride.

"Where would you be without me as your guide, Astor? Tryin' to figure out a way to walk with both feet in your mouth, I'd reckon."

Astor laughed heartily, and the attractive young Mrs. Astor, seated beside him, laughed, too—politely. Madeline wore a black silk-net beaded overdress designed not to draw attention to that "delicate condition" of hers.

The others seated at the captain's table included May, on Futrelle's other side, decked out in a pink silk-satin evening gown, white pearls nestling at the hollow of her slender neck. Next to May was Maggie Brown, and across the table, next to the Astors, was the shipbuilder Thomas Andrews, a soft-spoken gentleman with the rugged build of an athlete and the sensitive features of an artist.

At the far end of the table sat Ismay, playing host, while at the head of the table, of course, in a formal blue uniform bedecked with medals, sat the captain—Edward J. Smith, the beloved E. J., the so-called millionaire's captain, a favorite of wealthy, socially prominent frequent transatlantic passengers, many of whom wouldn't think of crossing the ocean with anyone else at the helm.

Smith was like a fiction writer's notion of a steamship captain—an unimaginative fiction writer at that, Futrelle thought, who would himself never dream of painting so clichéd a portrait: clear-eyed, stern-visaged, square jaw dusted with a perfectly trimmed snow-white beard, Smith was taller than most of his crew and as solidly built as a boiler-room stoker.

Where Captain Smith varied from the cliché of his own somewhat forbidding appearance was an avuncular manner that included a ready smile, rather urbane manners and a soothingly pleasant, softly modulated voice.

"Colonel Astor has every right to his rank, Mrs. Brown," the captain pointed out to her gently. "How many men in the Colonel's position would have traded the comfort and safety of their homes for the battlefield?"

"Oh, I know Astor's a patriot," Maggie said. "And believe me, I'm relieved he's a colonel, and not a captain…. Imagine where we'd be if he were in your shoes, Captain Smith."

"I'm not sure I follow, Mrs. Brown," the captain said with his easy smile.

"You got any idea how many times Astor here rammed his yacht into somebody else's canoe? Of course, he won his share of races, once the real captains started giving the Colonel a wide berth."

Astor was enjoying this immensely, and it did seem good-humored, but to Futrelle, Maggie Brown bordered on the overbearing. Still, in her way, she was a breath of fresh air in these stuffy quarters.

The dinner progressed through eleven amazing courses: oysters à la russe, cream of barley soup, poached salmon with mousseline sauce and sliced cucumbers, chicken lyonnaise, filet mignon with truffle on buttery potatoes, rice-stuffed vegetable marrow, lamb with mint sauce with creamed carrots, champagne sorbet, roasted squab, asparagus-salad vinaigrette, foie gras with celery, Waldorf pudding, cheese and fruit....

Conversation was pleasant and polite, though the food took center stage, and Maggie Brown said almost nothing, busying herself with eating everything in sight except the cut flowers in vases, stopping a waiter to ask for the occasional French translation.

Between courses, Futrelle mentioned to Astor that he had read the millionaire's science-fiction novel, *A Journey in Other Worlds*, and that he had enjoyed it, which was not a lie—such futuristic concepts as television, energy conservation and subway systems had been imaginative and fascinating, and it would have been bad form to mention to Astor how abysmal the prose itself was.

Maggie Brown, overhearing this, chimed in to inform any who didn't know (and this included the Futrelles) that "Astor here is quite the crackpot inventor—he holds all sorts of patents ... cooked up a bicycle brake, a pneumatic road-flattenin' contraption, turbines and batteries...."

Futrelle was impressed, and said so.

"I enjoy tinkering," Astor admitted.

Madeline said, "My husband could have given Edison a run for it, if his family's business responsibilities hadn't stood in the way."

"Money can be a curse," Astor observed. "Actually, I think a man who has a million dollars is almost as well-off as if he were wealthy."

Maggie Brown's eyes bugged out at that one; but even she couldn't think of anything to top it.

Between the sixth and seventh courses, Futrelle asked Andrews, "Is this a pleasure trip for you, Mr. Andrews? Enjoying the fruits of your labors?"

"Well," Andrews said, with the shy smile that caused so many to find him immediately endearing, "this trip is a pleasure … I'm proud of what we've accomplished. But I am working, I'm afraid."

Ismay said, "Mr. Andrews is heading up a guarantee group from Harland and Wolff." The White Star director was referring to the shipbuilding firm that, under Andrews's guidance, had constructed the *Titanic*.

"What is a 'guarantee group'?" May asked.

"My assistants and I move about, hopefully undetected," Andrews explained, "tracking down the inevitable snags, flaws and breakdowns that bedevil every new ship."

Maggie Brown asked, "Is there anything to be worried about, Mr. Andrews? We're not guinea pigs, are we? 'Cause if so, we're paying a pretty penny for the privilege."

"Actually, Mrs. Brown," Andrews said, lightly, "we're talking about such major problems as a plugged-up kitchen drain, or a malfunctioning ice machine."

"This ship is a marvel," Ismay said, at once dismissive and boastful. "And Mr. Andrews, God bless him, is a professional fussbudget … Earlier he told me he'd uncovered a troubling flaw in the ship."

All eyes turned to Ismay for this dire news.

"The coat hooks in the staterooms employ too many screws," Ismay said.

As his tablemates laughed good-naturedly, Andrews damn near blushed, touching a napkin to his lips, saying only in his defense, "The devil's in the details, Mr. Ismay."

"Well, you've given us a lovely ship, sir," Madeline Astor said. "Please accept our thanks, and our compliments."

Wineglasses were raised in an informal toast and Andrews finally went the entire distance, blushing like a rose. Captain Smith raised a water glass, however, as he was not drinking alcohol.

After dessert, Ismay spoke up. "I regret to inform you that this is Captain Smith's final crossing."

Astor asked, "Is that right, Captain?"

A smile emerged from the trim white beard. "Yes it is. I'll be sixty soon. Forty-five years at sea, thirty-two of them with White Star … I think it's time to turn the helm over to younger men."

Futrelle asked, "Do you like these big ships, Captain? Like the *Olympic*, and the *Titanic*?"

He nodded, but there was a graveness about it. "Modern shipbuilding has come a long way."

That wasn't quite an answer to his question, but Futrelle let it pass. He knew that Smith—whose career had been otherwise spotless—had had his first real accident earlier this year, with the *Titanic*'s sister ship, the *Olympic*, of which he was the captain at the time of a collision with a Royal Navy cruiser. Futrelle suspected, after the performance with the *New York*, that Captain

Smith had not mastered the finer points of seamanship needed to navigate the White Star's new "wonder ships."

"You should come back to command all the maiden voyages," Astor said. "It wouldn't be a White Star first crossing without you."

"I'll second that," Andrews said, raising his wineglass.

"And I," Ismay added.

The entire table raised their glasses to the captain, who smiled and nodded, then said, "I appreciate the sentiment, but at the end of this crossing, I'll have logged two million miles aboard White Star ships ... and I think I've earned some time ashore."

The captain thanked the group for its "splendid company," and invited the men to join him in the smoking room for a cigar and brandy, while the women stayed at the table for conversation and aperitifs.

The First-Class Smoking Room, on A deck, was a bastion of male supremacy, an exclusive men's club at sea where shipping magnates, rail and oil barons and millionaire industrialists could mingle in an atmosphere of free-flowing liquor, high-stakes card playing, and of course cigar smoke that was almost as rich as they were. The Georgian-style mahogany paneling, inlaid with mother-of-pearl, inset with stained-glass windows and etched mirrors, had the feel of a stately, prosperous Protestant church, an impression undercut by the green leather-upholstered armchairs and marble-topped tables, each with a raised edge around it to catch a sliding drink in rough weather.

The little group of men from the captain's table—Smith, Astor, Andrews, Ismay and Futrelle—stood near the jutting corner whose walls with backlighted stained-glass images of

Art Nouveau nymphs and sailing ships gracefully disguised and enclosed the casing of the ship's immense rear funnel.

Again, the captain declined to drink, but he clearly relished a Cuban cigar so seductively fragrant that confirmed cigarette smoker Futrelle began to question his own tastes.

"With the exception of the sea, and Mrs. Smith," Ismay said, "the captain's greatest love is a good cigar."

Smith raised an eyebrow, nodding his agreement as he held the Cuban before him, regarding it as if it were a treasure map. "Once I've retired, gentlemen, should you enter a room where I'm indulging in a fine Cuban such as this, I beg you keep still, so the blue cloud around my head not be disturbed."

That prompted some gentle laughter, and as Astor began a discussion of yachting with the captain, Futrelle turned away to take in the room.

Seated about the smoke-draped chamber were such luminaries as publisher Henry Harper, railroad magnate Charles M. Hays, Senator William B. Allison of Iowa, and military historian Colonel Archibald Gracie.

And so was at least one considerably less illustrious individual, a certain John Bertram Crafton.

Crafton was seated at a table for four, but only one other seat was taken, by a slender, respectable-looking clean-shaven reddish-haired man, perhaps forty years of age, in formal evening attire, indicating he—like the captain's party—had earlier supped in the First-Class Dining Saloon. Crafton still wore this afternoon's brown suit.

The blackmailer was leaning forward conspiratorially and his distinguished-looking companion was frowning in the manner so common to prospective Crafton "clients."

Noticing Major Butt and his friend Francis Millet seated near the fireplace, Futrelle excused himself and wandered over and sat between them.

"Gentlemen," he said. "I notice our old friend is spreading his typical good cheer."

Broad-shouldered Archie had a cigar in one hand and a brandy snifter in the other; his sneer sent his mustache askew. Gray-haired Millet sat across from the major, hands folded, his own brandy untouched.

"Somebody should toss that bastard overboard," Archie snorted. "Do I take it you've had the pleasure of Mr. Crafton's company, Jack? Are you now a fellow 'client'?"

"Oh yes—he dredged up my 'nervous breakdown' and I told him to stuff himself."

"Is that right?" Archie shook his head. "He's come after me with the same sort of rubbish ... only there wasn't much dredging that needed doing. This, uh ... papal visit is something of a camouflage. I've been recently hospitalized."

"I'm sorry to hear that, Archie—but you look well, now."

"Jack, I'm sure you can imagine the personal and professional pressure I've been under, with my loyalties divided between Teddy and Bill."

The major meant by that Theodore Roosevelt and William Howard Taft, two presidents whose loyalty he'd pledged who were now facing off against each other politically. Being pulled between two such powerful individuals could strain anyone, even someone as strong as Major Archie Butt.

Millet said, "Archie was briefly in an English sanitarium ... just to get away, to calm his jangled nerves, his ... depression."

Futrelle nodded toward Crafton, who was still quietly speaking to the distinguished stranger. "And he threatened to go to the yellow press with the story, I suppose."

Archie nodded. His eyes betrayed the depressed state in which he was still, to some degree, caught up.

"Did you pay him off, Archie?"

"Certainly not!"

"Forgive me for asking ... Who is that Crafton's sitting with?"

"That's Hugh Rood," Archie said. "I'm told he's a London merchant of some kind; import, export. Very well-off."

And barely had Archie's description of the man ended when Rood sprang to his feet and grasped Crafton by the lapels of his suit and dragged him halfway across the marble-topped table, spilling drinks, glass shattering on the fancy linoleum, every eye in the room turning toward the two men.

"Approach me again at your own risk," Rood shouted, his voice low-pitched, harsh.

And he backhanded the little blackmailer, viciously, the slap ringing in the room like a gunshot.

Crafton tumbled from his chair onto the floor, and the sound was like somebody dropping a bundle of kindling.

Captain Smith stepped forward, Ismay took a step back, but before anyone could do or say anything else, Rood strode from the room, his face burning.

Crafton, ever resilient, rose from the linoleum, shrugged, licked the blood from the corner of his mouth and smiled feebly, straightening his clothing. With surprising dignity, he said, "Mr. Rood has an unfortunate temper ... Captain, as a good Christian, I prefer not to press charges."

Then the ferrety little man took a halfhearted bow, and made a hasty exit, as conversation in the Smoking Room rose to a boisterous din of amazement, confusion and amusement.

DAY THREE

APRIL 12, 1912

FIVE

THE PROBLEM OF C13

AT TEN O'CLOCK, THE FUTRELLES were still in bed—actually, they were back in bed, having enjoyed a room-service break-fast—and, following some second-honeymoon calisthenics, they were still in their nightclothes, propped up with feather pillows, each lost in a novel.

They had decided the boat deck might be a bit chilly for deck-chair reading, and there would be time aplenty this afternoon for socializing. For all its amenities, the *Titanic* had no organized activities for passengers, who spent most of their time reading books, writing letters and playing cards.

Pools on the speed of the ship were another pastime, and each day in the Smoking Room, the prior day's run was posted; the ship had made 386 miles, from Thursday to Friday, despite her two stops for passengers and mail—yesterday's run would probably top five hundred. There was talk that Captain Smith and Ismay were trying to beat sister ship *Olympic*'s maiden-voyage performance.

May was reading the popular *The Virginian* by Owen Wister, which she'd bought in London; there had been something per-versely satisfying about purchasing a novel of the American West from a West End bookseller. Futrelle was absorbed in a book he'd discovered in the ship's library, contributed by some scamp as a grim joke: *Futility*, a science-fiction-tinged tale about the shipwreck of a luxury liner not unlike this one; in fact, the author—one Morgan Robertson, whose style was little better than the penny dreadfuls, but whose fertile imagination (like John Jacob Astor) made up for it—had even named his great ship the *Titan*.

The shrill ring of the nightstand phone drew Futrelle away from his novel—an iceberg had just struck the fictional wonder ship—and Futrelle answered it with a distracted, "Yes?"

"Oh, good! You're there.... This is Bruce ... Bruce Ismay."

As if there were any doubt which Bruce it might be.

Ismay was saying, "I had hoped we'd find you in your stateroom."

"Well, Bruce, you have," Futrelle said, hoping Ismay wasn't calling to say a full ship's tour with Andrews had been arranged; Futrelle had in mind a lazy day. "How can I help you?"

"Could you come to my suite, straightaway? And do please come alone. The captain and I would like to speak with you ... privately."

The captain? That fact, and something in Ismay's voice—a distressed edge—finally pulled Futrelle's attention away from the novel, which he laid folded open on the nightstand.

"I'll be there shortly," Futrelle said, and hung up.

May peeked over the colorful dust jacket of *The Virginian*. "I take it that was Mr. Ismay. What does he want now?"

"Possibly something to do with the book project," Futrelle said, reluctantly climbing from the comfortable bed.

"You don't sound convinced of that."

"I'm not." Futrelle was at the closet, choosing his clothing for the day. The brown houndstooth-check suit seemed appropriate, somehow. "I suspect something's wrong."

"Whatever could it be?"

He smirked to himself. "Let's hope it's not an iceberg."

"What, dear?"

"Nothing … just, when you've finished *The Virginian*, for your own peace of mind, I'd avoid this little novel I'm reading."

She gave him a puzzled look, shrugged and returned to her reading.

Within minutes, Futrelle was again knocking at the door to suite B52. This time a servant answered—a cadaverous liveried butler in his late fifties—who ushered Futrelle through the parlor of the grandiose stateroom. Soon the author had left Napoleon's Empire stylings behind for the mock-Tudor world of Ismay's private enclosed promenade, with its white walls with dark half-timbering.

Blond wicker chairs, mostly deck-style, mingled with the potted plants, so the sunny space provided plenty of places to sit; but both Captain Smith and J. Bruce Ismay were pacing, with all the anxiety of expectant fathers but none of the hope.

"Jack!" Ismay said. He wore a businesslike dark brown tweed; no knickers today. "Thank you for coming, old man. Sit down, won't you?"

Ismay pulled a wicker chair out into the walking area, and Futrelle sat; the White Star director drew up his own chair, while Smith—regal in a uniform as white and well pressed as that of a prosperous ice-cream salesman—stood with his hands locked behind him, staring absently out at the endless gunmetal sea.

Ismay was fussing. "Would you like coffee or tea, sir? Anything at all?"

"No. We had a late breakfast. Your room service is superb, gentlemen."

"Thank you," Ismay said.

The captain said nothing.

Awkwardness settled over the promenade like fog. Ismay looked toward Smith for help, but Smith's eyes were on the boundless waters.

"Something extremely unfortunate has occurred," Ismay said, finally. "One of our passengers has ... passed on to his final reward."

"Who died?"

Ismay twitched a wholly inappropriate smile. "Mr. John Bertram Crafton of London."

A humorless laugh that started in his chest rumbled out of Futrelle like a cannonball. Then he asked, "Murdered?"

Captain Smith glanced sharply over his shoulder, then stared back out at sea.

Ismay's eyes and nostrils were flaring like those of a rearing horse. "Why do you assume he's been murdered?"

"Oh, I don't know—perhaps because he appears to have been trying to blackmail the entire First-Class passenger list ... yourself included, Bruce."

Ismay swallowed thickly. "Our ship's surgeon indicates natural causes. Though a relatively young man, Mr. Crafton appears to have died in his sleep ... peacefully. Who knows— perhaps he had a heart condition."

Futrelle was cleaning his glasses on a handkerchief. "For that to be true, he'd've had to have a heart."

Ismay sighed, shifted in the wicker chair, crackingly. "If this *were* a case of murder ... and believe me, it isn't ... you would be in a particularly awkward position, Jack. After all, witnesses saw you suspending Mr. Crafton by his ankles over the Grand Staircase balcony."

"That was just a prank to make a point."

Futrelle thought he saw a faint smile cross the captain's lips, but—in his side view of the man—wasn't positive.

"In any case," Futrelle said, "I was hardly alone in my distaste for Mr. Crafton. I don't believe he was your choice for most favorite passenger, either, Bruce—and of course, Mr. Rood slapped him rather publicly, last night."

"Very true," Ismay said, nodding. "But, again, our ship's surgeon says this is definitely not murder."

"Well, that's a relief, because you'd certainly have a blue-chip list of suspects on your hands ... not to mention have a damper thrown over your highly publicized maiden voyage."

Fires lighted in the White Star's director's eyes, and his spine stiffened. "That will *not* be allowed to happen."

Futrelle shrugged. "If it's not murder, why should it? As I believe I pointed out, we are a little town, floating in this palace of the sea. People die in little towns every day, every night. A natural enough occurrence ... sad though it might be."

"Yes." Ismay lowered his head, his expression somber. "The loss of any one of our fellowmen is not to be taken lightly. As it is said in the Bible, 'His eye is on the sparrow.' "

"And, it would seem, the vulture ... So what does this have to do with me, gentlemen?"

The two men exchanged enigmatic expressions.

Then Ismay withdrew from the inside pocket of his suit coat a sheet of paper—White Star rounded-corner letterhead (found in every cabin on this ship) with its familiar wind-caught white-starred red flag at left of the legend: *On Board R.M.S. Titanic*. Oddly, the bottom of the sheet was torn away, leaving only three-quarters of the otherwise perfect specimen of *Titanic* stationery intact.

On the page, in a cramped, masculine cursive, had been penned the following list of names:

Astor

Brown

Butt/Millet

Futrelle

Guggenheim

Hoffman

Check marks were beside every name with the exception of "Brown."

Ismay asked, "And what do you make of this, Jack?"

Futrelle, studying the list, said, "Well, these, obviously, are the names of Crafton's blackmail 'clients.' "

"Yes. Including your own."

"With the exception of Mr. Guggenheim and Mrs. Brown ... and the lack of a check mark next to Maggie's name may indicate Crafton had not yet approached her ... I witnessed the late extortionist in action with each of these individuals. Are you talking to everyone on this list?"

A nonsmile twitched Ismay's lips; his mustache bobbed. "Thus far ... only you."

"Why? ... Let me answer that in part, myself: with the exception of your Second-Class passenger Mr. Hoffman, I'm the least socially prominent of the lot. Approaching Colonel Astor or Mr. Guggenheim ... that could be embarrassing. Delicate, at the very least."

A wan smile now formed under Ismay's mustache. "We value you every bit as much as anyone on this ship, Jack—a little more than most, actually."

"Why?"

Finally the captain spoke, though he still did not turn away from the view on the sea: "You have a background in newspaper work, sir, and criminology. Before this matter is closed, I would like you to have a look at Mr. Crafton."

Futrelle squinted; the sun coming in made it difficult to look at the captain for long. "I don't understand."

Smith swiveled on his heels, like a figure on a cuckoo clock; his hands remained locked behind him. "I want you to see the scene ... Mr. Crafton's body has not been moved, nothing has been disturbed."

Futrelle held up the White Star letterhead. "Other than this list."

Defensively pointing to the sheet still in Futrelle's grasp, Ismay said, "That was found on his dresser. Out in the open. Just like that."

"*Just* like this? May I point out, Bruce, that this letterhead has been torn."

"Obviously."

"And several names are missing."

"I don't follow."

Futrelle kept his voice gentle, as unintimidating as possible when he said, "I think you do. This is an alphabetical listing ... the missing names are Mr. Rood's, Mr. Stead's, Mr. Straus's ... and yours, Bruce. In order to remove your name from this list, tearing across the bottom, you had to remove Rood, Stead and Straus, as well."

Ismay was naturally pale, but he turned paler. "Well! I certainly didn't expect insults—"

"I didn't mean it as an insult. I don't blame you—in your position, I might have done the same. I might have destroyed the list in its entirety."

Ismay thought that over. "Then you are willing to be of help?"

"I'm certainly willing to look at the scene of the crime."

Eyes and nostrils again flared. "It's not a crime, damnit!"

"Then why bother having me view the scene? Believe me, I understand, Bruce, that your position in this is not enviable. The last thing on this earth that you desire is to have this maiden voyage blemished. I can well understand that you do not want the *Titanic*'s name forever linked with death."

Ismay considered Futrelle's words, then said, "So you will be discreet?"

"I have no desire for my wife and myself to be moved from our sumptuous stateroom into steerage, thank you."

Smith smiled—just a little, but a smile. He said, "We appreciate your cooperation, Mr. Futrelle."

"I won't go so far as to say it's my pleasure, Captain … but I do consider it my duty, a concept with which you're intimately acquainted."

They took the stairs down to C deck. Crafton's suite was C13, which was toward the forward end of the First-Class accommodations, on the port side of the ship, down a shallow hallway off of which were only a pair of rooms on either side. In a white uniform with cap, a bulbous-nosed, white-mustached, medium-sized old gent in his early sixties stood in the hallway to one side of the door marked C13, a black bag held before him like a big lumpy fig leaf.

Pausing there at the door, the captain said, "Mr. Futrelle, this is Dr. O'Loughlin, our chief surgeon. William, this is Jacques Futrelle."

O'Loughlin smiled, but his eyes didn't; he said, "I understand you're a famous author."

It occurred to Futrelle that if he were really famous, the chief surgeon would not have to be told that.

"I'm a writer," Futrelle said. "How was the body found, doctor?"

Ismay, looking furtively about, said, "Let's not discuss that until we're within the cabin, if you would, gentlemen?"

And the White Star director used a key to unlock the door, gesturing for Futrelle to go in, which he did, the other three men following.

It was a single, whitewashed oak-paneled room with a lavatory, like the Harrises' cabin, but minus the trunk closet—a brass double bed, green horsehair sofa, marble washstand, wicker cushioned armchair, a green mesh sack on the wall taking the place of a nightstand.

The figure on the near side of the bed, which was at left upon entering, was sheet-covered; no sign of struggle, or blood.

"I stripped the bed before making my examination," the doctor said, indicating the quilted bedspread and blankets which lay in a pile at the foot of the bed; on top of the pile sat the bed's two fat feathered pillows, both looking used.

Futrelle prowled the room, briefly, the three men getting out of his way as he did; he found nothing unusual, nothing that seemed out of place. He did not look in drawers, however, and stopped short of an actual search.

"To answer your earlier question, Jack," Ismay said, following him about, "Mr. Crafton was discovered this morning, just after nine o'clock, when a staff member came in to make up the room. As is common practice, the stewardess knocked, received no answer, unlocked the door and came in."

Futrelle was examining the door. "So the body was found in this locked room?"

"Yes."

"The door doesn't lock without a key, does it?"

"No—it can be locked from either side, but only with a key; there's no automatic locking device, as you do find in some hotels."

Futrelle, excusing himself as he brushed past the captain, approached the doctor, who stood near the bedside, poised to pull back the sheet.

"If you please, Doctor," he said.

"I warn you, sir—rigor mortis has set in."

"I'm a big-city newspaperman, Doctor. The dead are unfortunately not strangers to me."

The doctor nodded and drew the sheet to Crafton's waist.

In death, the blackmailer looked no less ferretlike, though easier to pity than despise. The late John Bertram Crafton stared at the ceiling with wide, dead eyes, his mouth drawn back in a grimace.

Futrelle tossed a smirk over his shoulder. "A peaceful death, did you say, Mr. Ismay?"

Crafton was a scrawny, even malnourished man with the scars of skin conditions and diseases upon his nearly hairless naked body.

"Did you strip him as well as the bed, Doctor?"

"No, sir. He's just as I found him—on his back, naked in bed.... No nightclothes or underthings."

Futrelle leaned in for a closer look. What he saw was hideous: the whites of Crafton's eyes were so clotted with burst vessels they were almost crimson.

"Petechial hemorrhaging, Doctor?"

Dr. O'Loughlin blinked in surprise; the nod that followed was barely perceptible.

Futrelle examined the corpse's hands, finding them—palms up—clawlike, a state grotesquely exaggerated by the rigor mortis.

Standing away from the corpse, Futrelle nodded to the doctor to cover Crafton back up, asking, "How many pillows was he sleeping with?"

"Just one," the doctor said.

"Where was the extra pillow? In its position near the headboard?"

"No. Halfway down the bed, as if …" The doctor glanced at Ismay, then shrugged.

"As if discarded," Futrelle said.

The captain stepped forward and said to Futrelle, "What was that medical term you used, sir?"

"Petechial hemorrhaging," Futrelle said. "A person being suffocated tries so hard to breathe, the blood vessels in the eyes burst. The clawed hands are another clear signal. Doctor, you may wish to examine under the fingernails for skin scratched from—"

"This is nonsense," Ismay said. His face was almost as red as Crafton's eyes had been.

"You're saying that this man was suffocated," the captain stated calmly.

"I have no doubt," Futrelle said. He nodded toward the pile of bed things. "With one of those pillows, most likely."

"Doctor," Ismay said, rage barely in check, "are these symptoms also consistent with heart failure or some other kind of natural cause?"

The doctor said nothing.

"Well, Doctor?" the captain asked.

"Perhaps," he said, with a shrug.

"Then as far as any of us are concerned," Ismay said forcefully, "this is death by natural causes. Is that understood?"

No one replied.

"Good," Ismay said.

Directing the question to all three of them, Futrelle asked, "Doesn't it concern you that you have a murderer aboard?"

Ismay's grimace was worse than Crafton's. "To have a murderer aboard, Mr. Futrelle, we would first have to have a murder."

"I understand your reluctance to involve passengers of prominence like Colonel Astor, Major Butt, Mr. Guggenheim and the rest ... but you might be endangering them, if a malevolent presence is aboard this ship."

Ismay sighed heavily. "Mr. Futrelle ..."

"What happened to 'Jack'?"

"Jack." And now Ismay spoke with withering sarcasm: "Let us suppose your diagnosis, and not Dr. O'Loughlin's, is the correct one; let's assume that years of medical school and years of the practice of medicine are no match for the expertise of a writer of mystery stories. What would be the motivation for Mr. Crafton's ... removal?"

"Oh, I don't know—possibly that he was a goddamned blackmailer."

"Precisely. This is not the work of Jack the Ripper, sir—if it's 'work' at all. Even if I wanted this matter investigated, I have limited security on the ship—the master-of-arms and his small staff. The 'suspects,' if you will, are wealthy individuals, traveling with retinue that could easily include a manservant or two, willing to dispatch an odious task of this nature. Someone like Major Butt, with his military background, would certainly have the stomach for it, himself."

Futrelle nodded. "We're certainly not lacking in possibilities for perpetrators."

Ismay threw his hands up. "For now, there is really nothing to be done. I ask everyone in this room—*everyone*, Mr. Futrelle

... Jack—to keep this unpleasant news to themselves. We won't be having stewards carting a body down the corridor, either. We will keep this room locked and the body will be removed to the cold-storage hold, tonight, when the ship is sleeping."

Futrelle regarded the cold-blooded Ismay with the dispassion of a scientist. "Not that anyone will be upset by the lack of his presence ... but how will you explain the absence of Mr. Crafton?"

Ismay was walking in a tiny circle in the tiny cabin. "Should anyone ask, he's taken ill, he is under Dr. O'Loughlin's care, staying here in his cabin. Though I hardly think on a ship this size, and with an individual so unloved, that this is likely to even come up."

"You may be right," Futrelle admitted.

Through all this, the captain had remained strangely silent.

In the hallway, with the room locked up tight, Ismay leaned in to Futrelle and whispered, "Now, I must ask you not to mention this to anyone, Jack—*anyone* ... including your lovely wife."

Futrelle grinned and patted Ismay on the back. "Do I look like the sort of man who tells his wife everything?"

Ten minutes later, in the sitting room of their stateroom, Futrelle had finished filling May in on all the details, including the more grisly ones.

They were sitting on the couch together, but May had her legs up under herself, and was turned toward her husband; she looked bright as a new penny in her casual day wear—white shirt with stiff collar and cuffs, blue woolen necktie, cream-color collarless cardigan and flared beige wool skirt.

She was not frightened or dismayed by the death of Crafton; if anything, she was exhilarated. She had been too long the wife of a newspaperman, too long the companion of a crime writer to be spooked by something so trivial as a locked-room murder.

"We should investigate," she said.

Futrelle smiled half a smile. "I'm sorely tempted."

"Do you think the murderer should be allowed to get away with this?"

"Frankly, considering the victim, I'm not sure the answer to that is obvious."

"As a good Christian, and a good citizen, you have a responsibility to put things right."

"I know. Besides, this is damned fascinating. Why was Crafton naked, do you suppose?"

"Perhaps sleeping that way was his normal practice."

"Possibly, but you know how cold it's been at night, even with these electric heaters. And not just anyone could have waltzed in there—whoever-it-was needed a key."

"That's not difficult, Jack—simply bribe someone on staff for the key."

"Ah, but that White Star Line staff member would eventually find out a murder had been committed in the room that key belonged to, and suddenly the killer finds himself either turned over to the law or being blackmailed from a new direction.... No, it's more likely Crafton let his murderer into his room, of his own free will."

May frowned and smiled at once. "*Naked?*"

The phone rang and made both of them jump; they laughed nervously, Futrelle saying, "Isn't it ducky we're taking this murder so lightly," and picked up the phone receiver.

"Futrelle here," he said.

"Mr. Futrelle ... Captain Smith."

He straightened, as if he were speaking to an officer—which of course he was. "Yes, Captain."

"Could you come to see me on the bridge? I'd like a word with you."

"Certainly." Futrelle decided to test the waters. "Could I bring my wife along? I'm sure she'd consider it a rare honor and treat."

"Perhaps another time. This I think should be in private. Straightaway, if you please."

"Yes, sir." Futrelle hung up the phone, turned to his wife, and said, "The captain wants to see me ... and not you."

"What does that mean?"

"It means, as my esteemed competitor's detective is wont to say, 'The game's afoot.' "

The bridge, on the boat deck, was a white chamber as spartan and well-scrubbed as an operating room, attended by a brace of crisply uniformed officers, youngish men with the weathered faces their profession bestows. The row of windows onto the gray, glistening ocean and the only slightly bluer sky above gave the room an open-air effect; along those windows was a row of the porcelain-based, double-sided clockfaces of gleaming brass-trimmed, double-handle-topped engine telegraphs, and of course the wooden wheel itself, an old-fashioned instrument attached to newly fashioned technology. Looking out over the bow of the ship conveyed a certain majesty, but nowhere near the actual size of the colossal vessel.

Captain Smith, pacing slowly, eyes on the horizon, suddenly looked less a symbol, more a man. Without Ismay around, Smith seemed considerably bigger—taller, broader, more formidable.

When Futrelle was announced, the captain smiled slightly and said, "Good of you to come, Mr. Futrelle … walk with me to the bridge wing, would you?"

On the outdoor platform near the small three-sided booth from which the ship's position was calculated by sextant, the captain leaned against the waist-high wall, regarding the sea with a stoic gaze. As they spoke, Smith rarely looked at Futrelle.

"Mr. Ismay wants the best for his company," the captain said, "and who can blame him? This ship was his dream—he first sketched it on a napkin. But it's my reality, Mr. Futrelle."

"Your concerns and duties aren't necessarily his," Futrelle said.

"Precisely. But he is the director of the line, launching the company's most important ship, and I am a lame duck of a captain, making his final crossing."

"All the more reason to do what you think is right."

Smith gave Futrelle a sideways look. "Right, as in proper? Correct?"

Futrelle shook his head. "There's no rule book for a situation of this kind. Ismay wants to avoid bad press, but simply ignoring the incident could court disaster."

"Elaborate."

"Crafton didn't just fall from the sky—even he had relatives and, presumably, friends. He certainly had business associates, in that extortion ring. Questions will be asked when we come ashore—and one may be why we didn't ask questions aboard ship."

Captain Smith nodded, barely. "I do believe Ismay's discretion is well-founded."

"Actually, so do I. Just too extreme."

Without looking at Futrelle, Smith asked, "Would you do me a service, sir? I can repay you only with my gratitude and friendship."

"Ask."

"Could you—in a circumspect manner, playing upon the lack of knowledge of those aboard as regards Mr. Crafton's demise—launch a sub-rosa investigation? Ask questions—innocent questions, on their face, but secretly knowing ones—to gather information so that I may make a decision before we reach New York."

"Not everyone is ignorant of this murder, you know."

"A handful know—ourselves, Ismay, the doctor and a single stewardess."

"And there's the murderer."

"So there is."

"And what if I should happen to ascertain the murderer's identity?"

The captain's face hardened. "Sir, I don't care what his social connections are or how many millions he has in the bank. If he's John Jacob Astor or some Italian beggar in steerage ... If Jesus Christ is the murderer, we'll turn Him over to the master-at-arms and slap Him in irons."

"I admire your backbone, Captain. But might I suggest we hear our Lord and Savior's side of it, first?"

And at last Smith turned and looked directly at Futrelle, and then he laughed and laughed; for so soft-spoken a man, the captain's booming laughter echoed across the forward well deck and forecastle deck, startling the smattering of steerage passengers risking the brisk air.

"We'll make no decisions until facts are gathered," Smith said. He slipped his hand onto Futrelle's shoulder again, and walked him slowly back toward the bridge. "There'll be no mention of this to Mr. Ismay, of course."

"Hell, no." He wasn't as deranged as the late Crafton had thought. "After all, we have an overriding reason to keep Ismay in the dark about the investigation, beyond his own White Star–based objections to it."

"What would that be, sir?"

"Why—he's a suspect himself, Captain."

"So he is."

And the two men smiled and shook hands.

SIX

INFORMAL INQUIRY

AT LUNCHEON, THE CAFÉ PARISIEN tended to be lightly frequented, and today was no exception.

The *Titanic*'s approximation of a sidewalk café on a Paris boulevard was designed more for a between-meal snack or perhaps an after-dinner aperitif; with sumptuous feasts available in the Dining Saloon and the à la carte Ritz, few passengers were willing to settle for the dainty sandwiches of the café's circular buffet.

The younger set had largely appropriated this sunlight-streaming trellised café on the starboard B deck—with its unobstructed ocean view—making it one of the livelier areas aboard ship. But right now the café held only a modest scattering of passengers, seated on the café's green wicker chairs at the festive round and square green-topped tables, taking advantage of the casually continental ambience, as the gently muted strains of the string trio playing in the reception room next door floated in.

Among this handful of passengers were the Futrelles and the Strauses, seated at a square table by the windows onto the ocean, tiny plates with tiny sandwiches before them all, accompanied by iced tea.

The Strauses had not selected their sandwiches from the buffet, however; a French waiter saw to it that they received kosher variations (the deviled ham Futrelle was nibbling at being wholly inappropriate). The waiter also made sure that the iced tea was sweetened, in the Southern style, as the two couples had Georgia backgrounds in common.

"What a good idea, getting away like this," Ida Straus said. She wore a black-and-white dress (mostly black) with fancy beadwork, typical of her conservative elegance. "They feed us so much on this ship! This makes a nice change.... Don't you agree, Papa?"

"Oh yes, Mama," Isidor Straus said, idly stroking his gray spade beard as he contemplated the minuscule sandwiches on his plate. His suit was dark blue, his shirt a wing collar with a tie of light blue silk; he too had a quiet elegance. "I only hope the Harrises and their friends don't mind eating alone."

"I invited Henry and René," Futrelle said, "but they declined—seems they exercised in the gym this morning, and worked up too much of an appetite."

Actually, Futrelle had explained to the Harrises that he needed to speak to the Strauses in private, supposedly to gather information for a story with a department-store setting.

"If you need an expert on department stores," Henry had said, "you're goin' to the wrong party .... Talk to René."

And René had added, "Henry B. is right—I probably spend more time in Macy's than Isidor Straus."

But nonetheless the Harrises graciously deferred, with no prying questions.

So far it had all been small talk. For such different couples, the Futrelles and Strauses had much in common, from Georgia to New York (Macy's was on Herald Square, after all, and Futrelle had worked for the *Herald*). Both couples agreed that the maiden voyage on the *Titanic* was proving a perfect way to top off their respective European trips. The Strauses had been taking a winter holiday at Cap Martin on the Riviera; the Futrelles had decided to cut their trip short when Jack, with his birthday looming, had gotten homesick for their two children.

"We plan to take Virginia and John traveling with us," Futrelle said, "when they're older, and out of school."

Straus nodded at the wisdom of that. "Let them be an age when they'll appreciate what you're giving them."

"We have six children," Ida said, "and as for grandchildren, we lose count."

It went on like that, with an excursion into mutual admiration. Straus—with no college education, an inveterate reader—was impressed by Futrelle's success in the writing field (though no mention was made of the Macy's magnate ever having read a Futrelle story or novel). Futrelle found it fascinating that Straus—who, with his brother Nathan, had started out with a china shop in Macy's basement and within ten years owned the store—had gone from the department-store business to Congress, becoming a close confidant of President Cleveland.

Straus was not a boastful man, and in fact downplayed his accomplishments. "I'm not interested in politics or business anymore. I'm at a stage in my life where my hobbies and traveling are more important."

"You're too modest," May said. She looked youthful in a boyish leisure outfit of white shirt with blue-and-green striped silk tie under a knitted green-and-brown waistcoat; her hat was a large-crowned light brown felt number with a curled brim. "After all, everyone knows your 'hobby' is helping people."

"You're too kind," Straus said, but he clearly liked hearing it.

Both Futrelles were well aware of Straus's philanthropy, particularly in the areas of education and aiding Jewish immigrants. Everything Futrelle knew about Straus made the man out a saint, albeit a Hebrew one; what in God's name could Crafton have had on this paragon of virtue?

It was time to find out; Futrelle caught his wife's gaze and narrowed his eyes in a signal imperceptible to all but her. May immediately began to dig in her purse.

"Oh dear," she said. "I've forgotten my medicine in our stateroom ... I need to take my pills with lunch."

The only medication May was taking was aspirin, but of course the Strauses didn't know that.

Futrelle began to rise. "Shall I go and fetch it for you, dear?"

"No, no, thank you, Jack—I'll run and get it." She turned to Ida with a smile. "I don't suppose I can talk you into keeping me company?"

And of course Ida could only say, "I'd love to," and soon the two women were winding through the mostly empty wicker tables and chairs.

Straus watched his wife depart with a fondness Futrelle found touching. "There goes as good a woman as ever a man was blessed with," Straus said. The old boy turned toward Futrelle. "And hang on to that gem of yours, if you don't mind a little advice."

"Smartest move I ever made," Futrelle said, "marrying that woman. Isidor ... now that we'll be alone for a moment, I need to ask you a question—in confidence."

The eyes behind the pince-nez glasses narrowed. "Your tone is serious."

"It's a serious matter."

Straus folded his hands, leaned forward. "Would it have to do with John B. Crafton?"

Straus's perceptiveness amused and surprised Futrelle. "Now, how did you know that, sir?"

"I know there is a rumor drifting about the ship that the famous mystery writer Jacques Futrelle held a man over the balcony of the Grand Staircase, and shook the change from his pockets."

Futrelle grinned. "That's more than a rumor, Isidor."

The old boy grinned back: the teeth weren't his (or actually they were—he'd purchased them).

"I'd have paid good money for a front-row seat to that show," Straus said. "You saw me give Crafton the heave-ho from our compartment, on the boat train, didn't you?"

"Yes—I had a front-row seat for that one, and it didn't cost me a dime."

Straus raised an eyebrow. "So we have more than a love for the state of Georgia in common. We share a dislike for that foul little man."

"We do. And I'd like to take the liberty of building on that common ground by asking a question or two … which if you do not answer, I'll take no offense. I only hope you take no offense in the asking."

"I'm sure I won't take offense. As to whether I'll answer your questions, I'll have to hear them first."

A waiter stopped by to replace their iced-tea glasses with fresh ones, and moved on.

Futrelle leaned in. "Is it safe for me to assume that Crafton approached you as one of his prospective 'clients'?"

"Safe indeed."

"My response to him was to hang him by his heels. Was your response, your full response, the one I saw on the train?"

The eyes behind the glasses narrowed. "I'm not sure I understand your meaning, sir."

"I mean ... forgive me ... did you pay him, or just send him packing?"

Now Straus understood; he nodded. "The latter. Not one penny in tribute to that scoundrel."

"I'm relieved to hear that. Have you seen Crafton today, about the ship, anywhere?"

Without hesitation, Straus said, "No. Not a trace. It's said another passenger slapped him last night."

"Yes. A Mr. Rood. I witnessed that, in the Smoking Room."

"Perhaps it's safe to assume that Mr. Crafton is ... what is the expression? 'Lying low'?"

"You may be right, Isidor. I can tell you I'm personally not at all concerned by his threats to me, and my reputation."

Briefly, Futrelle told Straus of the mental breakdown he'd suffered covering the war news at the *Herald*, and that he felt exposure of this ancient history could do him no professional harm whatsoever.

"The threat to me was equally trivial," Straus said. "You may be aware that my firm has a ... motto, you might say, used by Macy's rather extensively in its advertising: 'We never deal in old or bankrupt stocks ...' "

Futrelle, nodding, finished the familiar slogan: "... 'Macy's sells new and desirable goods only.' Yes, of course."

Straus's mouth pursed briefly, as if he were tasting something nasty, not sweetened iced tea. Then he said, "Well, Mr. Crafton claims to have documentary evidence that Macy's has been buying at public auction, selling items we purchased at close-out sales at full price, and so on. Furthermore, Crafton says he has proof that our advertising claims of having the lowest prices are often inaccurate and deceptive.... This is all poppycock, and even if it weren't, even if it were true, who would publish it? No one!"

Futrelle—newspaperman that he was—knew Straus was correct; Macy's advertised heavily in every New York City paper, and there was no way on God's green earth that those papers would expose a firm that was doing so much business with them.

"The only person who might do it is someone like that cantankerous crusader Stead," Futrelle said.

Straus chuckled and nodded. "Crafton said that he was negotiating with Stead to write the book which would expose my store's practices."

"That's nonsense! I saw Stead rebuff the bastard with a violence second only to my own."

Straus seemed faintly amused. "Nonsense indeed. Stead is a Salvation Army man, you know, and that group is among the charities we support."

Philanthropist Straus was as shrewd as he was generous: the Jewish philanthropist contributing to this Christian charity put the Salvation Army in the same position as the New York newspapers. Maybe the old boy wasn't exactly a saint; just another capitalist, granted a smart, good-hearted one.

Suddenly there was strength in Straus's face, and in his words, that belied his kindly demeanor: "I've known the likes of Crafton since I was a youth, running the European blockade for the Confederacy. He's a cowardly snake, and I say let him do his worst."

"I admire your attitude, sir," Futrelle said, just as the wives were returning.

Later, in their stateroom, Futrelle reported the conversation to May, as she reclined prettily on the chaise lounge. Her husband was pacing.

"Well," she said, "I think they're very sweet."

"They're a nice old couple," he granted. "But Isidor Straus is a tougher old bird than he appears."

"Capable of murder?"

"Who knows what a man of his accomplishments is or isn't capable of? And Crafton may have had something far worse on the old boy than false advertising."

"Such as what?"

"Don't forget Straus was in Washington politics—that's not exactly a bastion of morality and ethics. Businessmen like Straus run for office, saying they have the public at heart, but often are thinking of their own vested interests."

"You suspect him, then."

"He's a suspect. But if he did it, he's a better actor than Henry Harris could ever afford. When I asked old Isidor if he'd seen Crafton around the ship today, I saw no sign that he might know the man lay dead."

"Not to mention naked. But maybe that's the solution."

Futrelle frowned at his wife. "What is?"

She gazed at him with mock innocence. "He was naked because Mr. Straus was coming 'round to measure him for a new Macy's suit."

Futrelle laughed in spite of himself, and joined her on the chaise lounge; it creaked and squeaked under the weight of them—mostly, him.

"Careful, Jack! We might have to pay for this."

He kissed her sweet throat, then drew away, saying, "Did you ever hear of the man who asked every attractive woman he met if he could make love to her?"

"No! What did they say?"

"Most of them said no."

"Then why did he keep asking?"

"I said 'most of them'.... And maybe that's the kind of blackmailer we have here. Maybe there's no elaborate ring; perhaps Mr. Crafton even worked alone. Maybe his threats were empty, and the little blackguard was just a petty swindler looking for the occasional payoff."

"You mean, he's a nuisance and, if you're rich enough, it's worth some money to make him go away."

"Precisely. Think how many people were on that list of his! If he were getting big money out of any one of them, he wouldn't have needed so many 'clients' ... If I'd only waited to see how much money he wanted out of me, before I ..."

"Before you what?"

"Nothing."

She studied him as they lay side by side on the chaise, then asked, "What if I told you René said someone saw you hanging Mr. Crafton over the balcony by his feet?"

"I'd say René was getting that information secondhand ... because I definitely didn't see her there."

Her eyes widened and her grin was gleeful. "You did do it! Why, you reckless fool ..."

"I'll show you how reckless I am, if you'll let me."

She bounced off the chaise lounge. "I'm not about to spoil you with too much attention. Besides, I have a certain scrap of information I think you might like to have."

Watching as she smoothed out her brown ankle-length wool-tweed skirt, he asked, "Are you going to make me ask?"

Now she was straightening the blue-and-green tie, checking herself in the mirror, adjusting the cock of her brown felt hat. "I just don't want you to think you're the only detective in the family."

"What piece of information?"

She looked at him in the mirror. "When Mrs. Straus and I were fetching my 'medicine,' we ran into the Astors, and now Madeline is joining me for tea in the First-Class Lounge, in, oh … about fifteen minutes."

"No wonder you wouldn't let me get … reckless."

"You've been reckless enough for one day. Besides, I think you could use a little exercise, dear.…"

"What I have in mind *is* exercise, of a sort."

"… After all, Jack, writing is such sedentary work. Would you be offended if I suggested you attend the gymnasium this afternoon?"

"There will be less of me to love."

She shrugged, turned away from the mirror, perfectly pretty. "It's your decision. I just thought you might enjoy having a spirited physical-culture session.… I know *Colonel Astor* will be there."

Futrelle bounded up from the chaise lounge, and kissed his wife's cheek. "You are a detective, my love," he said, and slipped out of the stateroom.

On the starboard side of the ship, near the First-Class entrance, was the modern, spacious gymnasium, its walls a glistening white-painted pine with oak wainscoting, the floor gleaming linoleum tile, its equipment an array of the latest contraptions of physical training, or (in Futrelle's view) instruments of torture. With the exception of the white-flannel-clad instructor, the gym stood empty—morning was its busy time.

The instructor greeted Futrelle, who had met the robust little fellow on the purser's tour—T. W. McCawley, perhaps thirty-five years of age, with dark hair, dark bright eyes and a military-trim mustache.

"Mr. Futrelle!" McCawley said. He had a working-class English accent as thick as a glass of stout. "Good to see you, sir! Decide to come in and try your strength, t'day, did you?"

"I'm surprised you remember my name, Mr. McCawley."

"You First-Class passengers are my business, sir—and your health is my chief interest and concern."

"That's bully," Futrelle said, without much enthusiasm. The room's rowing machine, pulley weights, stationary bicycles, and mechanical camels and horses held no appeal for the mystery writer. His idea of exercise was sitting on the porch of his house in Scituate for a spirited session in his rocking chair. "Has Colonel Astor stopped by?"

"He's in the changing room," the instructor said, with a nod toward the door in question, "gettin' into his togs. There's a pair in there waitin' for you, sir."

"You sure you have my size?"

"And larger. No job is too big for T. W. McCawley."

The instructor's enthusiasm already had Futrelle worn-out.

But he headed for the changing room nonetheless, finding white flannels in his size, and John Jacob Astor, already bedecked in white flannel, seated on a bench, tying the laces of a pair of tennis shoes, and without the aid of valet.

"Colonel," Futrelle said. "What a pleasure running into you."

"Afternoon, Jack," Astor said; his voice was friendly enough, but his sky-blue eyes were glazed with their usual bored, distracted cast. "Your company will be appreciated."

Astor went on into the gym, while Futrelle climbed into the white flannels; he hadn't brought tennis shoes—the bluchers he'd had on would have to do.

"Join me for a spin, Jack?" Astor called out. He was pedaling away on one of two stationary bicycles near a large dial on the wall that registered the speed and distance of each bike.

Futrelle said, "Don't mind if I do," and hopped on.

The instructor was headed their way—as if any instruction on riding a bike were needed—when a young couple entered and McCawley did an about-face and attended them. The gym, unlike the Turkish Bath, did not segregate the sexes, and for about five minutes, the instructor ushered the young couple (honeymooners) around his dominion, eventually sending them off to their respective changing rooms.

During that time, Futrelle and Astor, aboard their bikes, chatted; this time Futrelle didn't bother with small talk, as the best way to deal with the remote millionaire was to directly engage his attention.

"I saw you talking to that fellow Crafton, in the cooling room yesterday," Futrelle said, barely pedaling.

Astor, who was in good shape, his legs working like pistons, said, "Did you?" It wasn't exactly a question.

"I wondered," Futrelle said, "if you'd had as unpleasant an experience with the louse as did I."

Astor kept pedaling, staring straight ahead; but he was listening, Futrelle could tell the man was listening.

"He tried to blackmail me," Futrelle said, and briefly explained.

Astor, hearing Futrelle frankly expose the mental skeleton in his closet, turned his cool gaze on his fellow rider, and his pedaling pace slowed.

"He had a similar scheme where I was concerned," Astor admitted. But he offered no clarification, and picked his speed back up.

"May I be so bold," Futrelle said, "as to ask if Crafton presented any real threat to you, Colonel?"

"Most likely not," he said casually, face bland, legs churning. "He claimed this fellow Stead was going to publish an exposé about the conditions of certain of our buildings."

Futrelle knew very well that the Astors—who owned much of Manhattan—numbered among their ample holdings not only the opulent Astoria Hotel but block upon block of notoriously wretched slums.

"Do you think Stead could be an accomplice of Crafton's?" Futrelle asked. This time he kept to himself Stead's vigorous rebuff of the ferrety little man on the boat train.

"Very doubtful. You see, Mr. Stead is aligned with the Salvation Army ..."

And as Astor caught a breath, Futrelle—fresh from hearing Isidor Straus sing so similar a song—finished for him: "Which is high on the list of those on the receiving end of the Astors' many charitable contributions."

"Quite so. Also, several other charities designed to aid former prostitutes and unwed mothers, pet causes of Mr. Stead's; my family, my mother in particular, has long been a supporter of these causes."

"So, this Crafton—you refused to pay the bastard."

"No. I paid him. He only wanted a pittance—five thousand."

Futrelle, on his bike ride to nowhere, was feeling light-headed; whether it was this exercise, which he wasn't used to, or encountering Astor's nonchalant attitude toward paying off a blackmailer, he couldn't be certain.

"Tell me, Colonel, have you seen Crafton around the ship at all today?"

"No." Astor suddenly stopped pedaling. His forehead was beaded with sweat but he wasn't breathing hard. "I can't say I was looking for him, either. He's rather disagreeable company, don't you think?"

Futrelle had stopped his pedaling, too. Astor was headed over to the rowing apparatus; he paused there and glanced at Futrelle, saying, "You mind if I have the first go, Jack?"

"It's all yours, Colonel," Futrelle said. "I've done all the traveling I care to, for the moment."

In his stateroom, Futrelle took a warm relaxing bath, and lounged in his robe, returning to the chaise lounge and the novel *Futility*, the title of which seemed to him to reflect his efforts. Trying to see beyond Astor's diffident mask was a hopeless task; like Straus, John Jacob Astor was a harder man than he might appear. Futrelle could well imagine the millionaire casually dispatching a manservant to smother a blackmailer with a pillow.

But he could also imagine Astor peeling off hundred after hundred from a fat wad of bills, to remove an annoyance, swatting the fly with money.

While Futrelle had been in the gym chasing Astor on a bolted-down bicycle, his wife had been sharing hot tea and buttered toast with Madeline Astor—and the Astors' mascot Maggie Brown—in the luxurious First-Class Lounge on A deck.

The extravagantly ornate lounge, modestly based on the Palace of Versailles, was primarily the province of ladies, the distaff equivalent of the Smoking Room, sans smoking of course. The high-ceilinged oak-paneled room—with its carved scroll-work and glowing overhead bonfire of a central chandelier—had boundaries defined by a fireplace (too grand to ever light) at one end and a bookcase (too elegant to ever open) at the other. The green color scheme of the lush carpeting and richly upholstered chairs was soothing, undermined by the busy nature of their rococo designs. Scattered games of bridge and canfield were under way at the most exquisitely carved tables ever used for card playing.

But May and Madeline and Maggie weren't playing cards; they were gossiping—or at least the latter two were ... May was secretly playing detective.

The women had already discussed how the becoming, "but in no way young" Mrs. Helen Candee had attracted a harem of middle-aged men, while all agreed that a certain handsome young Swede in the Candee coterie was the likely candidate for the one having the shipboard affair.

And it had been noted that Ben Guggenheim and his mistress had given up on the pretense of traveling separately, and a number of stewards had been heard to address her as "Mrs. Guggenheim."

"Have either of you seen this John Crafton around the ship?" May asked them casually.

"You mean that rat-faced little bastard with the gold-top cane?" Maggie Brown asked. She was bundled into a pale gray silk dress with black silk cuffs and trim, and a large wide-brimmed black velvet hat with ostrich feathers.

May, who had decided to be amused rather than disgusted by Maggie's dockworker vocabulary, laughed and said, "I think it's safe to say we're talking about the same party."

Madeline Astor—lovely in a pink silk suit with lilac satin bindings that matched the band and big bow of her wide-brimmed straw hat—leaned close and said, almost whispered, "You know, the little beggar tried to blackmail Jack and me."

Mrs. Astor meant *her* Jack, not May's. (Apparently John Jacob Astor did not require his wife to address him as "Colonel.")

"No!" May said, sounding genuinely shocked, thinking, *This detective work is easy.* "He must be trying to blackmail everyone on the ship! He did the same to my Jack and me."

And May quickly told them about the confrontation between Jack and Crafton, including her husband's "breakdown," and how he'd dangled the blackmailer over the balcony—which made Madeline titter, and Maggie squeal with delight.

Maggie, unabashed, turned to Madeline and said, "What d'he have on you, honey? I suppose he was threatenin' to tell the world that that bun was in your oven 'fore you walked down the aisle."

Madeline, who seemed quite used to Maggie's outrageous outbursts, tittered again, saying, "Exactly right. Oh, there was some nonsense about some of Jack's family's tenement properties … I didn't follow that. But this Craft character—"

"Crafton," Maggie corrected.

"Crafton," Madeline said, nodding. "Well, he claimed to have documents from the hospital in Paris, where I was examined, that would prove our supposed indiscretions. But it was just a bald-faced fabrication."

"Crafton was runnin' a bluff?" Maggie asked.

Madeline nodded. "Maggie, I'm five months pregnant ... John and I were married seven months ago. Our child was conceived in wedlock, much as that will disappoint the good people of Newport."

"So," Maggie said, eyes glittering with interest, "did the Colonel give the son of a bitch the boot?"

"No, I think he paid him, or anyway is going to."

"Why?" May asked, astounded.

"It's just easier that way. Jack is very sensitive right now to criticism, particularly about us. He very much wants to reenter society, and see me accepted ... I don't really care, myself, but it means a lot to Jack."

"Bunch of snooty high hats," Maggie snorted, though her apparent disdain for high society didn't jibe with her obvious desire to join it.

"Do you know Crafton?" May asked Maggie. "Frankly, it sounds like you do."

Maggie shrugged. "Slick little shrimp approached me, first night I come aboard. Said he wanted to talk to me about a 'business proposition.' I didn't like the look of him, but I said I'd try and work him into my dance card."

May narrowed her eyes. "But that meeting hasn't taken place."

"No, honey, not yet ... and I haven't seen 'im in a while—not today, anyway. How about you, Madeline?"

"I haven't seen him," Madeline said, with a little shrug. "I don't really ever care to see him."

"Y'suppose he was gonna try to blackmail yours truly?" Maggie asked, pointing a thumb to her formidable bosom.

Teasingly, May asked, "What have you done that you could be blackmailed over?"

Maggie roared. "What haven't I done?"

Dirty looks from nearby bridge players did not sway Maggie's enthusiasm, or her volume.

She continued: "Maybe he's got the goods on me sleeping with a younger man or two ... What he doesn't know is, my husband doesn't give a ding dong damn. We're separated, and we like it that way. I don't look in or under his bed, and he does me the same service."

An hour later, in their stateroom, May reported all this to her husband, who said, "It doesn't sound like Maggie Brown would've paid Crafton his dirty money."

"She's a tough old girl, Jack. I could see her doing it."

"Smothering Crafton with a pillow?" Futrelle smirked. "Or maybe her bosom."

May elbowed him, playfully; they were sitting on the couch together in the stateroom parlor.

"You know, I didn't like her at first," May said. "But Maggie Brown is a true eccentric, and about as genuine a person as you could hope to meet."

"In First Class on the *Titanic*, I'd have to agree with you ... Darling, you did well. Very well indeed."

"Thank you."

"Better than I did. Madeline Astor told you everything; her husband lied to me."

May shook her head, no. "Not really. He told you the truth, just not all of it—he was protecting his wife. Don't you think that's a noble objective?"

"People have been known to kill for noble objectives." Futrelle yawned. "We should be freshening up for dinner, soon. I think I'll run down to the barbershop for a shave."

"All right—just remember, we're meeting the Harrises at six-thirty."

The barbershop, which had two chairs, was right there on C deck, a short stroll from their stateroom, near the aft staircase. The small shop also served as a souvenir stand, offering pennants, postcards and toy life preservers; display cases showed off overpriced pipes and watches and wallets. Stuffed dolls of the Katzenjammer Kids, Happy Hooligan, Buster Brown and other cartoon characters hung from the ceiling, strung up like a comics-page lynching.

Both chairs were filled as the two white-smocked barbers attended their customers; Futrelle settled in on the black leather couch, to wait his turn. There was one patron ahead of him: Hugh Rood.

Crafton's Smoking Room adversary still had a distinguished look, his dark brown herringbone suit set off nicely by a brown-and-gold striped silk tie with diamond stickpin.

Futrelle introduced himself, and Rood—somewhat warily, it seemed—gave his name and accepted a handshake.

"I'd like to compliment you, sir," Futrelle said. He spoke softly; the barbers were chatting with their customers, in the time-honored way, and Futrelle could—by keeping his voice down—keep their conversation private.

The handsome, reddish-haired Rood smiled, but his eyes, which were as green as money, seemed wary, confused. "What have I done to deserve a compliment from you, Mr. Futrelle?"

"You did what a lot of us wanted to do—you slapped that bastard Crafton."

Rood's face went curiously blank for a moment, then his brow tightened and, scowling, he said, "Nothing less than he deserved."

"He's a blackmailer, you know." Quickly, he told Rood what Crafton had threatened to reveal about him.

"The man's a cad," Rood said.

"Might I ask why you slapped him, Mr. Rood? Did he have similar extortion designs, where you were concerned?"

The blank expression returned; then, rather coldly, he said, "Well, that's my business, isn't it?"

"Certainly. Forgive my impertinence. I didn't mean to be rude ... Mr. Rood."

Then a chair became available and Futrelle sat down for his shave. When Rood finally took the chair next to him, for a haircut and shave, Futrelle asked, "Say, have you seen him about the ship today?"

"Who?"

"Crafton."

"No."

"Funny. I haven't either. Where do you suppose he's gotten to?"

"I'm sure I don't know."

And that was the end of their conversation; and of Futrelle's shave. He paid the barber, tipped him well, said good-bye to Mr. Rood, who curtly said good-bye to him.

In the stateroom, as they dressed for dinner, Futrelle reported the encounter to his wife.

"Finally," she said, "we've got someone who's acting suspiciously."

"In a way," Futrelle said, frustrated, "Rood is behaving the least suspiciously of all ... That is, like a blackmail victim with something to hide, something he doesn't want to talk about."

"You mean like murdering John Crafton?" May suggested.

And they went down to dinner.

SEVEN

SECOND-CLASS CITIZEN

IN THEIR EVENING CLOTHES, FUTRELLE and shipbuilder Thomas Andrews—who was leading the way—might have seemed to have wandered astray, winding through the elaborate galley on D deck.

But no one bothered the pair, not a single question met them, as they threaded through the seemingly endless array of glistening white cabinets and stainless-steel fixtures, mammoth ranges, grill after grill, oven upon oven, a bustling domain of aromas and steam, of clatter and clang. Every member of the culinary army—cooks specializing in sauces, roasts, fish, soups, desserts, vegetables; bakers and pastry chefs; busboys and dishwashers—recognized Andrews as a frequent visitor.

In fact the only comment they received was from a cook who informed Andrews, "That hot press still ain't workin' worth a damn, sir. Playin' bloody hell with our sauces."

Andrews assured the cook he was aware of the problem and working on it, as the shipbuilder and Futrelle pressed on.

"I'm at your service twenty-four hours a day," Andrews told Futrelle. "The captain said, should you need passage to any restricted areas on the ship, I'm to provide it."

143

The ceiling above them was arrayed with hundreds of handle-hung water pitchers.

"I'll try not to impose—I know you're busy, Mr. Andrews."

"My friends call me Tom."

"Mine call me Jack."

They were passing by an immense open cupboard of stacked china.

Gently, Andrews asked, "Do you mind telling me what this is about, Jack? If I'm not overstepping my bounds."

The builder of the *Titanic* asking this of Futrelle seemed at once absurd and extraordinary.

"I'm not allowed to say," Futrelle said. "But it does have to do with a matter of ship security."

"Then this is more along the lines of your criminologist expertise than newspapering or fiction writing."

"I really shouldn't say any more, Tom."

"Understood."

After dinner in the First-Class Dining Saloon, Futrelle had excused himself from May, the Harrises, Strauses and their other tablemates to approach the captain's table. Futrelle and Smith had stepped away—out of Ismay's hearing, if not his sight—and the mystery writer had a word with Smith about his need to speak to a certain Second-Class passenger. The captain had immediately put Andrews and Futrelle together, and sent them on this mission, through the huge galley that served both First and Second Class—the First-Class Dining Saloon was forward of the kitchens, the Second-Class Dining Saloon aft.

Not seeking to collide with waiters or busboys, Andrews and Futrelle avoided the central double push doors into the Second-Class Dining Saloon and entered through a door to the far right. They stood in the corner, looking out over hundreds of heads of diners, well dressed but not in the formal attire that now made Andrews and Futrelle look like the restaurant's headwaiters.

The pleasant, commodious dining room—with its unadorned, English-style oak paneling—was smaller than its First-Class brother, but not much—just as wide (the width of the ship) and a good seventy feet long. The windows, here, were portholes, undisguised, and the feeling of being on a ship was more prominent than in First Class. Endless long banquet tables with swivel chairs fixed into the linoleum floor gave the dining room an institutional feel, but that was a seating style common in First Class on other liners. White linen tablecloths and fine china made for typical *Titanic* elegance, and the food itself—baked haddock, curried chicken and rice, spring lamb—looked and smelled wonderful.

"Do you see who you're looking for?" Andrews asked Futrelle, who was casting his gaze all about the room.

"No … we'd better take a walk."

They moved down the central aisle, attracting a few glances.

Then Futrelle spotted him, up near the piano at the aft end of the room: Louis Hoffman, seated between his two adorable tousled-haired boys.

"I need to approach him alone," Futrelle said.

Andrews nodded, and settled himself next to a pillar.

Hoffman and his boys were almost finished eating, the father helping the youngest boy scoop out the last tasty tidbits of tapioca from a cup. Again, their attire was not inexpensive: the boys were dressed identically, in blue serge jackets and bloomers and stockings; Hoffman a lighter blue suit with a dark blue silk tie and wing collar. He was a doting father, and watching him interact with his boys made clear the love this little family shared.

Futrelle almost hated to interrupt, particularly with the unpleasant subject he must broach; but he had no choice.

The chair across from Hoffman was empty and the mystery writer came around the long table and took it. The black-haired, dimple-chinned Hoffman glanced up with a smile under the waxed curled-tip mustache; but the smile faded and a frown crossed his rather high forehead.

"Mr. Hoffman, my name is Futrelle."

"Can I help you?" His accent wasn't English or German, but it wasn't French, either, which based upon the continental manner of the man's grooming had been Futrelle's guess, and after all Crafton had referred to Hoffman as a "Frenchman." Now Futrelle revised his opinion to something more like middle European—Czech perhaps, or Slovak …

"Papa!" the older boy said, and then the child spoke to his father in rapid French (apparently asking for more tapioca), and the father replied the same way (apparently gently refusing him).

Now Futrelle was thoroughly confused—"Hoffman" with his Slovak accent spoke French and so did his children.

"There's a matter of common concern to both of us," Futrelle said.

"How is that possible?" Hoffman asked curtly; his dark eyes were hard and glittering. "We have never met."

"But we have both met John Crafton."

Now the eyes narrowed. "The name is not familiar."

"Please, Mr. Hoffman. I saw you speaking with him on the boat deck, Wednesday afternoon … and Crafton mentioned you to me himself."

And now the eyes widened—but they were still hard, glittering. Gentle as he was with his boys, this was a dangerous man. "Are you calling me a liar?"

"Believe me, as another of Mr. Crafton's 'clients,' I understand the need for discretion ... Could we speak in private?"

Hoffman glanced from one boy to the other; even the youngest one, who couldn't be more than two years of age, was perfectly well behaved. As a fellow father, Futrelle found this remarkable.

"I do not leave my boys," Hoffman said. "They are with me always."

"Do they speak English?"

"No."

"Well, bring them along, then. Perhaps we could go to your cabin."

Hoffman considered that, then said, "No. We will speak in private. A moment please."

He rose and moved two seats down, to an attractive young blonde woman in her twenties, to whom he spoke in French. She smiled at him, nodding, speaking in Swedish-accented French! The only word Futrelle recognized in her response was "*Oui*," for despite his Huguenot heritage, he knew barely enough of the language to order in a French restaurant.

As the blonde woman took the father's seat between the boys, Hoffman smiled shyly at her and thanked her, then kissed each boy on the forehead, a gesture neither seemed to notice, so common was it from this doting father. Then Hoffman's benign expression dissolved into a glower, as his gaze fixed upon Futrelle; Hoffman nodded toward the exit and bid Futrelle follow him.

Futrelle glanced behind him, seeing Andrews frowning and stepping forward; but Futrelle gestured to him to stay put. Andrews nodded and fell back.

The cabin was farther aft on D deck, and neither party said a word as they made their way there, Futrelle trailing dutifully after the smaller man. Hoffman unlocked the door and gestured for Futrelle to go in, which he did.

The Second-Class cabin was cozy but not cramped, and Futrelle had been in First-Class quarters on other ships that did not equal these pleasant accommodations: bunk berths at left, a sofa bed at right, a mahogany dresser against the wall between the beds, equipped with a mirror and foldout washbasin. The walls were white, the floors linoleum-tiled.

"May I sit?" Futrelle asked, gesturing to the sofa.

Hoffman nodded, his eyes tight with suspicion.

Futrelle sat and then Hoffman sat, too, opposite, on the lower berth.

"First of all, Mr. Hoffman, I want to assure you I don't represent any police agency in any way."

Alarm leaped into the dark eyes, but Hoffman tried to keep his voice calm and casual as he replied, "Why should that bother me if you did?"

"Because you're traveling under an assumed name."

"Nonsense."

"You're a Slovak with two French-speaking boys named Lolo and Momon. But you boarded as an Englishman named 'Hoffman.' "

Eyes wild now, he sprang to his feet. "How much has he told you?"

Futrelle patted the air, as if trying to calm a child. "Nothing ..."

Hoffman's hand dropped into his suit coat pocket. "Are you with him?"

"What?"

"Are you part of this ... ring?"

"No!"

And Hoffman's hand withdrew from the pocket: in it was a small, but no less deadly-looking, blue-steel revolver.

The revolver's single eye was staring at Futrelle.

Hoffman's voice trembled with rage and something else, something worse: fear. He said, "You tell him, you tell your Crafton, the only price I'll pay him is bullets. Tell him that."

Futrelle rose, slowly, holding his hands, palms out. "I'm not with Crafton."

Now Hoffman jammed the gun into Futrelle's belly and said, "What, you think you can cut in on his game? Maybe you want to go over the side, yes?"

"No. Mr. Hoffman, I'm not a blackmailer. I'm in the same position you're in—damnit, I'm Crafton's prey, too!"

Hoffman thought about that, withdrawing the snout of the gun from Futrelle's belly, stepping back one step.

In a move so fast it surprised even himself, Futrelle slapped the gun from Hoffman's hand and it clattered onto the linoleum, thankfully not firing as it landed. Hoffman, startled but furious, threw a punch at Futrelle, but the larger man leaned back and the fist swished by harmlessly.

Then Futrelle—so much bigger than Hoffman—threw a punch into the man's midsection that doubled him over, sending him stumbling backward, into the berths.

Futrelle retrieved the little revolver. He checked the cylinder: it was fully loaded. Sweating, nervous, Futrelle said, "You've gotten on my bad side now, Hoffman. Sit down. Now."

Hoffman, clutching his stomach, desperately seeking to retain his fine Second-Class meal, sat back down on the lower berth.

"I'm not a blackmailer," Futrelle said, and he emptied the revolver's shells onto the linoleum floor, then tossed the empty gun at Hoffman, who he stood looming over. "I'm no friend of John Crafton's, either. Let me tell you how he threatened me. ...."

And Futrelle sat down again, on the sofa, and quietly told Hoffman about Crafton's threat to expose his mental breakdown. Slowly, Hoffman regained his composure and his manner softened.

"I'm sorry," Hoffman said, and then he began to weep.

More startled by this than when the man had drawn the gun on him, Futrelle found himself rising and settling next to the little man on the lower berth, easing an arm around his shoulder.

Gently, like an understanding parent, Futrelle said, "Tell me, Mr. Hoffman. What is this about? Crafton holds some threat over you and your boys, doesn't he?"

Hoffman, tears streaming, snuffling, nodded. "Do you have ... ?"

"Certainly." Futrelle withdrew a handkerchief and gave it to the man.

"My ... my name isn't Hoffman. I'm a tailor and yes, I was born in Slovakia, though for the last ten years I've lived in France. I married a beautiful young girl from Italy ..."

Yet another country heard from.

"... and we had our two beautiful sons. No man ever had a happier life."

Hearing those words from a man whose face was streaked with tears, his nose running, his lips trembling, could only mean a tragedy was about to be recounted.

It was, and a familiar one: "My business began to fail, my wife had an affair ... we separated. The boys went with their mother. Lolo and Momon, they came to stay with me over Easter, and I ... I stole them."

"You kidnapped your own children?"

He wasn't crying now; he had himself under control. "Yes. I have made arrangements for a new life in America. A former partner awaits me to go in business with him—and I am a good tailor, I will give my boys a good life."

"What about their mother?"

He lowered his head. "I still love her. If she comes to her senses and leaves this man, perhaps she'll come and find us one day, her little family."

And the weeping began again.

"How did Crafton find out?"

Bitterness edged Hoffman's voice. "It's his business to know the grief of others. My wife has posted a reward, there are circulars ... Crafton says if I don't make him a partner in the new business, he'll turn me over to the police. I'll go to jail for kidnapping my own flesh and blood."

Futrelle patted the man on the back, in a "there there" manner, and then he said, "When did you see Crafton last?"

Hoffman shrugged. "On the deck that day. He's like you—in First Class. He does not come bother me again—but he will in America. He will in America."

"No he won't."

Hoffman looked up at Futrelle with red eyes. "What do you mean?"

"If I tell you something, Mr. Hoffman ..."

"It's Navatril. Michel Navatril."

The little man offered his hand and Futrelle shook it.

"Mr. Navatril, I need your word that if I share a confidence with you, it will go no further than these walls and our ears."

"You have my word."

"John Crafton is dead."

"... How?"

"Someone murdered him."

"It wasn't me!"

"No. I'm fairly certain you'd have shot him and tossed him overboard. No, he was smothered with a pillow. Those in charge of the *Titanic* are keeping this news concealed, for the moment, for their own purposes. But you must be careful—you are known to be one of his blackmail victims."

"How could anyone know?"

"A list of 'clients' was in his room. You need to get off the ship, when it docks, and quickly disappear with your boys."

"You ... you're not going to ..."

"Turn you in? No. I don't know that what you did was right, Mr. Navatril, but I do know you love your boys ... and I'm convinced you didn't kill John Crafton."

"I would have liked to."

"An understandable sentiment ... Good luck to you."

And the two men again shook hands.

His manner considerably warmer, Navatril walked Futrelle back to the Second-Class Dining Saloon, where father rejoined sons and Futrelle rejoined Andrews.

"Did you do what you needed to?" Andrews asked as they headed out.

"Yes."

"No difficulties?"

"Nothing much."

By the time the two formally attired men wound their way through the galley, on the return trip, the hectic pace of the expansive kitchen had slowed into the cleanup phase, the execution of culinary arts replaced with the mundane reality of dishwashing, storage and garbage disposal. And in the now cavernously empty First-Class Dining Saloon, tables were being set anew with linen and china and silverware.

At the Grand Staircase beyond the Dining Saloon, Andrews disappeared with a nod, probably heading up to his stateroom, while Futrelle made his way into the spacious reception room, where the nightly concert was under way.

Like the two dining saloons, the reception room extended the width of the ship, yet for an area so expansive (over fifty feet in length, Futrelle guessed), the effect was of intimacy— the white-paneled walls so exquisitely carved in low relief, soft glowing lighting, the rich Axminster carpet, the casual cane chairs, the occasional luxurious Chesterfields, the round cane tables for parties of four amidst lazily leaning palms sprouting from an abundance of pots.

Violinist Wallace Hartley's quintet was clustered about the grand piano (there was no stage), playing a medley of numbers from Offenbach's *The Tales of Hoffmann*, which seemed ironically fitting to Futrelle, considering the tale he'd just heard from "Hoffman." The little orchestra was quite good at light classical—Puccini, Dvořák, Bizet—and late in the evening an area might be cleared for some informal dancing to ragtime, primarily by the younger passengers, struggling to perform that latest dance, the fox-trot, to a drummerless orchestra with no fox-trots in their repertoire.

Futrelle joined May and the Harrises at a little table near a window onto the serene ocean under a clear starless sky; faintly, ever so faintly, the thrum of the ship's motion could be perceived, like a gentle counterpoint under the main melody. The "concert" was informal, and muted conversation was common, as stewards circulated with coffee and tea, and scones (in the unlikely event anyone had saved room).

"She's a pretty girl," Henry was saying.

"Don't get any ideas, Henry B.," René said, kidding him on the square. She looked pretty herself in a green silk organdy evening gown with a diamond tiara trimmed with bird-of-paradise feathers.

"Who's a pretty girl?" Futrelle asked, settling into his chair.

"Dorothy Gibson," May explained. His wife looked especially comely tonight, in her cream silk-satin evening dress, her hair up, no hat. "Young cinema actress Henry and René met on the boat deck, this afternoon."

"Brazen little thing," René said, rolling her eyes. "She came up and introduced her*self*." This seemed to Futrelle an amusing judgment coming from such a modern, self-assertive woman.

"She has your typical obnoxious stage mother," Henry said, "who normally I couldn't abide. But this girl, Dorothy, has a, uh ... business relationship with Jules Brulatour, the film distributor."

"Business relationship," René said. "That's a new word for it."

"Anyway," Henry said, "I'm offering her a part in my next Broadway production."

"I hope she can talk," May said.

Henry waved that off. "With her looks she doesn't have to ... and with her connections, I'll be making my own cinematographs before the year's out."

"You're convinced these moving pictures are the future," Futrelle said, shaking his head.

"The future is here and now, Jack. And I'm gonna be looking for snappy stories ... if you should happen to know of any good writers."

"Nobody comes to mind," Futrelle said, and as he nodded to a steward that he would indeed like his coffee cup filled, the mystery writer noticed Ben Guggenheim seated nearby, sharing a table for four with the lovely blonde Madame Pauline Aubert, stunning and shapely in her pink-beaded purple panne-velvet dinner dress.

Guggenheim's was an odd shipboard situation; the renegade member of the iron-smelting dynasty, now in his dapper late forties, was not shunned exactly, and due to his station, he was treated respectfully. Futrelle had seen the Astors stop and chat with him just before dinner, and Maggie Brown appeared to be an old friend, possibly dating to Guggenheim's mining days in Colorado.

But no one sat with Guggenheim and his lovely lady in the reception room. The blue-eyed, fair-skinned, slightly plump, prematurely gray millionaire was, after all, Jewish, and the Jewish tended to sit together, by choice, or in the case of the dining saloons, by White Star's prearrangement. And could anyone imagine that model of married life, the conservative Strauses—Guggenheim's nearest social equivalent—sitting with a man and his mistress?

The little orchestra completed their *Tales of Hoffmann* medley, to much applause, and had begun playing the haunting "Songe d'Automne," when Guggenheim rose, patting his lovely companion on the shoulder and exchanging smiles with her, then heading out of the room.

Futrelle leaned in and whispered to May, "I need to talk to Guggenheim, and he's ducking out for a smoke or something."

She gave him a mischievous smile. "Shall I pay my compliments to Madame Aubert?"

"That would be awfully gracious of you, dear.... Let's both see what we can find out."

EIGHT

THE MUMMY'S CURSE

FUTRELLE CAUGHT UP WITH GUGGENHEIM stepping onto the elevator, behind the Grand Staircase; the uniformed attendant waited as the mystery writer stepped aboard.

Guggenheim smiled at him, nodding, saying in a fluid baritone, "The boys play well enough, but I felt the call of a cigar."

"I heard a similar siren song for a cigarette," Futrelle said. "Mind if I tag after?"

"I'd enjoy the companionship." To the elevator attendant, Guggenheim said, "A deck, if you please.... You're Futrelle, aren't you, the detective-story writer? Jacques Futrelle?"

It was then that Futrelle realized Guggenheim was mildly intoxicated—not falling-down drunk by any means, but the man had clearly not stinted on the wine during dinner, or perhaps an after-dinner brandy (or three) had done it.

"That's right. But I prefer Jack."

"Pleasure, Jack." The millionaire offered his hand, which bore several jeweled rings, a diamond here, a ruby there. "Ben Guggenheim."

They shook, and Futrelle said, "Is this elevator one of yours?"

Guggenheim, pleasantly surprised by Futrelle's question, said, "Why, no—I do business with White Star, but thus far they've not done business with me."

Futrelle had read a newspaper article about Guggenheim's new company, International Steampump, building the elevators at the Eiffel Tower.

"Sporting of you to give them your business, then," Futrelle said.

Guggenheim chuckled. "No choice—all the Cunard liners out of Paris were delayed because of the damned stokers' strike."

Soon they were poised at the rail of the open portion of the promenade, Guggenheim indulging himself with a Havana, Futrelle lighting up a Fatima. Stars seemed to have been flung like diamonds against the black velvet of the sky; brilliant as they were, the stars cast no reflection on the obsidian waters, far below. The cold was bracing and a pleasant contrast to the intake of tobacco smoke.

"Were you in Paris on business, Mr. Guggenheim?"

"It's 'Ben.' " The millionaire's handsome features had a softness to them, an almost baby-faced quality, his mouth as sensual as a woman's. "No, my business has its headquarters in Paris, and I have an apartment there.... Do you have children, Jack?"

They were alone on the deck, with only the night and the breeze to keep them company; even the deck chairs were folded up and neatly stacked against the wall.

"I do," Futrelle said. "A son and a daughter, both in their teens."

"I'm on my way home for my daughter Hazel's ninth birthday."

"There's a coincidence," Futrelle said. "I just had a birthday, and celebrating it without having my children around made me so homesick we hopped this boat."

Guggenheim blew a blue cloud of cigar smoke into the breeze for it to carry out to sea. "I really love my three little girls."

"It must be difficult, business keeping you away from your family so much."

"I miss my children; my wife and I ..." He turned to look at Futrelle and his eyes were half-lidded; he was tipsy, all right. "As you may be aware ... Jack? Jack. As you may be aware, since gossip seems to run rampant on this floating Vanity Fair, the attractive young woman with whom I'm traveling is not my wife."

"Madame Aubert is quite beautiful."

He sent another wreath of blue smoke out to sea. "I know I have a reputation as a playboy, and it doesn't bother me. It bothers my brothers—all except William—but I'm not in the family business anymore, not directly. Do you know that my brothers made an outcast of William because he married a gentile?"

"I wasn't aware of that." Futrelle wondered if Guggenheim had made the assumption he was Jewish because he and May regularly sat with the Harrises and Strauses in the Dining Saloon.

Guggenheim was saying, "My wife wanted to divorce me last year and they talked her out of it, my brothers. Said it would be bad for the family name. Family business."

"Ben, were you by any chance approached by this black-mailer—this fellow Crafton?"

Guggenheim looked at Futrelle as if for the first time; perhaps the millionaire realized he'd been rambling, somewhat drunkenly, and wondered if he'd said too much.

"I only bring this up," Futrelle said, "because he attempted to extort money out of me."

Guggenheim's oval face had turned blank, and still had a puttylike softness; but the eyes were hardening, if still half-lidded. So talkative before, Guggenheim now fell mute.

So, briefly but frankly, Futrelle told Guggenheim what John Crafton had threatened to reveal, and that he had refused to pay.

"I also refused to pay the bastard," Guggenheim said, won back over to Futrelle by his candor. Then he laughed. "For a blackmailer, he wasn't very well informed."

"How so?"

"First, he threatened to go to my family with my 'philander-ing.' To my brothers! Who know I've been friendly with ladies of ill repute since my days in the Rocky Mountains. And to my wife! As if she weren't already well aware of my proclivi-ties.... She has her gossip and tea and bridge and stocks and bonds, and I have my redheads, brunettes and blondes. Jack, do you know why you should never make love to a woman before breakfast?"

"Can't say I do, Ben."

"First, it's tiring. Second, over the course of the day, you may meet somebody you like better."

"I'll keep that in mind, Ben."

He shrugged. "Even my children know of Daddy's lady friends—I'm sure they all remember the live-in nurse we had around the house for several years. I've always been honest about my dishonesty, Jack."

"Not every man can say that."

"How well I know."

"Tell me, Ben—how did Crafton take your rejection of his 'services'?"

Guggenheim snorted a laugh. "He threatened to reveal my 'secret' to the newspapers. I told him to go ahead—the respectable publications won't touch it, and the yellow press doesn't matter."

To a man of Guggenheim's stature, a minor impropriety like a mistress could be common knowledge as long as he himself did not publicly confirm it. Sexual hypocrisy was a privilege of wealth, and even John Astor and his child bride would eventually be accepted by the nobs.

"Have you talked to Crafton since, Ben? Seen him around the ship?"

"No." He exhaled more smoke into the night. "Not that I was looking for him. There was a time ..."

"Yes?"

"A time I might have shot him."

"Really?"

A faint smile touched the sensual lips. "Happiest time, best days of my life."

"When was that?"

"Leadville, Colorado," he said fondly. "Ten acres of land, three shafts and one hundred men ... Sitting with a revolver strapped to my belt, by the shack near number-three mine. Keeping track of income and expenses, making out the payroll myself. Going down to Tiger Alley in the Row, dancing with the fancy girls for fifty cents a dance, three-card monte with the mule skinners and miners at Crazy Jim's ... corn whiskey at the Comique Saloon—twenty cents a glass. You know, I've made love to some of the most beautiful women in Manhattan, the loveliest ladies in Europe ... and I'd give it all up for one night with any one of those saucy belles at Peppersauce Bottoms."

Then Guggenheim sighed, pitched his cigar over the side, and said, "Shall we go back down to civilization, Jack?"

"If we must," Futrelle said, tossing his spent Fatima overboard.

When they returned to the concert (the little orchestra was playing the whimsical idyll "Glow-Worm" from *Lysistrata*) they found May sitting with Madame Aubert; so was Maggie Brown, in the shade of a wide-brimmed hat covered with pleated pink silk, her bosomy body bedecked in a pink silk gown with a silk posy at the white lace bodice.

Guggenheim introduced Futrelle to Madame Aubert and vice versa. In a French accent as thick as hollandaise, the blonde goddess said, "You have a charming wife, monsieur."

"Sit down, you two," Maggie said. "You're blocking the show for the suckers in the cheap seats."

Guggenheim laughed, following her command. "You haven't changed a bit since Leadville."

"You have, Goog," Maggie said. "I remember when your hair was brown and your belly flat as a washboard ... but to tell more would be indiscreet."

Futrelle borrowed a chair from a nearby abandoned table, and joined the little group. He whispered to Guggenheim, "This is civilization?" and the millionaire chuckled.

"Get a load of us now, Goog," Maggie said. "You look like a waiter at a fancy restaurant that wouldn't seat either one of us, and me, I'm wrapped up in the drapes and pretendin' to be a lady. Once upon a time you were a young buck who come west, leavin' Wall Street behind ..." She spoke to Madame Aubert, May and Futrelle. "Too depressin', he told me, too gloomy ..."

"And you were a feisty little red-haired blue-eyed number looking for a man with a gold mine," Guggenheim said.

"An uppity Jew and a hardscrabble Irish Catholic," she said, shaking her head. "How do you think we made out?"

She was smiling, but Futrelle had a hunch she missed Leadville at least as much as "Goog" did.

"You did fine, Maggie," Guggenheim said. "I haven't made my mind up about myself, just yet."

Madame Aubert didn't seem to take offense at Maggie's vulgar gregariousness, or begrudge the warmth between Guggenheim and the gaudy Denver matron; but Futrelle, studying Maggie's pleasant, slightly irregular features, could suddenly see her as she must have been, age nineteen, busty, blue-eyed, red-haired, in mining camp days. Years and pounds melted away, and there she was, in Futrelle's writer's imagination, a beautiful doll.

Which was the song Wallace Hartley's band began to play.

"That's my request!" Maggie squealed with delight. "I sent that up there on a napkin!"

Up front, tables were being moved aside to make room for dancing. The room was starting to clear out, leaving only the younger and/or more daring passengers.

Maggie clutched the millionaire's hand, like she was falling off a cliff, reaching for a branch. "Hey, cowboy—how's about dancin' with an old Rocky Mountain belle?"

He glanced at his blonde companion, who granted permission with a regal nod and smile, and Guggenheim walked Maggie Brown up to the impromptu dance floor.

As they cut a rug together, fairly stylish at that, Madame Aubert said, "You don't think it's possible? Could Ben and that woman, ever have … ?"

"No," Futrelle said flatly.

But in their stateroom, Futrelle said to May, "Oh, they were an item all right."

"Maggie Brown and Ben Guggenheim," she said, shaking her head, pleasantly amazed. "Who'd have thought it?"

"Well, I don't think Madame Aubert has much to worry about her meal ticket, tonight. That was too many years, and too many pounds ago."

May was sitting on the edge of their brass bed. "Pauline Aubert is quite the beauty. She was very nice, but not too revealing about herself and Mr. Guggenheim."

Futrelle sat next to her. "So you didn't find anything out about Ben and Crafton."

"Not from her, but when Maggie sat down, the facts began to fly. Or anyway, they did when Pauline excused herself to use the ladies' room, and Maggie began rattling off a litany of Ben Guggenheim's mistresses—there was a Marquise de Cerruti, this showgirl, that secretary, even a slender red-haired nurse who lived in their mansion with them! Just in case his 'chronically neuralgic' head needed a massage...."

"A man never knows when he's going to need a massage."

"Husbands had best get their massages at home."

"Sounds like Ben was at home."

"Keep that up, and you'll need a nurse ... Maggie says before he married his wife—Florette—he had his way with the most beautiful Jewish girls in Manhattan, and his share of gentiles, too."

"I gather it's a marriage of family fortunes."

"Of convenience, yes. I didn't bring Crafton up, but I doubt a man so openly living his double life can be victimized by any blackmailer."

"I agree," Futrelle said, and he told her of his conversation on the A-deck promenade with Guggenheim.

May rose to the dresser and took out her nightgown. She began undressing, asking, "Coming to bed, Jack?"

"Possibly. I'm suddenly getting the urge for a massage…."

"Maybe tomorrow morning … 'cowboy.' "

He decided not to share with her Guggenheim's opinion of morning lovemaking.

"I still haven't spoken to that fellow Stead," Futrelle said, and went to the door. "Archie Butt told me the old boy's been keeping to his stateroom. But I understand he's been down to the Smoking Room, this time of night, once or twice."

"Go on and see if he's there." She was in her nightgown, a vision. "I'll read till you get back."

"You don't have to wait up."

She drew back the bedspread, the sheets. "I'll want a detailed report—if nothing else, just to make sure you aren't out with one of your many mistresses … I'll be under the covers with *The Virginian*."

He let her have the last word—with two writers in the family, such surrenders were occasionally necessary—and wondered if the Ben Guggenheims of the world would still stray, if they had married for love instead of finance. The only answer he came up with, as he walked down the corridor, was that he couldn't imagine being with any woman but May; then he was at the aft staircase and walked up the two flights to A deck.

The private men's club that was the *Titanic*'s Smoking Room was filled with blue smoke and drinking men and a dull din of conversation. The frequenters of this mahogany-walled male preserve were still in evening dress, for the most part, having come directly from either dinner or the concert. The marble-topped tables were home to bridge and poker games and, though gambling was not legal, paper money littered the tables like confetti. A few tables were given over strictly to conversation, and at one of these—two actually, which had been butted together—William T. Stead was holding court.

The absurdity brought a smile to Futrelle's lips. Not just listening but enraptured were these men of finance and politics and wealth in their white ties and tails, supplicating at the figurative feet of a bushily white-bearded, Buddha-bellied old fellow in a shabby sealskin cap and a yellowish-brown tweed suit as rumpled as an unmade bed.

Among Stead's admiring audience were Major Archie Butt and his artist friend Francis Millet. Futrelle also recognized Frederick Seward, a New York lawyer, young Harry Widener, the book collector, and Charles Hays of the Grand Trunk railways.

"Jack!" Archie called out. "Come join us! Mr. Stead is regaling us with his supernatural lore."

Futrelle found a spare chair and pulled it up next to Archie, which was also right beside the great man himself, who immediately scolded Archie in a resonant, cheerful voice: " 'Supernatural' is your term, Major Butt—mine is spiritualism, where science and religion meet."

"Well, sir," Archie said good-naturedly, "could you take time, first, for Stead to meet Futrelle?"

"This is Jacques Futrelle?" A spark came to Stead's piercing sky-blue eyes, and a broad smile—wearing evidence of a course or two from dinner—formed in the thicket of white beard. "Jacques Futrelle—why, it's an honor, sir!"

"The honor is mine," Futrelle said, meaning it. He offered his hand and the two men shook.

Futrelle joined the unlikely acolytes of this untidy, ruddy, squat man who, in his early sixties now but looking older, was nonetheless a major figure in British journalism. Stead—for all his muckraking, in his *Pall Mall Gazette*, and with books that in explicitly exposing sin were often themselves decried as obscene— was the father of the New Journalism in England, the man who created the interview format for newspaper and magazine articles.

"I'm a great admirer of this fellow you work for," Stead said, eyes narrowed, nodding at Futrelle.

"Mr. Hearst?"

"Yes. William Randolph Hearst. The man understands newspapers! He's fearless."

Futrelle had to smile. "Not everyone shares your admiration of Mr. Hearst, sir."

"Not everyone understands the newspaper business, as do you and I, sir."

"That's kind of you."

"I must say, however, that you at times disappoint me, Mr. Futrelle."

"It's Jack—and why have I disappointed you, sir?"

Stead rocked back in his chair; his voice was teasing. "Well, Jack, I've read some of these 'Thinking Machine' stories of yours, and this detective you've conjured up, he's a debunker. You contrive tales that are ... if I must use your word, Major Butt ... 'supernatural,' and then your man explains the mystical occurrences away with mundane realities."

Futrelle shrugged. "That's just the pattern of the tales. Some of my stories don't resolve their otherworldly aspects."

"Then you must give me the names of those stories before this voyage ends—I would like to read them." He tented his fingers and stared over their structure at Futrelle, eyes nothing but glittering slits. "That dim, obscure world of the spirit is very real, Jack. Have you met Conan Doyle?"

"I have."

"Do you respect him, sir?"

"Of course. He was the inspiration for me to write."

"And you know that he shares my views on such subjects as clairvoyance, telepathy, psychometry, automatic writing ..."

Millet spoke up. "What the devil is automatic writing, Mr. Stead?"

"The devil has nothing to do with it." Stead withdrew a packet of Prince Albert cigars from his inside pocket and a kitchen match from an outside pocket and lighted up as he responded to the artist.

"I am one of those certain few gifted individuals who can merely pick up a pen and, with no conscious thought of my own, my hand will be guided by telepathic communication. I write automatically, as it were, as I receive thoughts from the unconscious minds of other people."

Intrigued but skeptical, Futrelle asked, "You could receive my thoughts? Perhaps when I was asleep, for example?"

Stead nodded. "Yes, conceivably. But most of what I receive comes from the other side."

Archie was frowning. "The other side of what, sir?"

"The veil. My most frequent visitor is Mrs. Julia Ames, a departed friend of mine, a Chicago journalist. Now and then I hear from Catherine."

"Catherine?"

Stead blew smoke. "The Second. Of Russia."

Smiles and chuckles rippled around the butted-together tables, but no one was bored, and the good-natured Stead took no offense.

"I understand your skepticism, gentlemen ... I would have shared it, not so long ago. I spent the better part of my life in pursuit of charlatans and sinners. But I assure you that I am not mad and not a fraud. Many of the most well-known and well-respected sensitives—mediums—of our day are among my closest friends. We have formed 'Julia's Bureau' and meet regularly, for séances."

The men exchanged glances and smiles, but they were still in his thrall.

Harry Widener, the independently wealthy bibliophile, spoke up. "Do you think you might hold a séance aboard this ship?"

Stead shook his head, no. "I have no plans. This is as serious as church to me, gentlemen—not a parlor trick." He withdrew and checked his gold-plated pocket watch. "It's getting on toward midnight, gentlemen ... perhaps we have time for one more example, to show you the power that can extend from the other side."

Archie laughed. "A ghost story?"

With a grandiose shrug, Stead said, "Call it that if you like—a tale told 'round our ocean campfire ... but a true one."

And the men at the table, however powerful and wealthy they might be, were like children, exchanging breathless glances, as the storyteller began.

"There is currently on exhibit, in the British Museum in London, a certain Eygptian relic—a mummy, the wrapped embalmed corpse of a priestess of the God Amen-Ra. The vividly painted coffin cover of this mummy is unlike any the curator of the museum had ever seen—the figure painted had anguish-filled eyes, a terror-constricted expression."

This melodrama had the men smiling—but they were listening. They were listening ...

"Experts on Egyptology were called in; their opinion was that this priestess had lived a tormented life, perhaps even an evil life ... and the coffin cover's portrait was designed, perhaps, to exorcise an evil spirit that possessed her soul."

The smiles faded.

"To learn more, of course, a translation of the hieroglyphics inscribed on the sarcophagus was necessary. And the translation of the inscription on that frightful mummy's coffin carried a tragic narrative of a beautiful young priestess who fell in love with the pharaoh. She poisoned the wife of the pharaoh, and all of the pharaoh's children as well, in a misguided, malevolent attempt to become the pharaoh's new queen. But she was discovered in her evil acts, gentlemen, and the vengeful pharaoh embalmed her alive, with screams that echoed through her pyramid ..."

Every man at the table was hanging on Stead's words.

"... but the inscription warned that should the priestess's body be disturbed, should it ever be removed from her tomb, and most importantly should her story ever be translated and spoken aloud—the evil she had once within her would be again unleashed, in a torrent of sickness, death and destruction, rained upon those who translated the sacred inscription, and even upon those who passed along the story ... as I have just done."

Stead cast a grave look around his listeners, even as he crushed out his cigar in a White Star ashtray.

The lawyer Seward asked, "What ... what became of those who translated the hieroglyphics?"

"Within months, dead to a man. The mummy and its coffin lid remain on display at the British Museum, gentlemen—but there is of course a new curator. And for reasons of safety, they do not post the translation; in fact, it has been burned."

Archie was leaning so far forward, he was all but sprawled upon the table. "Good God, man—you don't believe in this curse?"

Stead roared with laughter. "Of course not! That, my friends, is superstition, pure and simple. As Christians you should be ashamed if you even pondered the possibility. I have told you this tale to make a point—not the point you expected—but as proof that I am not superstitious."

And again Stead removed his gold pocket watch from its resting place in the shabby tweed suit and he announced, "I call to your attention, gentlemen, that it was Friday when I began this story, and the day of its ending falls on the thirteenth."

"But," Seward said, "if the curse is true—"

"Why," Stead said grandly, ridiculously, "this ship is doomed, and the first corpse should appear by morning."

Then the old man rose, nodding to his audience, bidding them pleasant good-byes individually, and exited from the Smoking Room like a tugboat with legs.

Futrelle followed him through the revolving door.

"Where are you headed, sir?"

"Ah, Mr. Futrelle! Jack! To my stateroom on C deck."

"I'm on C deck, as well. I'll walk with you, if you've no objection."

"Pleased and proud to be in your company, young man."

Soon they were on the staircase, and Futrelle said, "I witnessed you, on the boat train, in a brief altercation with John Crafton."

Stead frowned and paused. "Are you unfortunate enough to know the sorry specimen?"

"Yes, I'm afraid so."

"Surely you don't call him your friend!"

"No! He, uh … if I may be frank, sir, he tried to blackmail me."

Stead continued on up the stairs. "Why, in God's name? Forgive me … it's none of my business."

They were in the reception area of B deck, now, and the chairs were deserted.

"Could we sit for a moment, Mr. Stead? I'd like to share something with you."

Stead seemed a little surprised by the request, but he said, "All right," and they took chairs at a small table.

"I hope it's not another ghost story," Stead said.

"No," Futrelle grinned.

Then, once again, Futrelle told of Crafton's attempt to expose the mystery writer's supposed "mental aberrations."

"He is a man without conscience, without morals," Stead said, shaking his head bitterly. "You see, I'm to speak at the Men and Religion Forward convention, at Carnegie Hall, this April twenty-first—I go on between Booker T. Washington and William Jennings Bryan—and Crafton threatened to besmirch my appearance by making public, in the more scurrilous publications, my jail sentence."

Futrelle could hardly believe what he was hearing. "You were in jail?"

"You'd have no reason to know of it, Jack—you were a child when it happened, and it was news in England, not America."

"What were you jailed for, if I might ask?"

"Abduction of a thirteen-year-old girl for immoral purposes."

171

Futrelle could find no words to respond.

Astonishingly, Stead was beaming. "It does sound bad, doesn't it? But it's an experience of which I am inordinately proud, I must admit. You see, in order to demonstrate how easily young girls could be sold into white slavery, I arranged with several 'accomplices' to buy a child from her mother. This despicable deed done, we took the child to a house of ill repute, where she was accepted by the proprietress, and taken to a room where the next client would surely deflower the child—but, my point made, I then spirited the girl off, before any harm had been done to her. We sent to her France, where she was given a good life away from a mother willing to sell her into prostitution."

"So this was a ... stunt?"

Stead frowned at that characterization. "Much more than that, sir. Thanks to my efforts, the law was changed in England—the age of legal consent raised from thirteen to fifteen—and my book *The Maiden Tribute of Modern Babylon* exposed to one and all, for once and for all, this criminal vice, this foul child prostitution."

"Why did you go to jail?"

He shrugged and half a smile could be seen in the thicket of beard. "The mother brought charges. I'm sure we could have bought her off, Jack—but I chose instead to go to jail for three months. I wore my jail uniform proudly thereafter—until it fell to pieces."

Futrelle could only laugh and say, "Sir, you are a remarkable man."

"Perhaps, from this, you can extrapolate my reaction to a blackmail attempt from the likes of John Crafton."

"I witnessed your reaction—fairly strong for a pacifist."

Stead shrugged. "He hasn't contacted me since. I have not seen him since I came aboard, but then I've chiefly confined myself to my stateroom, going over the proofs of my new book."

"Sir, I feel it only fair to make you aware of another unpleasant action of Mr. Crafton's: he's told certain other 'clients' of his on this ship that you and he are partners."

The clear blue eyes widened. "What? That's a damned lie!"

"I know, sir. But you can see the cunningness of it—your presence on the ship, your reputation for exposing crime and corruption ..."

Stead was, after all, the author of such works as *If Christ Came to Chicago* and *Satan's Invisible World Displayed: A Study of Greater New York*.

"Jack, do you know who this fabrication has been foisted upon?"

"I know of Mr. Straus and Mr. Astor, only."

He laughed harshly. "They'll see through him. They know of my association with the Salvation Army. I would tarnish the name of neither of these good charitable families."

This was neither the time nor place to bring it up, but Futrelle could only wonder how this crusader could in good conscience overlook John Jacob Astor's wretched history as a slum landlord.

Then Stead unexpectedly answered the unposed question: "The Astors of this world did not create the class that is the poor. My enemies are those who are mandated to serve society, but who choose instead to profit from the misery of others: crooked police, the corrupt politicians, those Tammany Hall villains."

Futrelle rose. "Well, I think we can go on up to bed now, sir. I appreciate your hearing me out."

And Stead rose, as well. "I appreciate the information, Jack."

On C deck, Futrelle bid the old man good night.

"It's a monstrous floating babylon, this ship," Stead said, heading down the corridor, "isn't it, Jack?"

"Yes it is."

But as Futrelle entered his stateroom, where his wife was asleep with the light on and *The Virginian* in her arms, he wasn't sure whether Stead meant to compliment the *Titanic* or insult it.

And he wasn't sure if Stead knew, either.

DAY FOUR

APRIL 13, 1912

NINE

STEERAGE

EVEN ON THE *TITANIC*, A vessel whose motion was at best barely detectable, Futrelle found that the subtle pulse of steaming engines and rushing waters conspired to make shipboard sleep particularly restful, satisfying, deep and dreamless. The unexpected and unwelcome alarm of the shrill ringing phone awakened him instantly, nonetheless, and he snatched the receiver from its cradle before the gently slumbering May, beside him, was similarly disturbed.

"Yes?" he whispered.

"Jack, it's Bruce—Bruce Ismay."

At least he didn't say "J. Bruce Ismay." But Futrelle sat up, reading the signal of the frazzled edge in the White Star director's voice.

"Yes, Bruce," Futrelle said thickly, wedging his glasses onto his nose, as if seeing better would help clear the cobwebs from his mind and ears.

"Did I wake you? If so I apologize, but it's urgent that we see you, the captain and I."

"Certainly. Your suite?"

"No, Captain Smith's. It's on the boat deck, starboard side, near the wheelhouse. There's a gate separating the First-Class promenade and the officers' promenade."

"I know where that is."

"Good. Second Officer Lightoller will be waiting there for you."

"Give me five minutes," Futrelle said, hung up, and rolled out of bed.

May turned over and her eyes slitted open. "What was that?"

Her husband was at the closet, selecting his clothes. "Ismay again. Probably wanting to know how my inquiries went yesterday."

"What are you going to tell him?"

Climbing into his pants, he said, "Only what I see fit. I'm not getting Hoffman or Navatril or whatever-his-name-is into hot water. It's not my place."

She smiled sleepily at him. "You have a soft heart, Jack. That's one of the few hundred reasons why I love you ... What time is it, anyway?"

Slipping into his shirt, he walked over and checked the nightstand clock, an ornate gold item that would have been at home on a palace mantel. "After nine ... I guess we slept in."

She sat up, covers in her lap, her breasts perky under the nightgown. "Shall I get dressed? Shall we have breakfast when you get back, in the Dining Saloon? Or call room service again?"

Futrelle, otherwise clothed, was sitting on a chair, tying his shoes. "Why don't you call room service, darling. Then we can talk frankly, about whatever it is Ismay and Smith want me for."

Waiting at the forward end of the First-Class promenade on the boat deck, at the accordion gate, was crisply uniformed

Second Officer Lightoller, a tall man (though not as tall as Futrelle) with dark close-set eyes, pointed features and a jutting jaw.

"Mr. Futrelle?" The voice was deep, resonant.

"Officer Lightoller, I presume?"

"Yes, sir. This way, sir."

Futrelle stepped through, and Lightoller closed and locked the folding gate behind them: a near slam followed by the click of the key in the lock; there was something ominous about it. Then the businesslike Lightoller led Futrelle down the officers' promenade to a door marked CAPTAIN—PRIVATE, which in military terms seemed a contradiction, and the second officer knocked.

Smith himself answered, in his navy-blue uniform today, graced with the usual ribbons; but he was not wearing his hat, and the lack of it was somehow disturbing. So were the eyes in the comfortingly stern white-bearded visage: they seemed cloudy, troubled.

"Thank you for coming, Mr. Futrelle," Smith said, the soothingly soft voice touched with, what? Melancholy? Distress?

The captain motioned Futrelle in, instructing Lightoller to wait outside the door.

These quarters, with their white-painted walls and oak wainscoting, harbored the no-nonsense, spartan style characteristic of a naval man, leaving luxury to the First-Class passengers; maple and oak Colonial furnishings gave the spacious sitting room a New England air, as did the handful of modestly framed nautical prints. This sitting room was also a sort of office, as in one corner, by a porthole, sat a heavy Chippendale desk with many compartments, and a brass captain's-wheel lamp atop it. A doorway stood half-open for a glimpse into the bedroom.

In the midst of the room, Ismay was seated at a round table—a captain's table—and there it was, the captain's hat, crown down, like a centerpiece bowl awaiting flowers or fruit.

The White Star director—in an undertaker's black suit and tie—was pale as milk, if the milk had gone as sour as his expression, anyway; dark pouches lingered under bloodshot eyes and even his mustache seemed wilted.

Captain Smith gestured to a chair at the round table and Futrelle sat, and so did he.

"Would you be so kind," Ismay said, and despite his cadaverous appearance, there was nothing rude or anxious in his voice, "to provide an informal report as to the results of your ad hoc investigation, yesterday, Mr. Futrelle?"

Futrelle glanced sharply at Captain Smith, who said, almost sheepishly, "It became necessary to acquaint Mr. Ismay with our arrangement."

After a sigh and shrug, Futrelle said, "Well, as you both can guess, I had to be indirect in my questioning, and in my approach. Most of our suspects, if indeed that's what they are, are distinguished, notable individuals. If you are expecting a detailed list of alibis and denials of guilt, I have none."

"What did you learn?" Ismay asked politely. "What did you observe?"

"What," the captain added, "are your suspicions?"

"I spoke with Mr. Straus, Mr. Astor, Mr. Guggenheim, Mr. Rood, Mr. Stead, even Mrs. Brown. And I'd spoken frankly about Crafton with Major Butt prior to the blackmailer's death. I also spoke with Mr. Hoffman. By being frank with them about the nature of how Crafton intended to blackmail me, all but one of them was equally frank with me. Now, my friends, I see no reason to share with you what these reasons are; suffice to say, that while every one of these gentlemen, and the one lady, did have something in their past or present that Crafton conceivably could attempt to blackmail them over, none of these people seemed agitated enough to kill, none of their skeletons-in-the-closet seemed worthy of murdering the man over."

"Any one of them could have been lying," Ismay pointed out. "Any one of them could have withheld the true nature of the blackmail, substituting something else, something more trivial."

Futrelle removed his glasses and polished them on a handkerchief. "That's certainly true. But I am an experienced newspaperman, Mr. Ismay, and while I do not claim infallibility, I feel I know when an interview subject is evading the truth or outright lying to me." He snugged his glasses back on. "These men—and again, the one lady—seem to me to be telling the truth. None of them, in my at least somewhat informed opinion, had sufficient motive to kill the man."

"But someone did," Ismay said.

Futrelle cast another sharp look at Captain Smith, whose expression was unreadable. Then to Ismay, the mystery writer said, "You seem to have changed your opinion about Mr. Crafton dying of natural causes."

"You have no suspicions, then, sir," Ismay said, without addressing Futrelle's statement.

"I asked each of them if they'd seen Crafton aboard the ship yesterday—knowing, of course, that he was already dead, and hoping to catch the killer in a lie, or at least get some indication, some nervous flash in the eyes, some tic or gesture that might indicate I'd touched a raw nerve." He shrugged. "Nothing."

"You said, 'with the exception of one man,' " the captain pointed out.

Nodding, Futrelle said, "Yes, Mr. Rood wasn't very forth-coming. His reaction was the most consistent with someone who had something to hide—perhaps Crafton *was* blackmailing Rood over something worth killing for. And I suppose, if pressed, for the sake of argument, I would have to say our leading suspect is Mr. Rood."

"I would say that's highly unlikely," Ismay said, dryly.

"And why is that?"

The captain sighed heavily. "Mr. Rood was murdered last night."

"The devil you say!" In a quick chilling flash, the mummy's curse Stead had recounted filled his mind, but Futrelle still managed to ask, "What are the circumstances? Another bedroom entry, and smothering—"

"No," Ismay said. "He was struck a blow to the back of the head."

Nodding toward the outside, Captain Smith said, "He may have been shoved hard, backward, into the side of one of the lifeboats, here on the boat deck."

"What makes you think that?"

Ismay said, "His body was discovered, having been stuffed rather rudely into lifeboat seven … not terribly far from where we sit right now."

"A hasty, clumsy job of concealment," Captain Smith said. "One of Mr. Rood's arms, dangling from the side of the tarp-covered craft, caught the attention of a deckhand."

Futrelle sat forward. "My God, gentlemen. Has the word gotten out? This will cast a terrible pall across the ship."

"Mr. Rood's body was discovered before dawn," Ismay said, "and, after Dr. O'Loughlin approved it—the good doctor believes the murder took place sometime between midnight and five A.M.—the body was moved into the cold cargo hold, where Mr. Crafton's remains also currently reside."

"The lid, as they say, is still on," Captain Smith said. "Only a handful of crew know about this, including the master-at-arms, and all have been given strict orders to speak to no one of the affair, at peril of loss of their jobs."

"The lifeboat in question has been tidied up," Ismay said.

"Maybe so," Futrelle said, "and I would also like to see the 'lid' kept on, at least for the time being ... but we've gone well beyond a death in a stateroom that could possibly have been written off as a heart attack. We have a murderer aboard, gentlemen ... a violent one."

"You're correct, sir," Captain Smith said. "We have a new set of concerns, now, for the safety of our passengers."

Futrelle stood, and began to pace. "We understand why John Crafton, in all probability, was killed; he was a damned blackmailer. But why Rood?"

Ismay said nothing, but shot a telling look at Captain Smith, who was also mute and expressionless.

"Gentlemen," Futrelle said, sensing something was up, "did you conduct a complete search of Mr. Crafton's room, yesterday?"

After a few moments, Ismay nodded.

"Did you turn up anything of interest? Any documents pertaining to our late friend's blackmail victims, perhaps?"

"No," Ismay said.

"All right. Has Rood's cabin been searched?"

Again, Ismay paused but finally said, "Yes."

"And?"

"We found a room key that was not Rood's own."

"Really? Whose room key was it?"

"… Crafton's."

Futrelle's eyebrows climbed his forehead. "Rood had a key to Crafton's room? If he weren't dead, I'd say he was still our best suspect. What about blackmail documents?"

Ismay said nothing, and he avoided Futrelle's gaze.

But Captain Smith frankly said, "We did find certain documents, pertaining to our First-Class passengers."

Ismay, rather petulantly, added, "Yourself included, sir."

Futrelle sat down heavily. "Specifically, what?"

"Various items," Captain Smith said. "Statements from witnesses … photostatic copies of various records … in your case, of a hospital admissions book. Frankly, we haven't examined them closely."

"Good God, man—you haven't destroyed them, have you?"

"No!" The captain seemed rather offended by the suggestion. "These documents are evidence. When we reach port, the material will have to be read, have to be handed over to the authorities."

Ismay shook his head, moaning, saying, "The embarrassment to our passengers … On a maiden voyage, a catastrophe like this, it's unimaginable."

Futrelle didn't bother pointing out that the embarrassment Ismay was concerned about was his own, and his company's.

Instead, he said, "Where are the documents now?"

"In the purser's safe," the captain said. "Mr. Futrelle, as bizarre as the proposition might sound, could we have *two* murderers aboard? If Mr. Rood had obtained the extra key, and used it to enter and slay Mr. Crafton, it would explain the presence in Rood's room of these sensitive documents."

Futrelle smiled but he wasn't happy. "Rood wasn't Crafton's blackmail victim, gentlemen—he was his accomplice."

Captain Smith's eyes widened and he shook his head, no. "Have you forgotten that Rood assaulted Crafton in the Smoking Room!"

"Conveniently staged by the two of them," Futrelle said, "to cloak their collaboration."

The eyes of both men seemed to light up as they grasped the implications.

Futrelle continued: "And Rood was unforthcoming to me, yesterday, because he alone of those I spoke to knew that Crafton was dead, or was at least in a bad way. Rood may have entered his partner's cabin and seen the body, before that housekeeping stewardess discovered it; or he may have realized that the guard posted on Crafton's room meant that either his partner was in custody, or dead."

"So the motive remains the same," Captain Smith said. "Another blackmailer has been murdered."

"And probably by one of your First-Class passengers," Futrelle said.

Ismay thought about that briefly, then said, "Your suspect in Second Class—Mr. Hoffman—might have made his way to the boat deck, in the middle of the night. That is when our crew members would be most susceptible to a bribe from a Second-Class passenger who wanted to see how the other half traveled."

"What are we going to do, gentlemen?" Futrelle asked.

Ismay's eyes narrowed and his voice cut like a knife. "You, sir, are going to do nothing. You will cease and desist, where your investigation is concerned, and you will speak to no one of this, including your wife."

"That sounds suspiciously like an order."

"I apologize for the harshness of my tone. Perhaps, if you and your delightful wife were moved to Second Class, it would remove the temptation of talking about this matter with the First-Class passengers."

"Why not put us in steerage? Then I couldn't even talk to Hoffman."

Ismay smiled and half bowed. "Very gracious of you. Shall I make the arrangements?"

"Mr. Ismay," Captain Smith said sharply, "I don't appreciate any attempt to intimidate Mr. Futrelle. As you damn well know, his investigation was at my request. He's generously helped us, and I won't condone your rudeness to him. Must I remind you that I'm still the captain of this ship?"

Ismay nodded. "I apologize, gentlemen. The captain is quite right. Mr. Futrelle, I do thank you for what you've done, and request your cooperation."

Futrelle offered half a smile to the White Star director. "I was just about to say yes to your idea of writing a murder mystery set on the *Titanic*. I believe we have the right subject matter, now."

Ismay sighed, his eyes going to half-lidded. "Perhaps I deserve that. Can I count on your cooperation, Jack?"

"Bruce ... Captain Smith ... I'm at your service. Will you be launching an official inquiry? Perhaps by the master-at-arms?"

The captain shook his head. "No. But we will be heightening ship's security. These murders both happened after dark. Let's hope the daylight is safe."

"I don't think our passengers are in any danger," Ismay said. "The only victims have been blackmailers, and unless a third accomplice is aboard, who would be at risk?"

"I tend to agree," Futrelle said, rising, "but I applaud the captain's precautions nonetheless."

"I have suggested," Ismay said, "that we proceed with all possible speed into port. The sooner we have our passengers safely on shore, the better."

"With the extra boilers lit, we may be able to reach New York as early as Tuesday evening," Captain Smith said, rising, adding, "I'll see you out, Mr. Futrelle."

The captain walked with Futrelle down the officers' promenade, Second Officer Lightoller walking behind, keeping a respectful distance.

Staring out at the gray sea under the gray-blue sky, the captain asked, "Do you think there's anything we've overlooked, sir?"

Futrelle considered that for a few seconds, then admitted, "The only thing that comes to mind ... and it's probably nothing ... is the Allison family."

"The Allisons." Captain Smith nodded. "I've spoken to Hudson Allison; nice fellow. What connection could he have to any of this?"

"You wouldn't think anything ... but I know for a fact Crafton sought the Allisons out, was friendly to them. If you were to ask Hudson and Bess Allison about John Bertram Crafton, they would tell you what a friendly, charming fellow he is. Of course, their nanny was giving him the evil eye...."

Captain Smith stopped dead. "Their nanny? A woman named Alice something?"

"Why, yes ..."

Why in God's name would the captain of a ship the size of the *Titanic*, carrying thousands of passengers, remember or even ever know the name of one family's nanny?

The captain turned to Lightoller and asked, "Do you have that note, Mr. Lightoller, that came up from Third Class a day or two ago?"

"I believe I know where it is, sir. We didn't do a thing about that, though, sir."

"I know. Fetch it, would you?"

"Yes, sir."

Lightoller clipped off, toward the wheelhouse, and Futrelle said, "I'm afraid, Captain, you've got me thoroughly confused."

"A note came up from Third Class, I don't remember the name of the fellow, but the gist of it was that he knew something about the Allisons' nanny and wanted to know what it was worth."

"Sounds like you have a blackmailer in steerage, too."

Captain Smith twitched a frown. "We didn't follow up on it—it seemed just a crank note, and unclear as to its purpose at that. If the Allisons are satisfied with their nanny, why should the opinion of some lout in steerage be of any interest or concern?"

Lightoller was on his way back, a small piece of paper in hand.

The captain said, "Give that to Mr. Futrelle, would you?"

"Yes, sir," Lightoller said, and did.

"That will be all, Mr. Lightoller. I'll see Mr. Futrelle to First Class."

"Yes, sir."

Then the captain and the mystery writer were alone on the promenade.

"Mr. Futrelle, would you do me the favor of looking into this for me? Mr. Andrews will see that you get down to steerage ... *and* back again, despite Mr. Ismay's wishes."

"My pleasure. Does this mean I'm back on the case, Captain?"

A glorious smile appeared in the impeccably trimmed snowy beard. "It's my last crossing, Mr. Futrelle. What's Ismay going to do—fire me?"

The captain said he had alerted Mr. Andrews that Futrelle would be stopping by, and the writer made his way to the shipbuilder's suite on A deck, on the port side of the ship just off the First-Class aft reception area. Along the way Futrelle read the note, written in pencil, in a legible cursive hand and, despite a few misspellings, fairly literate, seeming to speak less of blackmail than Captain Smith had implied:

To the captain

I have notice on your fine shipp Miss Alice Cleaver nurse to young children of man and wife in first class who's name I don't know. Details on Miss Cleavers past history is of value to parents.

Untill I hear from you sir I remain your servant

Alfred Davies

Futrelle folded the note and dropped it in his pocket, then knocked on the door of A36. He was just ready to knock again when Andrews appeared, wearing coveralls, a distracted expression and the baggy-eyed look of a man who wasn't getting enough sleep.

"Good morning, Tom," Futrelle said. "Are those the required togs for Third Class?"

"Pardon?" Then he looked at himself. "Oh, this boiler suit … no, after I've put you and your Mr. Davies together, I have to go down to the stokehold, to speak to the chief engineer."

Beyond the gentle-faced man with the rugged build in the doorway, a glimpse of the sitting room of A36 showed it had been given over to an office: blueprints were pinned to a drafting table near a desk arrayed with charts rolled up like treasure maps, piles of paper bearing calculations and sketches, and a half-eaten breakfast roll.

As they went down the stairway to C deck, Futrelle said, "You must be the only man in First Class not having a good time, Tom."

He gave Futrelle half a smile. "Perhaps this is my idea of a good time."

"Glutton for punishment, are you?"

The oak and marble of the stairway was all around him. "I've seen this vessel grow, from a design on a cocktail napkin to construction in the shipyard, frame by frame, plate after plate, day upon day, for two long years."

"And you're a proud father."

"Oh yes—but a typically fussy one. Have you noticed that the pebble dashing on the promenade decks is simply too damned dark?"

"No."

"I have." Andrews grinned as the staircase emptied them into the aft reception area on C deck. "It's my curse, and blessing. An argument between stewardesses, a defective electric fan … no concern too trivial, no job too small."

"Including ushering me into Third Class."

"Are you free yet to tell me what this is about, Jack?"

"You'll have to get that from the captain, Tom. You may be this baby's parent, but Captain Smith is her headmaster."

Andrews used one of his many keys to unlock a door between the First-Class C-deck corridor, leading into the

Second-Class enclosed promenade, where protected from the wind and cold, a number of passengers were seated on benches, enjoying the glassy gray view. A few were on deck chairs, bundled only lightly in a blanket, reading books or writing letters.

"I've called ahead and Davies should be waiting for us," Andrews said, as they stepped outside, onto the deck and into the chill air. They moved down the metal stairs, into and through the open well that was the Third-Class promenade, where the benches were empty, and only a few children of ten or eleven were braving the brisk weather, chasing each other, squealing with delight. Futrelle had a flash of his own son and daughter at that age, and felt a bittersweet pang of loss.

Under the poop-deck roof and through a door to the left of the wide, five-banistered flight of metal stairs down into the Third-Class aft cabins, Andrews led Futrelle into the General Room, the steerage equivalent of a lounge.

About forty by forty, the sterile white-enameled walls were dressed up with framed White Star Line posters promising pleasure cruises these passengers were unlikely ever to take; the sturdy yellowish-brown teakwood double-sided benches, built around pillars, were brimming with a shipboard melting pot, though not much melting was going on. Various languages being spoken by isolated groups within the room floated like clouds of words, English and German mostly, but Finnish, Italian and Swedish too, and Far Eastern languages that Futrelle could not identity.

But these were not pitiful huddling masses. They were men and women, from their late teens to old age, many gathered in family groupings, not even shabbily dressed, simply working people heading to a new land for new work. The undeniable smell—not quite a stench—of body odor had to do with steerage's limited bathing facilities, not the emigrants' lack of grooming. A piano seemed to be the only possible source of entertainment, though it stood silent at the moment.

A steward in a gold-buttoned white uniform approached Andrews and said something to him that Futrelle could not hear, over the babble.

Andrews turned to Futrelle. "We've found Davies. They have him waiting next door, in the Smoking Room."

As Futrelle followed Andrews across the room, it was as if he were crossing border upon border, so rapidly and frequently did the language shift. Then through a doorway into the Third-Class Smoking Room, the atmosphere changed.

It was quiet in here—men were smoking, playing cards, in an agreeably masculine room with dark-stained oak-paneled walls and long, room-spanning back-to-back teak benches, and, scattered about, tables-for-four with chairs. If the inlaid-pearl mahogany world of the First-Class Smoking Room was an exclusive men's club, this was a lodge hall.

The room was only sparsely attended, but that was natural: the small adjacent bar hadn't opened yet; too early in the day. The only languages Futrelle caught were English and German.

A strapping young man in a well-worn but not threadbare black sack coat over a green woolen sweater sat alone at one of the tables, turning his black cap in his hands like a wheel. Clean-shaven, with a round, almost babyish countenance, his brown hair was already thinning, though he couldn't be more than twenty-four or -five years of age.

"I believe that's your man," Andrews said, nodding toward the lad. "I suppose I should keep my distance while you talk to him."

"It embarrasses me to ask that of you," Futrelle admitted, "but yes."

"I'll take a seat in the General Room."

Andrews headed out as Futrelle approached the table and the burly young man rose.

The mystery writer asked, "Son, are you Alfred Davies?"

"Yes, sir," he said. His voice was a pleasant tenor. He smiled shyly, displaying the crooked yellowed teeth so common to his class and country. "Did the captain send you, sir?"

"Yes, he did."

"About the nurse them people is usin'?"

"That's right."

Davies let out an enormous sigh, shaking his head. " 'Tis a relief, sir. I was afraid me message didn't get to 'im ... or that them above thought I was some lyin' or some such."

"My name is Jack Futrelle." He extended his hand and the boy took and shook it; though Davies didn't make a show of it, power lay in those hands and the arms and shoulders that went with them. "Let's sit, shall we, son, and talk?"

"Yes, sir," the boy said, and sat. "If you don't mind my askin', sir, what's your job with the ship?"

"I'm working for Captain Smith on a matter of ship's security."

He nodded; the soft, childlike features seemed incongruous next to that massive frame. "I see, sir. Well, then, you'd be the man to talk to, then, sir."

"You have information about the Allisons' nanny—Alice Cleaver?"

"I don't know the family's name, sir, but if it's the hatchet-faced wench I saw up on the boat deck, yes, sir, Alice Cleaver, sir."

"You were up on the boat deck?"

"No! We stay on our side of the chain, sir. But from the well deck y'kin see up top. And it's hard to mistake her, with that puss of hers, sir. Stop a clock, it would."

Futrelle grinned. "Maybe so. But the rest of her could start a dead man's heart beating again."

Davies returned the grin. "I guess that's why God made the dark, sir."

From his inside suit coat pocket, Futrelle removed his gold-plated cigarette case, offered a Fatima to the boy, who refused, then lighted one up for himself. "Where do you hail from, son?"

"West Bromwich, sir—Harwood Street."

"You boarded at Southampton, I take it."

"Yes, sir."

"And are you bound for New York, or points west?"

"Points west, sir. Place called Michigan—Pontiac, Michigan."

"What takes you there?"

"Me two brothers are working there, in the motorcar works. They say we can get jobs, too, good ones. Y'see, sir, we lost our jobs at the smelting works."

Smelting again—Guggenheim's business in First Class, Davies's business in Third.

Davies went on: "Me old dad's been a galvanizer since the Lord was in the manger. All us Davieses are ironworks men— puddlers, copula workers, the like. But times at home is gettin' hard, sir—you're American, sir?"

"Born and raised."

"*Is* it the promised land, sir?"

Futrelle blew out a stream of smoke, laughing gently. "As close as anything on this earth might come, son."

"I'm travelin' with my other two brothers—John and Joseph—and we'll send for our families, soon as we get settled."

They were hitting it off well—young Davies treating Futrelle respectfully, but feeling comfortable enough to say whatever was on his mind. So Futrelle stepped forward gingerly into the next topic …

"Alfred—may I call you Alfred?"

"Me mates call me Fred."

"All right, Fred." But Futrelle didn't give the boy leave to call him "Jack": the writer liked the deference he was being paid; it gave him the upper hand.

"Fred, this information you have about Alice Cleaver."

"Yes, sir?"

"The captain took your note to mean you expected to be paid for sharing what you know."

"No, sir! This isn't about money a'tall, sir. It's about babbies."

Futrelle suppressed a smile at the pronunciation, but the sincerity in the lad's eyes was unmistakable.

"Well, then, tell me, son. What is it you know?"

He leaned forward, the cap on the table, his hands folded almost as if he were praying. "Dad and Mum raised me to read and write, sir. I may work with me hands, but I like to read a book now and again, and of course the newspaper."

Encouraging words to the ears of a journalist like Futrelle, but he wasn't sure what it had to do with anything.

"'Twas in January, must've been 1910, no—aught nine—such a terrible thing." He was shaking his head; his eyes were wide and staring into bad memories. "Plate layers, workin' the North London Railway, they found something terrible sad."

"What did they find, son?"

"A babby. A dead babby ... a poor pitiful dead boy, who they say was tossed from a movin' train, the night afore. They arrested a Tottenham woman for the crime—it was her babby boy, y'see, her own son—and she wailed to the sky she was innocent, said she gived up the child weeks afore to a orphanage run by a 'Mrs. Gray,' I think the papers said ... you'd have to check that ... but there was no orphanage and there was no 'Mrs. Gray.' They convicted her, and only then she copped, 'cause it come out that her boyfriend, who'd put her in the family way, had run off and left her and the little one to fend for themselves."

The lad sighed, slowly shaking his head at the horror of it.

Sitting forward, chilled, Futrelle said, "And this woman, this mother who murdered her infant son ... is *Alice Cleaver*? The nanny entrusted with the Allisons' children?"

He nodded. "It was in the papers day upon day. 'Twas a story you followed. They put her picture in, and it's not a face a man would likely forget, is it, sir?"

"No it's not. Why in God's name isn't she in prison?"

"The jury asked for leniency, the judge took pity on her. She was a wronged woman, His Honor said, and hers was a desperate act. Her livin' with the memory of what she done was punishment enough, he said. She was set free."

Futrelle was flabbergasted; he stabbed out his cigarette in a glass White Star ashtray. "How could she have ended up the Allisons' nanny with that in her past?"

The lad threw his hands in the air, his eyes wide with the conundrum. "I don't know, sir. If you lived in England, you'd likely know about the case."

"That may explain it—the Allisons were just visiting London; they're Canadian."

"Sir, has anyone else said anything of this sad business to you? Your British passengers?"

"It's mostly Americans, in First Class, son ... and the few British among us are not likely to read the same papers as you. And even so, the only stories they'd be inclined to 'follow' would focus on themselves."

Davies hung his head. "P'rhaps 'twas wrong to point this out, a'tall. P'rhaps the poor pitiful woman only wants what we all want, down here in the hindquarters of this great ship: a new life, another chance."

Futrelle nodded gravely. "The promised land."

Then Davies looked up and his dark eyes were burning in his baby face. "But the little babby she's carryin' in her arms, it deserves a *first* chance, don't it? And with a crazy woman, a child killer, lookin' after the wee one ... well, it just don't seem right, sir."

"No it doesn't ... You're a good man, Fred."

"Sir, I hope to have children of my own, someday, and soon." The crooked smile turned shy; it was strangely ingratiating. "Monday last, day afore we left, I was married at Oldbury parish church—April eighth—to the prettiest girl in West Bromwich."

"Well, congratulations. Is your bride aboard this ship, son?"

"No, she's moved in with her mum till I can send for her." He laughed. "Y'know, we almost missed the boat! Got the wrong train out of West Bromwich, barely made it aboard, me brothers and uncle and me. But I've always been a lucky sod ... sir."

Futrelle stood. "I hope you do find the promised land, son."

Davies stood, too. "Thank you, sir. I hope I done the right thing, tellin'. Couldn't stand the thought of her hurtin' another babby."

Futrelle nodded; they shook hands again, and the mystery writer joined Andrews in the General Room, where someone was playing the piano—some lively English music-hall number—while many of the emigrants clapped along.

"Success?" Andrews said.

"Of a sort," Futrelle said.

The clapping around him was almost like applause.

Almost.

TEN

SHIPBOARD SÉANCE

EVEN FOR THE *TITANIC*, THE Reading and Writing Room spoke of uncommon elegance. Situated on A deck, just forward of the ornate First-Class Lounge (of which it was a virtual extension), the high-ceilinged Georgian-styled chamber, with its plush armchairs and sofas upholstered in pink-and-red floral design, its wall-to-wall deep red carpet, its sheltering potted palms, made an ideal retreat for the ladies.

During the day, however, the white walls combined with the many-paned high windows, including a bay window onto the sea, so blindingly suffused the room with light, its designated purpose—reading and writing—was made moot. Thus the chamber was little used, and after dark, when the First-Class passengers were dining or attending the nightly concert, the room lay as abandoned as a mining-camp ghost town.

So it was with little difficulty that Futrelle—with Captain Smith's sanction—secured the room for a private affair, a unique event, for a very select and honored list of guests: a séance.

Just before nine P.M., Futrelle, still dressed in his formal clothes from dinner, his stomach rather nervously trying to digest the latest parade of delicacies bestowed by the First-Class Dining Saloon, wandered about the room, setting the stage. He had been, in his professional life, only three things, and two of them were different branches of the same tree: reporter and fiction writer.

But his other job had been those two years in Virginia, running that repertory company—managing a theater, mounting productions, casting and even writing the plays himself. That was his common bond with his friend Henry B. Harris; and, with Henry's help, he would again stage an effective show.

Helping him prepare the room for his production was May, emerald earrings glittering, resplendent in a high-waisted black lace dinner gown, the low neckline and white corsage emphasizing the swell of her bosom, a matching corsage in her hair. With tapering fingers tucked into the long white gloves that began where her short-tiered black lace sleeves ended, she was drawing closed the dark curtains on one of the many windows.

"Oh Jack," she said, gliding to the next window, "I haven't been this nervous since the opening night of *The Man from Japan*."

"If it goes well, do you suppose Henry will want to purchase the cinema rights?"

With some effort, Futrelle pushed a large, heavy round oak table into the center of the room, to accommodate the ten people who would be seated here, in just a few minutes. Already, with the drapes closed, the room was darkening into a more appropriate setting for mystical doings.

"How can you joke?" she asked, approaching him. She was pale, and even trembling a little. "Aren't you frightened?"

"There's nothing to be frightened about."

"How about, unmasking a murderer?"

"That may not happen. If, in fact, we have a cold-blooded, premeditating killer in our midst, there may be no reaction at all."

"Oh, Jack, I'm suddenly cold. Hold me."

And he did, tight, whispering in her ear, "There's no danger, darling. After all, this is the safest ship on the ocean."

She drew away enough to arch an eyebrow at him. "The two men in cold storage may have a different opinion."

As usual, she had a point; but he felt confident that he knew which of his guests tonight would reveal guilt, and similarly sure that the individual in question would not react violently.

The most violent reaction he'd received had come, predictably, from the most indispensable guest: William T. Stead.

"Are you suggesting," Stead had bellowed, the sky-blue eyes wide with indignation, "that I submit my good name, my untarnished reputation as a medium, to the conducting of a fraudulent séance?"

"I am," Futrelle said, "but for a worthy cause."

Futrelle had been admitted to the parlor of C89, Stead's suite, the layout of which was identical to the Futrelles' own, though the furnishings were Queen Anne, a delicate setting for the rumpled grizzly bear within. Stead had converted the sitting room to a study; the table and floor were littered with galley proofs, foolscap filled with longhand, and wadded-up balls of discarded paper.

Stead's chin jutted, the white-thicket beard held high, extending like a pennant. "No cause is worth my reputation, sir. These are my religious beliefs you're asking me to betray, no, verily to *prostitute!*"

Futrelle remained calm. "You may have noticed, Mr. Stead, the absence of Mr. Crafton in our presence in recent days."

"A blessing."

"No—a murder."

And Stead's wide eyes hardened, then narrowed, and softened, and soon the two men were seated on the sofa, as Futrelle revealed his intentions, and his plans.

"I am your servant, sir," Stead said quietly, even humbly. He shook his big shaggy head. "But at least it does explain something that's vexed me about this voyage."

"What would that be?"

"The many warnings I've had."

"I don't follow you, sir."

He shrugged. "Several friends ... two extraordinary psychics, and a most respected clergyman ... independently warned that danger awaited me on the sea, in April. None of them knew I intended travel, yet two specifically indicated I should avoid any trip to the Americas. These feelings of foreboding they shared indicated I would meet danger, even death, on the *Titanic* ... and now I have."

"Why, with your belief in such things, did you still book passage?"

"The president of your United States requested that I attend a peace conference; I could not refuse." He laughed heartily. "Messages from the invisible world are not Marconi 'grams—they require interpretation, Mr. Futrelle, and I am not about to live my life by assuming the worst, and by capitulating to fear."

With Stead's participation, lining up the rest of the guests was, for the most part, child's play. The man may have had the grooming of a shipwreck victim crawled to shore, but W. T. Stead was a famous fellow, one of the best-known journalists on either side of the pond, and sitting at one of his séances would make an irresistible anecdote for the likes of Astor, Guggenheim,

Straus and Maggie Brown, all of whom said yes more or less instantly. So did Ismay, who did not begin to suspect the real purpose of the evening.

The trickiest invitation was Alice Cleaver.

Futrelle had determined not to inform the nanny's employers of her criminal background—not just yet, anyway. He had observed her with the Allison children and she had been a good and gentle nurse; there was no reason to suspect that she might snap and turn violent on the tykes, no call to think she might—like Jekyll into Hyde—again become the woman who had fallen to pieces when her common-law husband deserted her and her child.

The problem was—how to invite the servant of a First-Class passenger to a party? A party her employers would not be invited to themselves?

Mid-afternoon, Futrelle found Hudson and Bess Allison strolling on the A-deck enclosed promenade, with no sign of their nanny or children.

"Another beautiful afternoon," Futrelle commented casually as they paused at the rail by the window onto the gray-blue expanse broken by tiny whitecaps.

"Oh yes," Hudson said, adjusting his glasses, "but too chilly for the boat deck, don't you think?"

Even within the relative warmth of the promenade, pretty Bess was holding on to her husband's arm tight.

"Much too chilly," Futrelle agreed. "And where are your lovely children?"

"Lorraine and Trevor are with Alice," Bess said, "in the starboard Verandah Café."

"The kids seem to have taken over that little palm court," Futrelle said with a grin. "I hope you won't consider this forward, but I have an unusual request."

"Certainly, Jack," Hudson said, as if they were old friends; that was the way it was on a crossing.

"You're familiar with W. T. Stead, of course."

"Of course," Hudson said, and some small talk followed about what an interesting character the old boy was.

"Well, he's having one of his famous séances this evening," Futrelle said.

Hudson's youthful face lighted up, and Bess was smiling too. They exchanged glances and Hudson said, "Oh, wouldn't that be a riot to attend! You're not asking us to be part of it, are you? I think we'd say yes in a flash."

"That's not precisely it ... You see, Stead, as you say, well ... he's a character all right—and he has eccentric criteria in selecting his participants."

Hudson's smile had frozen. "Do tell."

"As a medium, he studies faces, and senses spiritual auras, listens to vibrations we earthbound mortals don't feel or hear." Then, with a laugh, Futrelle added, "Or at least he thinks he does."

The Allisons, quite confused, laughed along, albeit a little stiffly.

"Anyway," Futrelle continued, "Stead asked me to ask you, on his behalf ... he apparently noticed that we'd formed a friendship ..."

The Allisons both nodded, though Futrelle was overstating wildly.

"... so he's asked me to ask if you would allow him to invite your nanny, Alice, to attend the séance."

A moment of stunned silence followed; the couple had suddenly turned into a wax-museum exhibit.

Finally, Hudson managed, "Alice?"

"Our Alice?" Bess echoed. "Why ever for? She's the quietest girl you could imagine."

Futrelle shrugged, laughed softly. "Well, apparently still waters run deep—or at least, psychic waters do … If you need a baby-sitter for Lorraine and Trevor, I can provide one. Either my wife May, or Mrs. Henry Harris—you've met her … René?"

Hudson was trying to process this bewildering request. "Uh, well … dear, what do you think?"

Bess seemed on the verge of turning cross. "I'm disappointed that we weren't asked, frankly. Can't we even watch?"

"No, I'm afraid not. Mr. Stead is rather stubborn on that point: participants only, no spectators." Futrelle hung his head, shaking it. "I do apologize for being party to this rudeness …"

"No!" Hudson blurted. "Not at all. I suppose it's rather an honor to have our … nanny asked to attend such a special affair."

Bess asked, "When is this séance?"

"Nine P.M."

"Well, then," she said, accepting her lot in life as coming in second place to her own servant, "the children will be in bed asleep by then. Our maid can look after them, easily enough. Let's go give Alice the good news, shall we?"

Alice didn't consider it good news.

"A séance?" she said. Trevor was on a blanket at her feet, pawing at a rattle with which golden-haired Lorraine was gently teasing the toddler. "Y'mean, one of them spook things?"

"Yes, dear," Bess said patiently. "It's an honor. Mr. Stead is a very famous man."

"Do I have to?"

"It's a night off, for Lord's sake," Hudson said irritably. "Don't be sullen when you're being singled out for a treat, girl!"

"If I must."

Futrelle smiled at the young woman; the battered nose did such a disservice to her otherwise attractive features. The cobalt eyes were striking—and carried more intelligence than her dour manner betrayed.

"Alice," Futrelle said, "Mr. Stead senses a great sensitivity in you. He would greatly appreciate your presence."

Tiny Trevor said, "Goo! Gah!"

Lovely little Lorraine was laughing at her brother, letting him snatch the rattle from her.

Their nanny, who had once murdered a child younger than either of them, shrugged. "I'll come."

Futrelle had ruled out Hoffman/Navatril. It would have been clumsy, arranging an invitation for the Second-Class passenger, and the mystery writer doubted the man would come, under any circumstances. The doting father would not let out of his sight the children he'd kidnapped, which was one of the several reasons Futrelle did not believe him to be the murderer of Crafton and Rood.

Only one of those he asked refused his invitation to Stead's séance.

"I want nothing to do with that old charlatan," Major Archie Butt had said, taking a break between hands in an ongoing high-stakes poker game in the Smoking Room, a fragrant blue cloud of cigar smoke hanging over the table, as if threatening rain. Butt's friend Millet was playing, as were young Widener and railroad man Hays.

"Hell, Archie," Futrelle said, "you were hanging on his every word in here the other night."

The dimpled jaw jutted. "That's when I knew I'd had enough of him! That mummy balderdash! No, sorry, old man—afraid I have better things to do with my time … such as play cards or get bloody drunk or a sublime combination thereof."

It was clear the major could not be budged, and, disappointed, Futrelle had moved through the revolving doors into the portside half of the Verandah Café (it was the starboard half of the palm court that had been taken over by children and their nannies). He had just sat at a table in the shade of a palm so close it was tickling his neck when Millet—dapper in a gray suit and blue silk tie—came through the revolving door, looking for him.

The white-haired, distinguished-looking artist pulled up a wicker chair and sat, smiling shyly. "Glad I caught up with you, Jack."

"Surprised you left the table, Frank. It looked like you were winning."

Millet smoothed his salt-and-pepper mustache with a thumbnail. "I asked to be dealt out for a few hands. I … wanted a word with you, sir—in private."

A steward came by and the two men ordered coffee.

"I wanted to explain about Archie's reluctance to accept your invitation," Millet said.

"No explanation necessary."

"Well, he was damn near rude, and … look, there's something I've been wanting to let you know, anyway."

"I'm listening, Frank."

The reserved artist drew in a breath, gathered his courage, and said, "The story Archie told you about this fellow, this blackmailer Crafton, that was true, as far it went—Archie indeed has been suffering from nervous exhaustion."

"Being pulled between two friends as powerful as Taft and Roosevelt has to be an ordeal."

"It was, and it is ... but this Crafton is a scoundrel of the first rank. You need to be cautious around him, Jack—he's capable of spreading the most scurrilous slander."

"I'm aware of that."

"I don't think you are. This is ... embarrassing to even bring up."

"I don't tell tales out of school, Frank—and the only writing I do these days is fiction."

Millet nodded, sighed again and, with a tremor in his voice, said, "Well, as you know, Archie and I are close friends—we're also both lifelong bachelors. This son-of-a-bitch Crafton was threatening to humiliate us, in the most damaging, defamatory manner imaginable ... Do I have to be more specific, Jack?"

Looking at this esteemed American artist—a man decorated for bravery under fire in both the Civil War and the Russian-Turkish conflict—Futrelle felt a flush of rage toward the late Crafton.

Through his teeth, Futrelle said, "Crafton was going to try to paint Major Archibald Butt as, what—Oscar Wilde? It's preposterous."

Millet avoided Futrelle's gaze, hanging his head. "All I can say is, Archie puts up a good front, but something as potentially emotional ... and revealing ... as Mr. Stead's séance—good fun though it will probably be—would be a trial for him. So I apologize for my friend."

"Again, none is necessary—but he's lucky to have as good a friend as you."

Now Millet met Futrelle's eyes. His voice was soft, his expression almost bashful. "You haven't asked me if there's any truth to his slander."

"I wouldn't dignify the accusation with any consideration whatsoever. Besides—it's none of my damned business, is it?"

Millet just thought about that for a moment; he seemed quietly shocked by Futrelle's reaction. Then he smiled and nodded, saying, "You're a good man, Jack."

Their coffee arrived, and the two sat drinking it, talking of more pleasant subjects, including mutual admiration for each other's prose (Millet was, in addition to a fine artist, an author of short stories, essays and an eminent translator of Tolstoy, among others). Millet expressed a typical expatriate's view of his fellow countrymen, or at least countrywomen.

"An inordinate number of obnoxious, ostentatious American women on this voyage, don't you think, Jack? Have you noticed how many of them carry tiny dogs with them, like living mufflers?"

"I have," Futrelle admitted. "But it's their husbands they lead around like pets."

The two men had a hearty laugh, finished their coffee, shook hands and went their separate ways.

But Futrelle was dismayed by Butt's refusal to attend, particularly now that he knew the major's murder motive was the only one that truly rivaled that of the person Futrelle had pegged as the killer.

Only belatedly did it occur to him that Millet had the same motive.

And the artist seemed as unlikely as Butt to accept an invitation to a séance; so Futrelle decided not to bother offering one. The performance the mystery writer was staging was meant for only one person, and if he had misjudged the guilt of that person, the evening ahead would be purely entertainment, just another exotic shipboard trifle to amuse the rich passengers.

Just before nine, the audience of his show—who were also the star players—began to drift in, the men in their evening clothes, brandies and cigars in hand: Guggenheim and Straus, the handsome playboy and the reserved patriarch, an unlikely pairing but joined in business and ethnicity; Astor and his mascot Maggie Brown (in a blue silk beaded dinner gown and a feathered chapeau you could row to shore in), laughing it up together, her raucous presence unloosening the real-estate tycoon into near humanity.

Futrelle and May mingled with the millionaires and Maggie, and it was quickly established that Madame Aubert, Ida Straus and Madeline Astor were attending the evening's concert.

Before long, Ismay entered, accompanying the lovely brunette actress Dorothy Gibson. Ladies' men Astor and Guggenheim seemed immediately mesmerized by her oval face and languid eyes and creamy complexion, not to mention the hourglass figure ensconced in gray silk chiffon over dark blue silk, double pearls riding the swell of a bosom well served by a low scooped neckline.

Futrelle approached Ismay and the actress, saying, "Miss Gibson, it was kind of you to consent to join us."

"Don't be silly," she said, in her rich, warm contralto. Henry Harris should have no worries over how this moving-picture player would do with a speaking part on Broadway. "When I learned Mr. Ismay was to be a member of our party tonight, I imposed upon him to escort me."

"Only too happy," the White Star director said, his smile echoed by the upturned ends of his waxed mustache.

"Mr. Stead should be here any moment," Futrelle said.

Ismay said, "I hope he'll give us full instructions; this is my first séance, I'm afraid."

Miss Gibson, clutching her escort's arm, said, "I doubt any of us are veterans, Mr. Ismay. I just hope I don't embarrass myself by screaming or tearing at the drapes."

"I've attended a few sittings," Futrelle admitted, "as story research. I wouldn't be overly concerned."

Maggie Brown, overhearing this, wandered over and said, "I sat with Eusapia Palladino once. She brought my parents back to talk to me."

"That must have been thrilling," Miss Gibson said.

"It was all right," Maggie said. "Kinda made me wonder why they didn't say somethin' all those years they was sittin' in my back parlor, freeloadin'."

Futrelle's laughter was partly in response to the irascible Mrs. Brown's latest outburst, but also to the endearingly unladylike chortling of Miss Gibson.

Not joining in on the fun was Ismay, who had no discernible sense of humor; he was instead glancing around the room at the other guests, as they milled about. "Uh, Jack, a word with you, please? If you'll excuse me, Miss Gibson ..."

Maggie Brown and Miss Gibson fell in together, for a spirited show-business conversation (Maggie had theatrical aspirations), while Ismay buttonholed Futrelle near the bay window.

"I suppose," Ismay said, "it's pure coincidence that everyone here was on Mr. Crafton's 'client' list?"

"Well, that's not quite true, Bruce. Dorothy Gibson wasn't on it, and for that matter, the, uh ... torn list you showed me didn't include Mr. Straus, Mr. Stead or yourself ... if you'll recall."

Ismay's frown was so tight it distorted his features. "What is this about? What are you up to?"

Futrelle patted Ismay gently on the back, almost as if comforting a baby. "Don't be so suspicious, Bruce. Enjoy yourself—*of course*, many of the names on Crafton's list are present. He selected only the very best people for his blackmail victims; there's bound to be some overlap."

Ismay's frown lessened but did not leave. "Should I believe you?"

Futrelle gestured to the double doorways that connected to the lounge. "Look, here—here's our host, and a participant he chose himself...."

And the great man, dressed in a brown tweed suit that may have been pressed once or twice since the century turned, rolled in like a cannon on wheels. On Stead's arm, looking feminine and almost pretty, like a new schoolmarm out west, was Alice Cleaver—her figure, every bit as hourglass fetching as Miss Gibson's, was draped in her Sunday best: a dark blue tailored suit with a white shirtwaist and a ruffled skirt. She wore a small fluffy-flowered hat and a timid but not fearful expression.

"Who is that woman?" Ismay whispered. She was obviously not of the same social standing as the Astors, Guggenheims, or for that matter Maggie Brown.

"Her name is Alice Cleaver," Futrelle said.

"That doesn't tell me anything."

"She works for the Allisons, First-Class passengers—their nanny. Stead noticed her and sensed some psychic vibrations or some such about her." Futrelle shrugged. "I don't understand the mumbo jumbo myself."

Stead was ushering the girl about the room, introducing her to her celebrated séance mates. To their credit, they were all quite gracious to her—of course, her shapely figure hadn't been lost on either Guggenheim or Astor. But whatever the reason, propriety or lust, they were putting her at ease, and Futrelle was grateful to Stead—who never looked to Futrelle more like

Santa Claus in those white whiskers than he did right now—for making the young woman feel welcome.

Futrelle wanted Alice Cleaver relaxed, not skittish, otherwise his experiment would be meaningless.

Now that everyone was present, Futrelle approached Stead, who still had the Cleaver woman on his arm, and asked, "Are you ready to begin, sir?"

"Certainly." Stead raised his voice, its deep, pleasing resonance filling the chamber; he opened his arms like an effusive preacher welcoming his flock. "Take your seats at the table, if you please!"

May had set place cards as if at a formal dinner, and the guests dutifully took their designated positions; a steward circled the table, gathering brandy glasses, offering an ashtray for cigars, Stead having requested no drinking or smoking during the sitting. Then the steward exited, pulling the double doors shut one at a time behind him, two reverberating thuds, sealing them in, quieting the dull din of conversation.

The large round table was covered with a white linen tablecloth and in the middle sat a hurricane oil lamp with a pale floral shade, already lighted. Set out on the table in front of Stead's seat was a pad of foolscap with three sharpened pencils. Smiles and nervous laughter tittered about the table, but talk had ceased, the atmosphere not unlike the last moments before a church service got under way.

The rumpled, bewhiskered, professorial journalist-turned-medium was the last to take his place, with Miss Gibson to his right, Ismay next to her, Maggie next to him, then Astor, Alice Cleaver (opposite Stead), Futrelle, Guggenheim and Straus, with an empty chair between Straus and Stead for May, who stood poised at the electric-light switch, awaiting the signal.

"Before we douse all lights but this lamp," Stead said, his voice calm yet commanding, "I must caution you against your preconceived notions of a séance. This table is unlikely to levitate; you will hear no rappings, no hooting trumpets, nor will you witness the materialization of ectoplasm or floating disembodied hands."

Respectfully, Straus asked, "What can we expect, sir?"

"Such manifestations as those I mentioned," Stead continued, in a measured, soothing manner, "are associated with a physical medium. I, ladies and gentleman, am a mental medium; I bring only spoken or written messages, messages from the world beyond the impalpable veil.... Are there any further questions before we begin?"

"You said physical manifestations are 'unlikely,' sir," Futrelle pointed out. "That seems to be leaving a door open."

"At a séance," Stead said gently, "many doors may open. You were invited here—all of you—because I sensed in you a certain receptivity to psychic energies. While I know, from experience, that I am not a physical medium ... one of you may hold that power."

"My word," Ismay said. "Wouldn't we know?"

Stead shrugged. "This ability may lay sleeping; tonight it could awaken ... I have seen it happen—not often. But I have seen it. Further, you should be warned that nothing may happen—we see, we hear, on any given night, only what the spirits may be pleased to share with us."

Guggenheim asked, "Are these spirits 'ghosts,' sir?"

"If that word pleases you. Are you a Christian, sir?"

"No. But I believe in the same God as the Christians."

Astor said, "I am a Christian, sir."

"And I," Ismay said.

Stead said, somberly, " 'If a man dies shall he live again?' Does not Christ promise us immortality? I have witnessed immortality, or at least the persistence of the personality of man after the dissolution of the vessel."

Maggie frowned. "What, the *Titanic*?"

"No! This vessel, this corporeal vesture. We no more die when we lay our bodies aside at 'death' than when we take off an overcoat."

"Who are these spirits?" Miss Gibson asked. "Why aren't they in heaven?"

Stead smiled patiently. "Perhaps they are, my child, returning to us from the other side, with wisdom to impart, or perhaps offering consolation for mourning loved ones. Others may be in a limbo world...."

"Purgatory," Maggie said.

"That is one religion's word for it. This is a science in its early stages; we are taking tentative steps into the unknown ... but I assure all of you, none of these spirits means us harm."

Maggie squinted at him. "The bad ones went straight to hell, you mean."

Despite his solemn demeanor, Stead chuckled softly. "Perhaps so—I know of no instance when a sitting like this one has been visited by a demon. A tormented soul, possibly ... an inhabitant of that limbo world to which you refer, perhaps some recently deceased party who has not come to terms with his new, noncorporeal state. Now—if there are no further questions ..."

And there were none.

"Mrs. Futrelle, if you would, the lights?"

The room fell dark but for the glowing oil lamp, the orb of its canary shade casting its flickery jaundiced reflection upon the nine faces, eerily highlighting bone structure while other features lurked in pools of shadow. Those seated there might have been spirits themselves, albeit well-dressed ones, phantasms in fancy evening dress. Stead especially looked unearthly with his clear blue eyes and prominent nose and bushy whiskers washed in yellow.

His sonorous voice intoned, "My friends, I beg you to clasp hands ..."

And, as May took her seat next to Stead, the group joined hands, forming a human circle, each one eager for the comfort of mortal flesh. Alice Cleaver's palm was cold and clammy against Futrelle's.

"... and we will wait, and allow the spirits to come to us, and to speak through me ... I may release your hand, Miss Gibson, should I feel the stimulus to write."

"Yes, sir," she said meekly.

Silence fell like a cloak over the room, not really silence, but the ordinary sounds of a steamer at night, suddenly heightened: the creak of woodwork, the remote thrum of engines, the muffled movement of stewards and passengers, the shimmer of the nearby glass dome over the stairwell as the ship created its own wind carving through the night at twenty-some knots. Somewhere a clock was ticking, a mechanical heartbeat, deafeningly soft ...

"William," a voice sweetly said.

Stead's own voice!

But this was higher-pitched than his normal tone, and feminine, coming from lips in a ghostly yellow face that had gone slack, eyes closed as if in sleep, or death.

The sweet female voice from the rough male form continued: "Why have you not saved my usual seat at your table? Am I not wanted here?"

Then the old man's bulk shuddered, and—his eyes remaining closed—he said in his own voice, "I apologize, dear Julia. I felt our purpose tonight was beneath you."

Futrelle—whose left hand was being gripped firmly, to the point of discomfort, by Alice Cleaver—was afraid the old boy, in the grip of his conscience and delusions, would spoil everything.

But Stead suddenly fell silent, releasing Miss Gibson's hand, and he grasped a pencil and, with eyes still closed, head raised, he began to write, quickly, fluidly. He seemed to have written about a paragraph's worth, when he reached for Miss Gibson's hand again and looked down at what he'd just written.

"My great and good friend, my spirit guide, Miss Julia Ames, has imparted a message for me, which I will share with you. She says, 'Let me say to my dear friend and helper, who goes forth across the sea, rest assured that you will be left in no uncertainty when comes the clarion call. All questions soon will be answered.' "

Futrelle, like any good producer, was getting irritated with Stead, to whom he attempted to send the following psychic message: *Stick to the script, you old goat!*

Then the quiet room was again loud with the ticking clock, the thrum of engines, the rattle of the glass dome, the distant movement of people elsewhere on the ship....

Just when Futrelle thought he would scream not from fright but boredom, Stead said, in his own voice, "I sense a spirit in this room."

Darkness and ambience had begun playing sly tricks; their own faces in the campfirelike glimmer of the lamplight seemed to float about the table.

"A child ... a very young child," Stead said quietly. "So young he has not learned to speak ..."

Alice Cleaver's hand gripped Futrelle's even tighter. With his head lowered, but his gaze secretly shifted her way, Futrelle could see her, staring at Stead, the blunt-nosed mask of her face frozen with fear, the cobalt eyes wide and staring and glittering in the hurricane's yellow glow.

"... but I sense forgiveness ... absolution ... this baby, like the baby Jesus, embodies forgiveness ..."

The grip loosened, just a bit; and Alice Cleaver's lower lip trembled, her eyes brimming with tears.

"... though he died by violence, the baby boy is at peace, and he loves his mother...."

Tears trickled down the homely face, glistening in the lamplight.

But another woman at the table was reacting, too: the woman next to Stead, Dorothy Gibson—her eyes closed tight, her head weaving as if loose on her neck—was in a trancelike state, trembling, a trembling that ascended to tremors, as if the young woman were a volcano intent on erupting.

All eyes in the darkened room were on the beautiful face in the yellowish luster of the lamp, a beautiful face that began to contort as if in excruciating pain.

Then, in a deep, male voice, Dorothy Gibson spewed the words: *"I forgive no one!"*

Stead, still holding on to the convulsing girl's hand, asked gently, "Who are you, spirit? Why are you troubled?"

Miss Gibson shivered, as if fighting the spirit within her, then the male voice said, "My name is John."

Alice Cleaver blinked away the tears; she, too, was trembling, but the tears had halted, and her eyes were wide and wild with fright.

Patiently Stead asked, "What is your last name, John?"

The deep male voice erupted from the girl: "Crafton!"

Astor said, confused, "Crafton isn't dead!"

Maggie said, "Yeah? When'd you see him last?"

"That's just wishful thinking," Guggenheim said, but he didn't sound so sure.

"Quiet," Straus said, fascinated by the bizarre tableau.

Ismay's eyes were narrowing in mistrust; then he glared across the table at the mystery writer. "Futrelle ..."

And Alice Cleaver's grip on Futrelle's hand was evincing the strength he'd suspected she had....

"I can't breathe!" the male voice screamed, and everyone at the table jumped in their seats, as Dorothy Gibson's face reddened, the pretty features twisting into a mask of anguish. The deep voice flowed out of her: "Stop! Please stop.... Can't breathe! *I can't breathe ... you ... are ... killing ... me!"*

Alice Cleaver screamed.

Releasing Futrelle's hand as if it were a stove's hot burner she'd touched, the young woman sprang to her feet and ran into the darkness.

"Please keep your seats," Stead said gently, just loud enough to rise over the murmured confusion of his guests. "May—the lights ... this sitting is over."

Ismay was rising, but Stead stood and reached across the exhausted Miss Gibson and clutched Ismay's arm. "Be seated, sir! Do not follow them ... I beseech all of you."

In the meantime, Futrelle had pursued the young woman into the darkness, her sobbing leading the way; even in the dark, Futrelle had enough sense of his bearings to know she wasn't heading for the double doors into the lounge, but to the side door, the corridor door.

Then a momentary slash of light cutting through the blackness—as that door opened and closed—confirmed his suspicion.

The nanny was running down the corridor, forward of the Reading and Writing Room, and Futrelle was after her, following her into the reception area—empty of passengers, not even a steward in sight—as the Grand Staircase yawned before them. His glasses had fallen off his face, and her hat had tumbled to the floor, like a big bread crumb marking her path.

She all but flew up the stairs, her ruffled skirt rustling, hard soles of flat shoes echoing like gunshots, running up onto that very balcony where, not so long ago, he had dangled the blackmailer down over.

Then she was through the door onto the boat deck, and he was only seconds behind her, and when he burst through the door, onto the deserted deck, the cold night air was little brittle icy daggers stabbing at him, and the girl ...

... the girl stood at the rail, between two lifeboats, her leg slung over the side, propped there, as she was trying to decide.

"That *would* end it, Alice," Futrelle admitted quietly.

"Stay back, sir! Stay away."

"I can't obey that request, Alice." He shrugged. "If you're going to jump, you're going to jump ... but do it knowing I stand here not as your judge, or as any threat to you."

"My life is over," she said, and her eyes were tormented, her face streaked with tears, her lips trembling. "I got to go join my baby."

But she didn't jump. He knew she might, but didn't really think she would: everything he knew about this young woman indicated, however sad and sick and even twisted she might be, that she was, first and foremost, a survivor.

So Futrelle moved gingerly forward until he was standing at the rail next to her. He glanced over its edge. "The water's so black it doesn't even reflect the stars. They say it's cold—near freezing."

"Don't touch me. Don't try to stop me."

The sky was a dark blue, cobalt not unlike this poor girl's eyes; no moon, but the stars were so vivid, so limitless, it was if the night had countless tiny holes punched in it and tomorrow was streaming through.

Futrelle leaned casually against the rail, as if he were just taking the air and not talking to a woman perched between the deck and the depthless ocean as if astride a mechanical horse in the nearby gym.

Gently, unthreateningly, he said, "John Crafton tried to blackmail me, too, Alice."

"... Pardon, sir?"

"Just about everyone in that room downstairs, at the séance, was one of his victims. I had a mental breakdown, Alice—I was hospitalized—and John Crafton was going to defame me with that knowledge, in front of the world."

Her lower lip quivered, shivered, whether from cold or emotion, he couldn't hazard a guess; the eyes welled with fresh tears. "He was a beast."

"Everyone has secrets, Alice—many of us have terrible secrets. Things we've put behind us; things for which we pray God has forgiven us."

She nodded, haltingly. That flat-nosed face could have been pretty if someone, perhaps as long ago as her childhood, hadn't struck her some dreadful blow.

He kept his voice casual. "Even Mr. Guggenheim, Mr. Astor, the richest men on this ship, richest in America herself, have secrets ... same as simple people like you and me, Alice. They were Crafton's prey, as well."

Her chin was quivering now, too. "He ... he didn't want my money."

"He wanted something else, didn't he, Alice?"

She nodded pathetically. "I had twenty dollars Canadian the Allisons give me. I sneaked out, late at night, went to his room like he asked ... he opened the door, and yanked me inside, and ..."

Tears streamed down her face and her body was racking with sobs, and Futrelle lifted her off the railing and into his arms and patted her back, comforted her, holding her gently.

"He was naked, wasn't he?" Futrelle whispered.

"Yes, sir."

"You tried to give him that money, Alice?"

"Yes ... He stood there, naked as a jaybird, pale as a frog's belly, and he laughed at me. Laughed!"

She drew away so that she could look at him; her expression said that she was telling the truth.

"Like I said, sir—he didn't want money. He ... he told me to get undressed; said he wanted to watch. Said if I didn't give him my favors ... every night of this voyage ... he'd tell the Allisons about my baby."

"I understand."

"He ... he climbed in bed. He kept saying, take them off, take them clothes off ... and I say, 'Let me give you a kiss first,' and he said somethin' like, 'Now that's a girl,' or 'That's more like it,' and I leaned over and I put the pillow on him."

Her voice and her face had a blankness now, an emptiness; her eyes were half-lidded, staring dully into the awful memory of it.

"He was a scrawny thing ... not strong. Weak as a kitten, or a cat, anyways. And I was never stronger. I held them feathers on him, and he fought, he did thrash, but I pushed down, I held him down, and ... and finally he didn't struggle no more."

She began to sob again and he gathered her to him, and patted her back, and said, "He was an evil man, Alice. You were protecting yourself."

Nodding desperately, she said, "I was protectin' my honor! I ain't the best girl in the world, I guess I know that better than anybody, sir ... but I ain't no man's white slave! So I smothered the son of Satan, and I'd do it again, gladly."

"You did do it again, didn't you?"

Her eyes flared. "Pardon?"

"Crafton's partner-in-crime: Mr. Rood."

She swallowed. "Don't know 'im, sir."

"Alice ... I'm your only hope. Either you trust that I have your best interests at heart, or you'd best go back to that rail and jump."

"I don't ... don't really wanna die, sir. Will they hang me?"

"I've told you: I'm not your judge. I'm your friend—and another victim of that vile pair. What happened with Rood?"

"He told me to meet him on the deck, middle of the night—two A.M., when the ship was asleep. He said if I didn't meet 'im, he'd tell on me to the Allisons. He knew all about my baby, too. He said he even had the pictures from the papers to show the Allisons. I need that job, sir! I need the chance the Americas give."

"You're getting off the subject, Alice. Tell me about that night on deck with Mr. Rood."

"He ... he knew his partner was dead. He said he seen the stewardess come tearin' out of his friend's cabin, white as a ghost, and he quicklike slipped in and seen the body. And he knew I done it—or anyways, he figured I done it, 'cause his friend told him what he was goin' to do to me. I think ... I think I was to be both their white slaves, by crossing's end."

"Is that what he wanted from you up here, Alice? Your 'favors'?"

She was staring at the deck. "No. No, he ... he wanted the money."

"What money, Alice?"

"I did somethin' bad in that room, somethin' I shouldn't—and I ain't talkin' about riddin' the world of that blackhearted bastard. But there was this money on his dresser, just sitting there, this great wad of paper money. When Mr. Crafton was dead, when I just stood there catchin' my breath, I seen it there, sir, that money ... and I snatched it up. Took it with me. Figured ... I earned it."

"And Rood wanted that money."

She nodded. "He started in to get rough with me, sir ... he begun to shake me like a doll, till my head was rattlin' ... it was right there, it happened."

She pointed, like a child picking out a toy in a store window; but she was singling out one of the davit-slung lifeboats.

"That's where it happened, sir ... I grabbed him and I shoved him, shoved him hard ... didn't mean to do it so hard, I was just ... tryin' to get loose of him."

"You're saying that's what killed him?"

She nodded. "Caved the back of his head in, it did, sir."

"There must have been blood."

"There was, sir. He didn't have no pulse, sir. So I hid him in the boat."

"You did that yourself? Slung him up in there?"

"Yes, sir. You said it yourself, sir ... I'm a strong girl."

Something didn't sit right with the second half of her story; but Futrelle had a feeling this was the only story he'd get out of her. She had calmed down—the hysteria was over, the tears too, and she had gone from the girl unhinged by his manipulated séance to the battle-scarred survivor she innately was.

Still, she was beaten down, a flat-nosed girl in her blue Sunday dress. "What now, sir? See the captain? I'll turn myself in, if you like. Will they hang me, sir?"

"Let's find a bench and sit, Alice."

They did. The deck remained theirs alone; theirs, and the cold night and the glittering stars.

"I'm going to try to help you," he said.

She gazed at him, puzzled. "Why, sir?"

"Because men like Astor and Guggenheim and the rest ... even men like me ... can fight the likes of a John Crafton in all sorts of ways, including just throwing money at him. But a girl of your station, you don't have the same choices. It troubles me that violence follows you, Alice ... but I told you I was not your judge."

"But the captain ... ?"

"The captain and Mr. Ismay, well ... I'm going to try to keep this from coming out. I can't promise you I can manage it. But I promise I will try."

"Why?"

"You were wronged, Alice. To see you spend a day in jail for removing a cancer on society like Crafton or Rood, I simply cannot countenance."

She beamed at him, happiness seeming out of place on the battered face. "Oh, sir ... what do you want from me?"

"Nothing!" Futrelle backed away, held his palms out. "Not a thing! Not your money, not your favors ..."

She frowned in confusion. "I don't understand. From where you sit, sir, I must be a murderess and a thief."

"I see only a blackmailer's victim, who fought back. If I'm successful in shielding you, I only want one thing, one promise ..."

"Yes, sir?"

"Upon arriving in Canada, you will leave the Allisons' employ, immediately ... and use that bankroll of Crafton's to begin a new life, with a new name."

"Yes, sir!"

"And find some profession other than nanny. I don't want you around children ... understood?"

"Sir, oh sir ... you *are* my judge, my kind and generous judge ..."

"Do you promise?"

Tears were welling in those pretty eyes again. "I promise, sir."

"Then let's get down off this deck," he said, "before we catch our death."

DAY FIVE

APRIL 14, 1912

ELEVEN

SMOOTH SAILING

THE WIND CAME FROM THE southwest, moderate but with a bite in it. The Futrelles were on the boat deck walking off an enormous First-Class Dining Saloon breakfast (Jack had perhaps ill advisedly taken two servings of the grilled mutton chops and bacon). The couple could not have found the clear, cool morning more delightful: to the horizon stretched a smooth shimmer of blue-gray sea under a faded blue sky blessed only with fluffy white unthreatening clouds.

"I hope I did the right thing," Futrelle said, his breath pluming. He was in his topcoat.

May, wrapped up in her black beaver coat, was holding on to her husband's right arm with both of hers. "I know you did, darling. And even if you didn't—you erred on the side of compassion ... and there's nothing wrong with that."

"Well, it remains to be seen if the captain will go along with my suggestions."

"Surely he will," she said.

And as they walked, they caught a glimpse of the man himself, Captain Smith undertaking his full inspection of the ship, that sacrosanct ritual of all passenger ships at sea. In his white uniform with its medals and gold-ribboned cuffs, the captain led a parade of his department heads—chief officer, chief engineer, chief steward, the purser, even old Dr. O'Loughlin, all in dress uniform. From boat deck to boiler room, bow to stern, every accessible nook and cranny was to be inspected.

What Futrelle knew, that no one else did, was that the inspection team was running half an hour late; the captain would have to shake a leg to finish before the church service at eleven A.M. that he was set to lead.

The captain's usual meeting of department heads, at ten A.M., had been canceled so that the captain could attend a meeting with Futrelle and Ismay, which the latter had called.

"I've informed Captain Smith of the doings in the Reading and Writing Room last night," Ismay said, the irritated contortions of his mouth making his mustache do a funny little dance.

The three men were again seated at the round table in the parlor of Captain Smith's suite near the wheelhouse. A steward, who had long since disappeared, had served coffee and tea—Futrelle took the former, and was stirring cream and sugar in—while Ismay and the captain had taken the latter, though neither had touched theirs.

"Really?" Futrelle said with a facial shrug. "It was just an evening's entertainment."

"I don't think so," Ismay said.

The captain said, "From what Mr. Ismay tells me, I gather you may have flushed out our murderer."

And here Futrelle and the captain shared a secret: Smith had been aware of Futrelle's scheme and had agreed to it, arranging the use of the Reading and Writing Room for the séance. But Ismay wasn't aware of that, and Futrelle was happy to cover for the captain.

Who was saying, "Yet Mr. Ismay says you refused to confirm your discovery, last night, when he confronted you, afterward."

"That's right."

The captain frowned. "You mean you did flush out the killer?"

"I mean, that's right, I did refuse to confirm Bruce's suspicions."

Ismay slapped the table and cups of coffee and tea jumped, spilling a little. "If we do have a murderer on this ship, we must act, and act at once!"

Futrelle sipped his coffee and smiled above the rim of the china cup. "Why? Because now that Astor, Guggenheim and the other nobs are in the clear—and it's just a servant girl in question—this won't be so embarrassing?"

Ismay scowled, folding his arms in disgust. "I won't stand for your insults, Futrelle."

"Well, then," Futrelle said, setting down the cup, starting to rise, "why don't I just leave and go on about my business?"

"Sir," the captain said, reaching out to touch Futrelle's arm. "Please. Sit down, sir. Let's dispense with personalities and concentrate on facts."

"All right." Futrelle sighed, shrugged, sat back down. "The fact is, if there's been *any* murder on this ship—even if the culprit isn't part of the Smart Set—it's going to blacken your great ship's maiden voyage, Bruce ... and your final crossing, Captain."

"Be that as it may," the captain sighed, "we have two murders, and there's no sweeping them under the carpet."

Futrelle leaned forward, dropping his casual, offhand tone, suddenly forceful. "This girl, Alice Cleaver, acted in self-defense. Crafton tried to rape her ..."

"What?" Ismay cried, eyes widening.

"... and, later his partner Rood began to manhandle her in a similar fashion."

Furrows carved into the captain's brow. "Details, man," he said.

Futrelle provided them, leaving out only that Alice Cleaver had helped herself to the cash on Crafton's dresser, some of which may have been payoff money Ismay gave the blackmailer, Futrelle surmised.

"I sympathize with this woman," Ismay said, and his concern seemed genuine enough. "But it's not our place to judge. In any case, with these mitigating circumstances, she'll probably get off."

"I don't think so," Futrelle said. "Not with her past. Can you imagine the sensationalist press having at this? 'Baby Killer Kills Again—on the *Titanic!*' There's some nice publicity for you."

"Good Lord, man," Ismay said, "there are children entrusted to her care, even as we speak!"

"She's pledged to leave the Allisons' service, upon reaching port."

"Mr. Futrelle—why do you want to see this woman go free?" the captain asked.

"Because it's the Christian thing to do. I realize this is a British vessel, but we're in the middle of the North Atlantic, gentlemen. We're a jurisdiction unto ourselves, out here. Let's serve justice, not serve this girl up to corrupt New York coppers and hungry yellow journalists. Let's give this unfortunate girl the opportunity my country gives anyone: a second chance."

"I don't see how we can," Ismay said, obviously wishing he could, wringing his hands. His bleak expression indicated he'd begun to gather the extent of the devastatingly bad press guaranteed his ship if this came out.

"Whatever you decide," Futrelle said, "I'm going to advise that you destroy that packet of blackmail documents."

Ismay laughed once, without humor. "Damn it all, man! Earlier you were adamant that they *not* be destroyed."

"Earlier I thought they'd be needed as evidence."

"They are evidence," the captain reminded both men.

"Precisely," Futrelle said. "And into the hands of the police, those New York police I mentioned earlier, you will have placed defamatory material on the cream of your First-Class passengers. Have you read this material, gentlemen?"

Ismay avoided Futrelle's gaze. "We, uh ... glanced at the distaseful tripe."

Captain Smith said, "We didn't dignify the bilge with a close examination."

"Well, if you had, you'd know that, at the very least, some of those involved will be embarrassed ... others, like Major Butt, a fine man, would be ruined."

Captain Smith reared back; his eyebrows were climbing his forehead. "Sir—would you have us sweep this entire affair under the carpet?"

"Why don't you dump it to the bottom of the sea?"

Ismay was amazed. "Including the two corpses in our cold-storage hold?"

Futrelle nodded. "Exactly what I'd suggest."

Captain Smith said, "Sir, you were the one who warned that these men, however vile, had associates, families...."

"Mr. Crafton died of a heart attack, in his sleep—natural causes. Mr. Rood, apparently despondent over his friend's death, drank rather too much and took a spill on deck, taking a fatal fall. Dr. O'Loughlin fills out the reports, you bury the bodies at sea, and ... if you can trust the handful of crew who know about this unfortunate situation … sit back and wait to see if the White Star Line gets sued by any family members for negligence. If they do, settling with them will be a small price to pay for the large embarrassment you avoid."

Ismay's expression—a mixture of confusion and irritation, mixed with dismay—melted into blankness; but his eyes were moving with the rapidity of his thoughts.

Captain Smith wore the faintest frown and his eyes moved not at all—unblinkingly so—but it was clear he too was considering Futrelle's suggestions and the various ramifications.

A knock at the door prompted the captain to say, "Come!"

Second Officer Lightoller stuck his head in. "Sir, my apologies for interrupting, but even if we begin our inspection immediately, we'll be seriously late for church services."

Rather dismissively, Smith said, "Well, then, cancel the boat drill."

"Sir?"

"It's just a formality, after all; we've got a calm Sabbath day at sea for our passengers, and we won't interrupt it."

Lightoller didn't seem to like the sound of this order, but he said, "Yes, sir," and disappeared.

Captain Smith stood. "Mr. Futrelle, I appreciate the manner in which you've aided us in this unfortunate matter. Mr. Ismay and I will take your suggestions under advisement."

Futrelle rose. "I would appreciate it if you'd inform me of your decision. We should, as they say, get our stories straight."

"We have another full day of travel," the captain said. "Mr. Ismay and I will discuss this further, and you'll have our decision tomorrow, by mid-afternoon."

"I hope at the very least you follow my advice to burn those blackmail documents—including that torn list found in Crafton's cabin."

Ismay and Smith exchanged glances, then the captain said, "I believe you may be assured of that, sir."

Futrelle sighed heavily. "I admit I'm relieved—not for myself; the documents aren't so damning in my case. But you'll do a great service to a number of people undeserving of such aspersions."

Ismay stepped forward. "Mr. Futrelle ... I apologize if I seemed rude. This has been an unusual situation, to say the least, and we do appreciate your generous counsel."

"Do I assume correctly that you've changed your mind about commissioning me to write a murder mystery on the *Titanic*?"

"That is a fair assumption, sir," Ismay said wearily.

And the White Star director offered his hand, which Futrelle shook; then the mystery writer and the captain shook hands, and the meeting was over.

With the boat drill canceled, church began on time—eleven A.M.—and though there were several pastors aboard, Captain Smith himself conducted the nondenominational Christian service himself. Held in the First-Class Dining Saloon, it marked the only occasion when Second- and Third-Class passengers were allowed into the First-Class area.

This rare instance of *Titanic* democracy meant that, present in the same room at the same time, were the Astors, Maggie Brown, Dorothy Gibson, Ismay, the Allisons with their children and nanny Alice, "Louis Hoffman" and his two cute boys and even the smelting-works lad, Alfred Davies.

And, of course, the Futrelles.

Captain Smith made a fine fill-in pastor, reading psalms and prayers, including "The Prayer for Those at Sea," leading hymns accompanied by Wallace Hartley's little orchestra.

Afterward, Futrelle—moving quickly to the rear where the Second and Third Class had been seated—managed to talk briefly to both Hoffman/Navatril, and Davies, filing out.

To the former he whispered, "You are in no danger of discovery if you do as I suggested previously, and on leaving this ship, promptly disappear."

Hoffman gratefully clutched Futrelle's arm and whispered, "God bless you, sir."

"Good luck to you—and your boys."

To Davies, Futrelle merely said, "I've passed your information along."

The strapping lad seemed concerned. "I seen her sittin' up front. She's still with them kids, sir."

"Only until crossing's end. All is well."

"If you say so, sir."

"I do." He patted the boy's shoulder. "See you in the promised land, Fred."

Davies grinned his crooked yellow grin, which suddenly seemed almost beautiful to Futrelle. "See you in the promised land, sir."

The tranquillity, the reflection, of Sunday-morning service was already dissolving in the clatter of dishes and silverware and the scraping of chairs and tables, as stewards rushed to set the room up for luncheon at one. The noon siren prompted Futrelle to temporarily abandon May—who was on her way back to their suite—so that he could hie to the Smoking Room, to see how he made out in today's pool.

The figures for yesterday's run—though Futrelle came up a loser—were impressive: 546 miles.

A familiar voice behind him said, "Twenty-two and a half knots—impressive for a vessel this size."

Futrelle smiled at his friend Archie Butt, one of many in the crowd of men checking out the bulletin board. "Are you a winner, Archie?"

"Hell no. But I hear the engines are turning three revolutions faster today … you may wish to figure that into your bet for tomorrow's pool."

For all his joviality, this military man—who, with his jutting, dimpled jaw and erect carriage might have walked off a recruiting poster—had the saddest eyes Futrelle had ever seen.

"Archie—a private word?"

"Certainly."

And, taking the major to one side, Futrelle told him that Crafton was dead, and that his blackmail documents were to be destroyed. He also told his friend that he could give him no details, and he must not repeat this to anyone, except Frank Millet.

Major Butt said nothing, at first. Then a smile appeared under the trim mustache and he swallowed, rather thickly, and said, "Jack, you've given this old soldier a new lease on life."

"I'm sure May would like an invitation to the White House."

Archie laughed, and the laughter carried to his eyes, where a veil had been lifted. "I'll pull some strings."

Luncheon was the usual feast, a buffet beyond imagination, and Futrelle took the opportunity to whisper into regular tablemate Isidor Straus's ear the same information he'd shared with Archie Butt. Straus merely smiled and nodded.

Early afternoon, a cold snap made a ghost town of the open decks. Even in the open promenades, passengers who'd taken to deck chairs were bundled up, often warming themselves with cups of beef broth, courtesy of the ever-attentive stewards. In the public rooms and cafés of the great ship, passengers took to letter writing, cardplaying, reading, and conversation.

Throughout the long, lazy afternoon, Futrelle gradually talked to the other Crafton "clients," passing along the same gratefully received information about the blackmailer and his documents, gently refusing any details or explanations regarding the séance of the evening before.

His remark to Ben Guggenheim was typical: "For the rest of your life, you can brag about sitting at a séance on the *Titanic*, with none other than W. T. Stead as the medium. Isn't that enough? Must you also understand what it was about?"

Guggenheim—who'd been walking the enclosed promenade with the lovely Madame Aubert, when the Futrelles came upon them—accepted Futrelle's terms, gladly.

"My only condition," Guggenheim said, "is that Crafton remain dead."

Only Maggie Brown, having a light dessert in the Parisien café, gave the writer a hard time.

"You can't tell me that séance wasn't a put-up job!" she said. "You coached that little Gibson girl! You wrote her damned lines, didn't you, Mr. Thinkin' Machine?"

"You're right …"

"I knew it!"

"… I can't tell you that."

"Jack, nobody likes a wiseacre!" But she was grinning at the time.

Futrelle found Alice Cleaver, as usual, in the Verandah Café, watching golden-haired Lorraine playing with a top that was mesmerizing baby Trevor.

The nanny sat so somberly, her black livery might have been mourning clothes. Then she noticed him approaching, and smiled nervously as Futrelle took the chair at the wicker table next to her.

Almost whispering, Futrelle said, "I've spoken to the captain. I believe your chances are good."

"Oh, sir ..."

"No tears. No scene. And no guarantees—we'll know tomorrow, sometime. Until then—everything as usual, my dear."

The beautiful eyes in the blunt-nosed face welled with tears. "Mr. Futrelle ... I owe you everything."

He patted her hand. "You owe me your best efforts toward making a better life for yourself."

The writer and the nanny sat quietly and watched the two lovely Allison children capering. They were served tea and scones by the good-looking young steward who, days before, had been exchanging winsome glances with the broken-nosed beauty. He had a small bruise on his jaw—maybe she'd slapped him for his freshness, the shipboard romance foundering on the rocks. At any rate, the towheaded boy remained businesslike, and Alice didn't bother acknowledging his existence.

Suddenly the nanny blurted, "Mr. Futrelle, do you think God will ever grant me another child of my own?"

"I don't know, Alice. Do you want Him to?"

She was pondering that as Futrelle took his leave.

Once Futrelle had made the rounds of the Crafton clients, he and May retreated to their stateroom, where fully dressed they flopped onto the bed to read their respective novels—May,

The Virginian, her husband, *Futility*. Futrelle had a shorter book to finish, and drifted off into a nap; May, the Western saga finally completed, slammed the covers shut and woke him, on purpose.

"For having nothing to do," she said, "the days certainly go by quickly."

"Nothing to do?" he muttered sleepily. "I only solved two murders."

"I thought *we* solved them."

"You're right. That was ungracious. We."

"I'm starting to think of this suite as home."

"Dangerous thinking—this is *nicer* than home."

She laughed a little. "Oh, Jack, this has been a wonderful second honeymoon ... exciting ... romantic ..."

"Especially romantic," he said, and he kissed her.

They were still kissing when the nightstand telephone rang; it was Henry Harris, wanting them to join him and René for some cards before supper.

"How 'bout we meet on the Grand Staircase balcony?" Henry suggested. "Half an hour?"

"All right. But make it an hour ... we'll need to dress for dinner."

"It takes you an hour to dress for dinner?"

"Not me. You know how women are."

Then he hung up and went back to what he and May had been doing.

Dorothy Gibson joined the two couples for poker on the balcony; dressed in their evening clothes and looking like a million dollars, they played penny-ante stakes and had a wonderful time. And it gave Futrelle the opportunity to thank the young actress.

"You were superb last night," Futrelle told her, shuffling the cards.

May pretended to misunderstand and said, "Would you care to explain that remark?"

There was general laughter, and Dorothy said, "I was afraid I was overdoing the deep 'man's voice.' "

"No, it was splendid," Futrelle said, dealing. "Henry, I think you may have your next Broadway star on your hands."

"Henry B. will kindly keep his hands to himself," René said.

Miss Gibson was embarrassed by that, but everyone else laughed.

Henry said, picking up his cards, "Why don't you write a movin'-picture script for Dorothy, Jack?"

"Henry B.," René said, "quit hounding the man. Jack, why don't you?"

The bugler announced dinner.

"There's nothing to do on these damned ships but eat," René said. "So—shall we?"

Everyone agreed with her on both counts, but as they were going down the stairs, René's high heel caught her dress and she went tumbling down half a flight of stairs. Futrelle's first thought was that Crafton's ghost had tried to shove him and caught René instead.

Everyone rushed to her side, and found her laughing and crying and swearing, all at once.

"First critical thing I've said about this ship," she said, "and the damned thing decides to break my arm."

Her arm indeed was broken, her self-diagnosis confirmed by Dr. O'Loughlin, and a Dr. Frauenthal—a joint specialist who was traveling First Class—agreed to set it in plaster. Dorothy Gibson went off to join her mother in the First-Class Dining

Saloon, but the rest of the group decided to wait to eat until René could join them, agreeing to meet for a late dinner in the à la carte restaurant, the so-called Ritz.

Just before nine P.M., the Futrelles were the first to take their seats at the table in the luxurious restaurant, which—with its Louis Seize decor, from its floral-pattern plaster ceiling to the gilded, finely figured French walnut paneling, from its crystal chandeliers to the rose-hued Axminster carpet—might have been the dining room of some fine hotel in Paris.

The passengers dining at the spacious Ritz were dressed to the nines, as traditionally the second-to-last night out was the final opportunity to dress up (last night out was for packing and formal dining attire was set aside). The men in their white tie and tails, the women in the latest Parisian gowns, pale satins and clingy gauze, arrayed in glittering jewelry, were in high spirits, the air ringing with giddy laughter and wafting with the sweet aroma of flowers.

"You know, Jack," May said, admiring the vase of American Beauty roses that was their table's centerpiece, "something has been troubling me."

None of the rich, fashionable women around them had anything over May: she was ravishing in her gold silk-satin gown, its short sleeves decorated with strands of glass beads, her hair up and adorned with bird-of-paradise plumes.

His wife's beauty made him light-headed; or was it the wine he was sipping? "What, darling?"

"It's about the Cleaver girl."

Futrelle smirked. "Whatever could you find troubling about a nice girl like Alice?"

"That fellow—Rood? He was a big man, wasn't he?"

"Yes, well, tall, anyway. Not heavyset."

"But, still … how could she have lifted him into that lifeboat?"

"She's got considerable strength, dear."

"Perhaps, but—"

"Here are the Harrises."

René was making a rather dramatic entrance, in a short-sleeved gown showing off her new cast, Henry following dutifully after. Word of her accident had traveled around the ship, and the passengers in the restaurant applauded her.

As Henry pulled out a chair for his wife, Futrelle said, "I thought the show-business expression was 'break a leg'?"

"I believe in setting trends," she said, though she was obviously suffering.

A private party in honor of Captain Smith's approaching retirement was under way, and both the captain and Tom Andrews stopped by to compliment René on her "spirit" and "spunk," respectively.

Futrelle chatted briefly with Andrews, who looked surprisingly fresh.

"Tom, what's wrong?" Futrelle asked. "You actually look like you've had some sleep!"

Andrews grinned, leaning a hand on the writer's chair. "Well, it's just that I've finally caught up with all the problems on this little rowboat. I believe she's as nearly perfect as human brains can make her."

"Judging by the human brains I've encountered," Futrelle kidded him, "that's not much of a testimonial."

Andrews laughed at that, graciously, and went back to the party honoring his captain.

The dinner was eight amazing courses, trundled over by the usual succession of white-jacketed waiters, bearing exotic dishes with French appellations that translated to quail eggs with caviar, spring pea soup, lobster thermidor with duchess potatoes, filet mignon with wild mushrooms, mint sorbet, quails with cherries, asparagus with hollandaise sauce and fresh fruit salad.

Familiar faces were dotted around the elegant restaurant: Archie Butt and Frank Millet were among the jovial guests at the Widener family's party for Captain Smith, who had long since retired to the bridge; John and Madeline Astor, at a table for two, the expecting couple huddling romantically; and Ismay and Dr. O'Loughlin, in a side alcove, huddling in a different manner, a serious, businesslike fashion at odds with the gaiety all around. Futrelle could only wonder if the good doctor was being enlisted to carry out the mystery writer's suggested course of action, i.e., the signing of certain documents, specifically death certificates for the late Crafton and Rood.

The Futrelles and the Harrises took their time with the endless meal, sipped their wine, told stories on each other, filling the air with laughter and forgoing the evening concert for each other's company. By the time the night was over, Futrelle had agreed to write both a Broadway play and a cinema script for the producer, and René—who had been holding court throughout the evening, as virtually every passenger dining in the Ritz stopped by to celebrate her pluck—grandly announced that having a broken arm was a definite social asset.

Despite the now bitter cold, Futrelle and May took one last stroll on the boat deck, in their elegant evening wear, without their coats; it was now eleven o'clock, but they were warmed by wine and each other.

"It's been a wonderful second honeymoon," he told her, as they paused at the rail, the sky was again flung with stars, the preternaturally calm ocean stretching out like the skin of a vast black pudding.

"You were wonderful, Jack," she said, not very drunk. "Brilliant as Professor Van Dusen himself—and braver than Sherlock Holmes."

"Well, you're a much prettier Watson, my darling. Also, smarter."

Her laughter was brittle yet musical, like a wind chime echoing in the sea air.

"The only thing missing is the children," he said.

"We'll be with them soon enough. Maybe next crossing, we'll bring them along."

"Capital idea, my love. Are you freezing? I'm freezing."

"Walk me home."

They entered the Grand Staircase balcony, being careful to watch their step, avoiding René's fate (and Crafton's ghost), and the sounds of the orchestra playing their medley from *Tales of Hoffmann*, with its romantic echoes of Venetian gondolas and lantern-lighted balconies, floated up the stairwell from several decks below. On the next landing, they waltzed briefly, laughing like young lovers, then stopped and embraced and kissed the same way.

He walked her to their stateroom door, and said, "Do you mind if I go to the Smoking Room, for a cigarette before bed?"

"Not at all. Just don't expect me to be awake when you get back ... that wine went straight to my head."

"I love you, darling," he said lightly, and they shared a peck of a kiss.

The Smoking Room was lightly attended, the concert tonight going a bit long, apparently; the usual card games were under way, and smoke floated like blue fog. Archie and Millet were playing bridge with young Widener and Hays. Nearby, in a leather armchair, in the glow of a table lamp, reading a book, sat a bewhiskered oversize gnome in yellow brown, rumpled tweed: W. T. Stead.

Futrelle pulled a chair around. "May I join you for a moment, Mr. Stead?"

Stead looked up, pleasantly. "Certainly, sir. I'm rereading Angell's *The Great Illusion*, that magnificent antiwar tract; it may provide inspiration for my speech at Carnegie Hall."

"I didn't see you about the ship, this afternoon, Mr. Stead. You were even missing from morning services."

"No, I've been indisposed."

"Indigestion?"

"Conscience … I ill used my powers of mediumship last night, Mr. Futrelle."

"Toward a good end."

"Perhaps." He shook his head. "But the ends do not justify the means."

"I apologize if I coerced you into corrupting your sense of ethics."

Stead managed a small grin, patting his belly. "I'm a big boy, Mr. Futrelle. No one forces me to do anything I don't care to do."

"Mr. Stead, what was that business last night with the message from 'Julia'? You were padding your part, a bit, weren't you?"

His response was matter of fact: "That was a real message from the other side, Mr. Futrelle—perhaps scolding me for my actions."

"Ah."

" 'Ah' indeed."

"Well, you should know soon enough, if helping me was right or wrong."

"Why do you say that, sir?"

Futrelle shrugged. "Your friend Julia said you'd be hearing a 'clarion call,' soon—and get all the answers you've been seeking. Doesn't sound like a scolding to me."

"Perhaps you're right, sir. I hope you are."

A steward leaned in and said, "Can I get you anything, sir? A brandy, perhaps?"

Futrelle glanced up; it was the boy from the Verandah Café, with the bruised jaw and the tow head.

"You know," Futrelle said, rising, "you can. Would you mind stepping out on deck with me for a moment?"

"Sir?"

"Won't take but a few seconds. The privacy will benefit both of us."

The steward, smiling nervously, backed up. "Sir, I'm working...."

"And I'm a First-Class passenger, and I'd like some help out on deck."

"... All right, sir."

Futrelle smiled down at Stead. "Thanks for your assistance, last night; that was a service only you could have provided. Now, get back to your book, and see if you can't come up with a formula for world peace."

Half a smile blossomed in the white-thicket beard. "I'll see what I can do, Mr. Futrelle."

Futrelle motioned to the young steward to go through the revolving doors, into the Verandah Café, which they did.

Though the café was empty, the writer said, "Out on the boat deck, if you please."

"Isn't this private enough, sir?"

"The boat deck, if you please."

The boy lowered his head, his eyes peering up like a beaten dog's. "All right, sir. If you insist, sir."

Out in the bitter cold of the still night, under a thousand stars but no moon, Futrelle lighted up a Fatima, smiled meaninglessly at the lad, who stood before him, with the blankly apprehensive expression of a teenager guilty of numerous infractions, wondering which one his parent knows about.

Smart in his white jacket with gold buttons, he was a handsome boy, with wide-set dark brown eyes, a strong nose and full, nearly feminine lips. He was shaking. It might have been the bitter cold. Futrelle doubted that.

"What's your name, son?"

"William, sir. William Stephen Faulkner."

"Do they call you Bill?"

"They call me William."

"Where are you from, William?"

"Romsey Road, sir. Southampton."

Futrelle exhaled a stream of Fatima smoke. "William, has Alice told you what I'm trying to do?"

The boy frowned. "What? Who?"

"Please don't insult my intelligence. Your girlfriend—Alice. I'm trying to help her. Like you tried to help her."

A nervous smile formed. "Sir, you … you must have me confused with someone else. If you'll excuse me."

The boy began to go, but Futrelle gripped his arm. "For God's sake, son, don't make me turn you in. Give me a reason not to."

Their faces were an inch apart; the brown eyes were wide with alarm. "Sir! What … what do you want from me?"

Futrelle let loose of him, took a step back. "The truth, William. What happened on the boat deck, with Alice and

Rood, that night? You were there, weren't you? In the shadows, waiting to protect her. Surely you wouldn't have allowed her to meet such a dangerous individual by herself, not after what she'd been through with Crafton."

His mouth hung open in amazement. "How can you know this?"

"Alice told me," Futrelle lied. "But I want to hear it from you, son."

The young man stumbled toward the rail, held on. The boat well yawned below; beyond that, the poop deck. No one was out on such a chill night as this—just this boy and the mystery writer.

"He grabbed her arms," the boy said numbly. "He was sha-kin' her, shakin' her …"

The boy demonstrated, grabbing the air.

"That's when you stepped in?"

He nodded, swallowing. "I … I grabbed him, pulled him away from her—and he swung at me, got me here … that's how I got this jaw, sir … and as I was gettin' up, he pushed me down. I came up hard, rammin' into him, shovin' him back, and …"

"He hit his head."

The boy sighed heavily and nodded. "There was a lot of blood; I sneaked back, later, with a bucket, and cleaned that up. Alice didn't scream or nothin'. She was calm, almost like she was in a trance. She helped me hide 'im in the boat … it took the both of us to do it.…"

"I know."

"You know that?"

"That's how I knew she had help, son. She couldn't have lifted that body up into that hanging boat, not by herself. And you were her only friend on the ship, weren't you?"

He shrugged, then nodded; hung his head. "She's not a bad girl, sir. 'Tweren't her fault, none of it."

"Did you unlock Crafton's door so she could go and smother him, and rob him?"

His eyes popped in horror. "No! Oh my God, no, sir—she come to me ... my quarters is right in First Class, y'know—and she took me to that room and showed me what she'd done. Him all dead in bed.... She was cryin'...."

"Did you know she'd taken the money off that dresser?"

His gaze dropped. "Well ... yes, sir, I did, sir ... I figured she had it comin', what hell he put her through."

"What did you do, William?"

"Nothin', sir. Just grabbed Alice and used my key to lock the door behind us."

So much for the locked-door mystery.

Another swallow; then Faulkner looked up, pitifully. "Do we ... do we go talk to the captain now, sir?"

"I don't think so."

He seemed on the verge of crying. "What do you want me to do, sir?"

"The story you just told me?"

"Yes, sir?"

"Never tell it again."

The boy's eyes tightened, then they widened, and his face exploded into a winning smile. "Yes, sir. You're a hell of a bloke, sir."

"One other thing ..."

"Sir?"

Futrelle pitched his Fatima into the sea; it arched and spit sparks, like a tiny flare. "I'm going back into the Smoking Room. I'll have a brandy."

So, nestled into a comfortable armchair, Futrelle sat and smoked a Havana cigar Archie Butt offered him, and sucked the rich smoke into his lungs, and enjoyed the snifter of brandy the attentive young steward brought him. He had nearly nodded off when something jarred him awake—an unexpected jostle that was the first sign since he'd boarded that he was on a ship, not in a hotel. The muffled sound of agitated voices, like distant cannon fire, drifted in from outside.

Wondering idly what that had been, Futrelle rose, stretched, took one last sip of brandy, crushed out the remainder of his cigar in a White Star ashtray. Perhaps he'd go out on the cold deck, before going back to his warm wife in their warm bed, and see what the fuss was about.

He certainly couldn't have felt more at ease, or frankly more self-satisfied. A pair of damned blackmailers were dead, a mystery or two solved; the young lovers responsible would likely meet a merciful fate at the hands of Captain Smith. All was right with the world, the little city on the big ship safe once again, with naught but the promise of calm seas and smooth sailing ahead.

THAT NIGHT REMEMBERED

MY ANONYMOUS PHONE CALLER NEVER contacted me again, and my attempts to contact the various official expeditions to the *Titanic*'s wreckage on the ocean's floor, two and a half miles under the Grand Banks, have been fruitless. My letters about murders on the ship, and the possible existence (and discovery) of two canvas-body-bagged corpses in the cold cargo hold, apparently have been viewed much as I originally did my midnight caller: the work of a crank. (My phone calls have resulted in hang-ups, bum's rushes and being put on hold until a dial tone clicks back in.)

Of course, I have no way of contacting any unofficial expedition—doubtful as the existence of such an effort might be, considering the shortage of deep-diving submersibles like Robert Ballard's *Alvin* and IFREMER's *Nautile*—and confirming my caller's story now seems unlikely or even hopeless.

Researching the story told me by May and Jack Futrelle's daughter, Virginia, that April afternoon in Scituate, has been considerably more successful, as the narrative you've just concluded I hope indicates. Virtually everything Mrs. Raymond told me about the murders fit neatly into known history, and answered a number of questions that have baffled researchers (why Captain Smith canceled the Sunday lifeboat drill, for instance, and the seemingly needless rush to port).

Unfortunately, I had only that one long afternoon's meeting with Mrs. Raymond, who passed away later that same year.

What we do know is: who survived, and who did not, and—despite the tumult of that terrible night—we have at least some idea of the circumstances surrounding those who lost their lives so tragically and, almost invariably, heroically.

For the record, at approximately 11:40 P.M., the *Titanic*—at a speed approaching twenty-three knots—side-swiped an iceberg, despite the ship's captain and crew having received numerous warnings of ice in the area. With too few lifeboats aboard and a slowly dawning realization by crew and passengers of the extent of the damage to the ship, a disaster worsened into tragedy. By 2:20 A.M., the *Titanic* was gone, taking many of her passengers and crew with her, putting more than fifteen hundred people either in or under the icy waters.

Archie Butt and Frank Millet, with several other passengers, aided in the loading of women and children onto lifeboats; when all of the lifeboats had been dispatched, the gentlemen returned to their card game in the Smoking Room until the slant of the table no longer allowed. Stories of Major Butt on deck fighting off swarthy steerage "rabble" with a walking stick or even a firearm appear to be one of the many yellow-journalistic inventions that pervaded early coverage of the disaster.

Archie Butt was last seen standing solemnly to one side on the boat deck, stoically awaiting his fate like the good soldier he was. He was apparently in the company of his friend Francis Millet; both men died in the sinking, Millet's body recovered by the crew of the *MacKay Bennett*, whose grim task it was to salvage as many *Titanic* corpses as possible from the icy Atlantic.

Captain Smith's fate remains clouded, as do conflicting reports of his demeanor on deck. The press of the day made him out a hero, but considering the source, the reports that he fell into a dazed, near-catatonic state are more credible; still, witnesses recalled seeing him with a megaphone, directing lifeboats to return to pick up more passengers (an order ignored). One story has him committing suicide with a pistol, but more credible is the eyewitness account of a steward who saw his captain walk onto the bridge, shortly before the forward superstructure went under, presumably to be washed away—a suicide of sorts, at that.

Another crew member reported seeing Captain Smith in the freezing water, holding a baby in his arms, moments before his ship made her final slide into the sea. Legend has it that the captain swam to a lifeboat, handed the child over, and swam off to go down after, if not with, his ship. The last reliable reports of Smith have him, in the water, cheering the attempts of crew members to struggle onto the top of an overturned lifeboat, calling, "Good lads! Good lads!" An oar offered to Smith was out of the captain's reach, as a swell carried him away.

Some of the most famous stories of that night—the ones sounding most like legend—are true.

Isidor Straus, offered a seat on lifeboat number eight in consideration of his age, refused to go when other, younger men were staying; and Ida Straus refused to leave her husband's side.

"I will not be separated from my husband," she said. "As we have lived, so will we die together."

And they did; in one final indignity, however, the ocean took Mrs. Straus's body, while her husband's was recovered, to be buried in Beth-El Cemetery, Brooklyn. Forty thousand attended the memorial service for the couple, with a eulogy read by Andrew Carnegie.

Benjamin Guggenheim, at first protesting the discomfort of a life belt, later abandoned it for his finest evening wear. With his valet, he awaited death in style, announcing, "We've dressed up in our best and are prepared to go down like gentlemen." Oddly, his final thoughts—or at least his final thoughts of how he might like to be remembered—had to do with his long-suffering wife, writing the following note: *If anything should happen to me, tell my wife I've done my best in doing my duty.*

This may have been small solace to Mrs. Guggenheim, after Madame Aubert—rescued with the others in lifeboats by the ship *Carpathia*—came ashore announced as "Mrs. Benjamin Guggenheim." As a further indignity, Guggenheim's business affairs were in disorder, his steampump company doing poorly at the time of his death, leaving his children to make do with trust funds of only half a million or so, each.

Thomas Andrews, one of the first to understand that his ship was doomed, circulated through the *Titanic* dispensing various stories to various passengers, depending on how well he felt they might bear up under the truth. He worked manfully to see to it that as many women and children as possible were gotten into the lifeboats; but despair, finally, overtook him.

Andrews was last seen in the Smoking Room, staring at a serene nautical painting, his life belt nearby, flung carelessly across a green-topped table. His arms were folded, his shoulders slumped. When a steward, moving quickly through the room, asked him, "Aren't you even going to have a try for it, Mr. Andrews?", the shipbuilder did not even acknowledge the question.

William T. Stead was also seen in the Smoking Room, seemingly absorbed in the book he was reading, unconcerned about the brouhaha (he had taken a break from his book and was one of the few on deck at the time of the collision with the iceberg). He continued this until near the end, when he was spotted standing calmly at the rail. He had never mentioned to his fellow passengers that he had premonitions of drowning, and that he had—like Morgan Robertson, the author of *Futility*—written a story about an ocean liner striking an iceberg, with lives lost because too few lifeboats had been aboard.

"This is exactly what might take place," he had predicted in 1886, "and what will take place, if liners are sent to sea short of boats."

His body was not recovered.

Third-Class passenger Alfred Davies lost his life in the disaster; so did his uncle and two brothers. Their father described them, at the memorial service, as "fine big lads" and "the best of sons."

In lifeboat number six, Maggie Brown, by standing up to an obnoxious crew member who'd taken charge, found her place in history as the "Unsinkable Mrs. Brown." Never reconciling with her husband, over whose money she and her children battled for years, Maggie reveled in her celebrity until her death by a stroke in 1932. A Broadway musical loosely based on her life spawned a 1964 MGM motion picture starring Debbie Reynolds, who looked not much like Maggie (who somehow, after her death, became "Molly"); but then neither had Maggie wielded a handgun on a White Star lifeboat.

First-Class passengers Emil Brandeis and John Baumann were lost in the sinking; the body of the former was recovered, the latter's was not.

J. Bruce Ismay worked bravely and hard, seeing that women and children were shuttled onto lifeboats; but he carved himself a place in history as a coward by stepping into one of the last lifeboats, collapsible C, and choosing not to go down with his ship—not even watching the great ship slip under, turning his back to the sight, much as the world would turn its back to him. By June 1913, he had "retired" from White Star, and was vilified throughout the remainder of a life that has been described as reclusive; his wife said the *Titanic* "ruined" him. Ismay's charitable acts—and there were a number of these—included establishing a fund to benefit the widows of lost seamen. He died in 1937.

Charles Lightoller performed professionally, even heroically, going down with the ship, but swimming to capsized collapsible B, and scrambling on top. He was a company man at the two official inquiries, protecting both the late Smith and the very much alive Ismay; but nonetheless fell prey to the White Star Line's unofficial policy of sabotaging the careers of surviving *Titanic* officers. He did become a commander in the Royal Navy during World War I, and provided heroic volunteer duty at Dunkirk in World War II. He died in 1952, not living to see himself portrayed as the hero of the film of Walter Lord's epic version of the *Titanic*'s story, *A Night to Remember*.

Lightoller was the one who allowed Michel Navatril, a.k.a. Louis Hoffman, to place his sons Lolo and Momon on collapsible D, the final lifeboat launched. Michel Jr. (Lolo was the boy's nickname) recalled his father's final words to him: "My child, when your mother comes for you, as she surely will, tell her that I loved her dearly and still do. Tell her I expected her to follow us, so that we might all live happily together in the peace and freedom of the New World."

Navatril's body was recovered; he had a revolver in his pocket.

The two boys—briefly celebrities as the unidentified "*Titanic* orphans"—were returned to their mother in France. Edmond

Navatril (Momon had been his nickname as a child) fought with the French army in World War II, escaping from a prisoner-of-war camp; however, due to health problems suffered during his captivity, he died at age forty-three. Michel Jr., who became a professor of psychology, lives in France.

Bertha Lehmann, the Swiss girl who was the only person Navatril ever trusted to take charge of his sons out of his own sight, boarded the same lifeboat as the Navatril boys. She lived in Minnesota and Iowa and raised a number of children; she died in December 1967.

John Jacob Astor IV guided his wife Madeline into lifeboat number four, but Lightoller refused Astor's request to accompany and protect his wife, who was after all in a "delicate condition." Lightoller firmly refused and Astor accepted this judgment, but did ask the number of the boat, whether to locate his wife later, or to register a complaint against Lightoller, will never be known.

Astor then assumed a casual, confident manner, lighting up a cigarette, tossing his gloves to his wife and assuring her that the sea was calm; saying, "You'll be all right. You're in good hands," adding that he would see her in the morning. He stepped away and receded onto the boat deck.

When older boys were being turned away by Lightoller from lifeboats as "men," Astor impulsively grabbed a girl's large hat off a nearby head and shoved it onto a boy's, saying, "Well now he's a girl," gaining ten-year-old William Carter a seat and his life. One of his last acts, apparently, was to go to the kennels and let out all of the dogs there, including the Astors' Airedale Kitty, whom Madeline Astor claimed to have seen, from her lifeboat, running about the boat deck as the ship was sinking.

Astor was seen at the railing with Archie Butt and others, but did not drown; his crushed, soot-covered remains, recovered, indicated he'd apparently been killed by the falling forward funnel. In the pockets of his blue serge suit were $2,400 in American money and smaller amounts in French and English currency.

Madeline Astor was granted the income of a five-million-dollar trust and various mansions, as long as she did not remarry; but she married again, anyway, having two more sons by elderly stockholder William Dick, and married yet again—after a divorce—in 1933, to an Italian prizefighter, divorcing him five years later, also. Presumably her son John Jacob V, who had his own five-million-dollar trust fund, saw to it his mother didn't starve. She died in 1940, in Palm Beach, Florida—a suicide, according to some sources—rarely speaking of the tragedy, and younger than her husband had been when he died.

Henry B. Harris, ushering his wife René to where Lightoller was restricting seating on the collapsible D, was told his wife could come aboard, but that he could not. He said softly, "I know—I'll stay," bade her farewell, and stepped back into the crowd.

René sued White Star for a million dollars, receiving only $50,000 (the standard payoff for a First-Class death aboard the *Titanic*—steerage was a thousand dollars). Plucky as always, she bucked the standard sentiment that a woman could not be a theatrical producer, and had a long and prosperous run doing just that; for years she had hit plays running in her own theaters, living a life strewn with yachts, Central Park penthouses, various homes and various husbands (though always using only "Harris" as her surname). The stock-market crash of '29 sank her finances, but not her spirits; when she died, penniless, in a one-room apartment in a welfare hotel, at age ninety-three in 1969, she was still (in the words of Walter Lord) "radiantly blissful."

Wallace Hartley and his orchestra—the full eight members playing together for the first time on the deck of the sinking ship—performed until the ship went down. Some say the impromptu concert ended around half an hour before the final plunge; even if this is so, their cheery on-deck ragtime is an enduring legend, and fact, of the tragedy. Despite adamant opinions to the contrary, their last number probably was "Nearer My God to Thee."

Actress Dorothy Gibson—one of the twenty-eight persons in boat number seven, capacity sixty-five—sailed the *Titanic* to fifteen minutes of fame. One month after the sinking, a moving picture starring and written by Miss Gibson—*Saved from the Titanic*, in which the silent-film star's costume was the very dress she'd worn that memorable night—appeared in theaters to huge crowds. It was her last success. She married film distributor Jules Brulatour, divorcing two years later (with a hefty $10,000 a year in alimony), dying in obscurity in Paris in 1946.

Official records list John Bertram Crafton and Hugh Rood as having gone down with the ship; neither body was recovered by the *MacKay Bennett*.

One of the enduring mysteries of the night the *Titanic* sank is whether Alice Cleaver behaved as a heroine, or a villain. Hudson Allison had left the family's C-deck suite to find out what exactly was wrong; soon his wife Bess was in mild hysterics, and Alice Cleaver seized up baby Trevor into her arms, wrapped the nightgowned child in a small fur blanket, and assured the boy's mother that she would not let the child out of her arms much less her sight.

Alice then rushed out, apparently passing Hudson in the hallway; but the stunned parent seemed not to recognize either Alice or his boy. The nanny hurried onto deck, where, with the help of steward William Stephen Faulkner, she made her way to lifeboat eleven. As she climbed into the boat, Faulkner held the child for her; rather than accept the child from the young man, Alice pulled him into the boat after her. Because he was holding a baby in his arms, this was allowed.

The Allisons—Hudson and Hugh and golden-haired Lorraine—were lost in the sinking; Lorraine was, in fact, the only First-Class child to die. Even as newspapers were praising the blunt-nosed nanny for her courage and quick thinking, the families of Hudson and Bess Allison accused her of an act tantamount to murder.

Mrs. Allison's mother asserted that the Allisons had obviously stayed aboard the ship, searching for their baby, and missed their chance at a lifeboat. Space was the birthright of their gender for Bess and Lorraine, and Hudson Allison—with the baby in his arms—could just as easily stepped into that lifeboat as the young steward.

After all, Hudson Allison's only crime was hastily accepting a last-minute replacement for the position of nanny, without sufficient time to check references. (His body was recovered but not his wife's, or his daughter's.)

Lending credibility to the theory that Alice Cleaver was more coward than heroine were the lies she told reporters, giving her name as Jane Andrews. Obviously, the nanny did not wish to see the glowing reaction of the press tainted by knowledge that the woman who saved the Allison baby off a sinking ship was a mother who'd thrown her own baby off a train.

Alice Cleaver lived out her life in North America, fading into obscurity, dying in 1984. What became of her relationship with William Stephen Faulkner—the only person she would let near baby Trevor, on the rescue ship *Carpathia*—is unknown.

Baby Trevor was raised by his aunt and uncle, George and Lillian Allison, and grew to manhood, only to die in his teens of ptomaine poisoning. His parents' fortune became the object of a struggle between his aunt and uncle and a woman who claimed to be (but never was able to prove she was) his now grown-up sister, Lorraine.

May Futrelle, rescued in lifeboat nine, never remarried. She spent the rest of her life in Scituate, mostly in the home she'd shared with her husband. While their children's education was well provided for, May felt a responsibility to pay back $17,000 in cash advances that had gone down on the ship, along with Jack's half a dozen new "Thinking Machine" stories.

She oversaw the publication of her husband's final post-humous works, as well as aggressively sought reprinting of his earlier work. The straightforward, journalistic style of Futrelle's "Thinking Machine" stories allowed his wife to keep many of them in print, for many years; and of course "The Problem of Cell 13" became an acknowledged classic of the mystery genre.

Active with the Authors' League of America and first chair-woman of the American League of Pen Women, May published a number of her own novels, and was a pioneer in conducting writers' workshop-style clinics for beginning writers, leading to a CBS radio show in the thirties, *Do You Want to Be a Writer?*

Well into the 1960s, she was pushing the republication of her husband's fiction—witness the best-selling 1959 Scholastic Book Club collection of "Thinking Machine" stories—and shortly before her death in 1967, May signed exclusive rights for radio adaptations of twenty-eight Futrelle "Thinking Machine" stories, many of which were presented on *CBS Radio Mystery Theater.* She is buried in St. Mary's Cemetery in Scituate.

Throughout her life, as her daughter Virginia reported, May would carry out the ritual of tossing a bouquet of fresh flowers into the sea on the anniversary of the tragedy. The memories of that last night remained vivid and with her always.

Futrelle had come rushing into their stateroom, saying, "Get dressed at once—throw anything on. The boat is going down."

She recalled the screams of women and shrill orders of officers on deck, "drowned out intermittently by the tremendous vibration of the *Titanic*'s bass foghorn."

Futrelle remained calm, telling May, "Hurry up, dear, you're keeping the others waiting," kissing her, then lifting her like a bride over the threshold and placing her into the lifeboat, one of the last to leave.

"There's room," May said frantically, looking about the boat as it began to lower. "Look! Come with me! There's room!"

"I'll be along later," he said.

Her last memory of him, she carried with her—to that cliff, from which she tossed her flowers, and to her grave.

Their lifeboat had not been in the water for more than a few minutes when the *Titanic* made its final plunge. Over the years she came to question whether or not it was only her imagination …

… but she always swore that she'd seen Jack, standing, clinging to the rail with one hand.

And waving good-bye to her with the other.

A TIP OF THE CAPTAIN'S HAT

The basic idea for this novel, as my prologue indicates, extends back to my childhood enthusiasm for Jacques Futrelle's "Thinking Machine" tales, and my fascination with the notion that he—and a number of his stories—went down with the *Titanic*.

In response to the new interest in the tragedy, spurred of course by James Cameron's successful film, I began to tinker with the notion of a mystery aboard the ship, with Futrelle as the detective, and offhandedly mentioned all this to Elizabeth Beier, the wonderful editor at Boulevard Books with whom I've worked on a number of movie tie-in novels. She at once saw the possibilities in my idea, and *The Titanic Murders* became my only novel to date sold on the basis of a single, casual phone call.

The writing of the book, however, has not been a casual affair. The idea evolved from a drawing-room mystery involving the real-life Futrelle and a typical Agatha Christie–style fictional cast into using only real passengers as my players (and suspects). This of course took the book into the more demanding arena of historical fiction (as opposed to simply a "period" mystery).

I have accordingly attempted to stay consistent with known facts about the *Titanic* and her maiden voyage, though the many books on this subject are often inconsistent, particularly on smaller points, and the various experts disagree on all sorts of matters, both trivial and profound. When research was contradictory, I made the choice most beneficial to the telling of this tale. Any blame for historical inaccuracies is my own, reflecting, I hope, the limitations of this conflicting source material.

The characters in this novel are real and appear with their true names; the blackmail threats made to the various players are grounded in reality. The epilogue's litany of whatever-happened-to these real people is strictly factual. Nothing is known of either John Bertram Crafton and Hugh Rood, however, beyond their presence on the ship and their deaths in the disaster; they could just as likely have been clerics as crooks, saints as sinners, and were chosen from among the anonymous deceased because of the melodramatic felicity of their names. I would say that I intend no offense to their memories, but unfortunately no memories of them appear to endure.

My fact-based novels about fictional 1930s/1940s-era Chicago private detective Nathan Heller have required extensive research not unlike what was required of this project. I called upon my Heller research assistants, Lynn Myers and George Hagenauer, to help me in my attempt to re-create the maiden voyage of the great ill-fated ship. Throughout the writing of this novel, they were in touch with me on an almost daily basis, and without them this journey would not have been possible.

Lynn, a longtime *Titanic* buff (which I am not—or at least was not, until this project came along), focused on the ship itself, discussing various minute details and digging out the answers to innumerable nitpicking concerns of mine. He also shared his library of *Titanic* reference works, including numerous rare, period items, and provided videotapes of several documentaries and one of the *Titanic* films (*S.O.S. Titanic*). A police booking detective, Lynn also provided details about death by smothering.

George focused more on the people, and worked with me to gather background on the famous passengers (and, in the case of this story, suspects). In particular he was helpful in gathering, and interpreting, materials on John Jacob Astor, Isidor Straus, Benjamin Guggenheim and especially W. T. Stead.

Jacques Futrelle, while a major figure in the history of mystery fiction, is unfortunately little known (or read) today. I was blessed by the existence of a fascinating, well-done book on Futrelle's life, the unique *The Thinking Machine: Jacques Futrelle* (1995) by Freddie Seymour and Bettina Kyper, a biography supplemented by five "Thinking Machine" stories—including "The Problem of Cell 13" and "The Grinning God," a collaboration between Jack and May. In addition, coauthor Bettina Kyper—who knew both May and Virginia Futrelle intimately—generously shared further information with me over the phone. Other information on Futrelle was culled from E. R. Bleiler's introduction to *Best "Thinking Machine" Stories* (1973) and the introduction to the Futrelle story collected in *Detection by Gaslight* (1997) edited by Douglas G. Greene. Further Futrelle information was drawn from *Encylopedia of Mystery and Detection* (1976) by Chris Steinbrunner and Otto Penzler and *Twentieth-Century Crime and Mystery Writers—Second Edition* (1985) edited by John M. Reilly.

A vital research tool to this book was Philip Hind's extensive website, *Encyclopedia Titanica*, which (among many other things) features First-, Second- and Third-Class lists that include many biographies of passengers (and not just the famous ones); crew members, too. The wealth of information Mr. Hind has assembled is equaled by the clarity of his writing. My son Nathan helped me with Internet research and guided me through the use of the CD-ROM game from Cyberflix, *Titanic—Adventure Out of Time* (1996), which allowed me to tour the ship.

Also, since no major biography of Maggie Brown exists (at least that I know of), I was grateful and relieved to discover the *Molly Brown House Museum* website, which provided a lengthy, in-depth and well-written biographical essay, with many pictures, of the Unsinkable Mrs. Brown.

I would also like to acknowledge and praise musicologist Ian Whitcomb's delightful CD, *Titanic—Music As Heard on the Fateful Voyage*, which includes renditions by "The White Star Orchestra" re-creating the authentic period music in the precise instrumentation of Wallace Hartley's ensemble. In addition to providing an ineffable sense of mood, Whitcomb's CD includes a voluminous, detailed, informative booklet.

Three first-rate book-length narratives about the sinking of the *Titanic* were key references in the writing of this novel.

Walter Lord's *A Night to Remember* (1955) remains a riveting, beautifully written account (and his 1987 follow-up, *The Night Lives On*, answers many questions and explores various controversies that his earlier, you-are-there-style classic did not, including material on the Ballard expedition's discovery of the wreckage).

Geoffrey Marcus's *The Maiden Voyage* (1969) is a more detailed account and includes much material Lord ignored in favor of focusing on the night of the disaster; extensively researched, it stands beside *A Night to Remember* as a definitive work.

A similar, and similarly excellent, in-depth look at the tragedy is found in Daniel Allen Butler's *"Unsinkable"—The Full*

Story of RMS Titanic (1998), a clear-eyed, readable narrative including up-to-date material on the expeditions as well the public's enduring fascination with this subject, and its impact on popular culture.

The *Titanic* obviously lends itself to oversized volumes that combine pictures and text; few pictures of the *Titanic* exist, however, and most of these books are filled chiefly with photos of her sister ship, the *Olympic*. The majority of the known photos of the real ship were taken by Jesuit Father E. E. O'Donnell, who took passage on the *Titanic* from Southampton to Queenstown, where he disembarked. In 1985, the same year that Robert Ballard discovered the ship's wreckage, a cache of Father O'Donnell's photos turned up, with their glimpses of life on and around the doomed ship. They have been well gathered, with a 1912 article by O'Donnell himself, in *The Last Days of the Titanic* (1997). O'Donnell spoke to Futrelle aboard the ship and took a photograph of the mystery writer standing on the boat deck.

Titanic—An Illustrated History (1992) by Don Lynch, featuring paintings by famed *Titanic* illustrator Ken Marschall, is an excellent coffee-table-style book, and both its text and elaborate illustrations (including a foldout cutaway painting of the ship that greatly aided me in gaining my bearings) were vital to the writing of this novel.

Similarly helpful was *Titanic—Triumph and Tragedy* (1994/1998), by John P. Easton and Charles A. Haas, a fastidiously detailed nuts-and-bolts account, voluminously illustrated with rare photos, a mammoth undertaking well done.

The Titanic—The Extraordinary Story of the "Unsinkable" Ship (1997) by Geoff Tibballs is a comparatively slender volume but extremely well assembled, with effective, well-researched text and nicely chosen pictures, which were of great help to me—this *Reader's Digest* trade paperback is a handsome, user-friendly volume, particularly for the more casual *Titanic* buff.

A similar volume is *Titanic* (1997) by Leo Marriott, which features a gallery of paintings not seen elsewhere, and many large illustrations that were useful for imagining the ship; unfortunately, the book has no index, which limits its effectiveness as a research tool. Even more maddening is *Titanic Voices—Memories from the Fateful Voyage* (1994), by Donald Hyslop, Alastair Forsyth and Sheila Jemima, which collects photos and letters and other rare documents and information about the disaster; prepared for the Southampton City Council, the book is oddly skewed and, even with three authors, no one bothered to assemble an index. Still, it was beneficial, sometimes uniquely so.

Two excellent "picture books" that combine the story of the disaster with haunting photos of the wreckage are *The Discovery of the Titanic* (1987) by Dr. Robert D. Ballard and *Titanic—Legacy of the World's Greatest Ocean Liner* (1997) by Susan Wels. The latter—a Discovery Channel book—is stronger on history, the former focusing on Ballard's expeditions.

A number of vintage books (or reprints thereof) were consulted: *The Sinking of the Titanic* (1912), Logan Marshall; *Sinking of the Titanic—Thrilling Stories Told by Survivors* (1912), George W. Bertron; *The Truth About the Titanic* (1913), Colonel Archibald Gracie; and *Wrecking and Sinking of the Titanic—The Ocean's Greatest Disaster* (1912), no author given ("told by the Survivors").

Particularly useful, in my attempt to re-create what it must have been like to be a First-Class passenger on the great ship, was *Last Dinner on the Titanic* (1997) by Rick Archbold with recipes by Dana McCauley, a lovely, eccentric combination of history lesson and cookbook.

Other relatively recent books, taking more specialized looks at the *Titanic* story, were also of help: *Down with the Old Canoe—A Cultural History of the Titanic Disaster* (1996), Steven Biel; *Her Name Titanic* (1988), Charles Pellegrino; *The Titanic Conspiracy* (1995), Robin Gardiner and Dan Van Der Vat; *Titanic—Destination Disaster* (1987/1996), John P. Eaton and Charles A. Haas; *The Titanic Disaster* (1997), Dave Bryceson (the story as reported in the British press); *The Titanic—End of a Dream* (1986), Wyn Craig Wade; and *Total Titanic* (1998), Marc Shapiro.

A number of biographies and studies of society in the early 1900s were consulted, including: *The Age of the Moguls* (1953), Stephen H. Holbrook; *And the Price Is Right* (1958), Margaret Case Harriman (the story of the Strauses and Macy's department store); *The Astors* (1941), Harvey O'Connor; *The Astors* (1979), Virginia Cowles; *The Astor Family* (1981), John D. Gates; *The Case of Eliza Armstrong—A Child of 13 Bought for 5 Pounds* (1974), Alison Plowden (the W. T. Stead "white slavery" case); *Crusader in Babylon—W. T. Stead and the Pall Mall Gazette* (1972), Raymond Schults; *The Guggenheims—An American Epic* (1978), John H. Davis; *The Guggenheims—The Making of an American Dynasty* (1976), Harvey O'Connor; *The Guggenheims and the American Dream* (1967), Edwin P. Hoyt, Jr.; *Peggy—The Wayward Guggenheim* (1986), Jacqueline Bograd Weld; *The Inheritors* (1962), John Tebbel; *My Father* (1913), Estelle W. Stead; and *Who Killed Society* (1960), Cleveland Amory. Also useful was a March 15, 1998, *People Magazine* article, "Sunken Dreams" by Jeffrey Wells, Joanna Blonska and Jason Lynch.

Further material on W. T. Stead was culled from *The Wreck of the Titanic Foretold?* (1998), edited by Martin Gardener, reprinting Morgan Robertson's prophetic *The Wreck of the Titan* (originally published as *Futility*) as well as Stead's own prophetic sea-disaster writings.

Midway through the writing of this novel, by which time I had become intimate with the material via research, I went for a third time to James Cameron's *Titanic*, and was very impressed by the verisimilitude of the art direction and the quality of the screenwriter's research. I also viewed several other *Titanic* films: *Titanic* (1953); *A Night to Remember* (1958); *S.O.S. Titanic* (1979); and the television miniseries *Titanic* (1996). Surprisingly, every one of these productions has its merits, most obviously the adaptation of the Lord book; all but the first of these (and even it's not bad) take pains to be accurate, and the mini-series in particular is underrated and has art direction that rivals Cameron's, despite a considerably smaller budget.

In addition, I screened numerous documentaries, the most useful of which was A&E's *Titanic* (1994) written and directed by Melissa Peltier; others viewed included *Secrets of the Titanic* (1997) written and directed by Dennis B. Kaye, codirected by Dr. Robert D. Ballard; *Titanic* (1997) written by Linda Cooper and produced by Dick Arlett; *Titanic: Secrets Revealed* (1998) written by Lois DeCosia and directed by John Tindall; *The Titanic Tragedy* (1997) written by Tom Gredishar, Randy Jackson and Mariangela Malespin, directed by Geoff Chadwick; and Ray Johnson's *Titanic Remembered* (1992) and *Echoes of Titanic* (1995).

My talented wife, mystery writer Barbara Collins—the May to my Jack—helped me through this difficult, demanding project, providing frequent impromptu library trips, poring over blueprints and photos in an attempt to help her directionally dyslexic husband find his way around the ship, and offering insightful criticism and needed praise, while keeping a constant lookout for looming bergs, growlers and field ice.

ABOUT THE AUTHOR

Max Allan Collins is the *New York Times* best-selling author of *Road to Perdition* and multiple award-winning novels, screenplays, comic books, comic strips, trading cards, short stories, movie novelizations, and historical fiction. He has scripted the *Dick Tracy* comic strip, *Batman* comic books, and written tie-in novels based on the *CSI*, *Bones*, and *Dark Angel* TV series; collaborated with legendary mystery author Mickey Spillane; and authored numerous mystery series including Quarry, Nolan, Mallory, and the bestselling Nathan Heller historical thrillers. His additional *Disaster* series mystery novels include *The Lusitania Murders*, The *Hindenburg Murders*, *The Pearl Harbor Murders*, *The London Blitz Murders*, and *The War of the Worlds Murder*.

GAYLORD

15843100R00166

Made in the USA
Charleston, SC
24 November 2012